The Jewelry
of Grace

This book is dedicated to my nephews,

Octavian and J.J.,

and to my nieces,

Sky, Brigitt, Liz, Savannah, Becca and Danielle.

4

Prologue

The two sides of the desk could not be more different, as the two phases of Williams' adult life could not have been more dissimilar.

On the right, there were dozens of papers. Some old, some new, but all crumpled, smeared, disorganized, scattered around his workspace. No matter if he took the time to settle the files in order, he understood what they told him.

His family's debt had grown too large to handle.

On the left was only a jewelry box. It was closed, but he knew what was under the lid.

His legacy.

"William," Joan called to him. "Grace is going to bed."

He switched off the lamp and left the den. Walking into his daughter's room, William saw her half-asleep already.

"I love you, daddy," Grace said, straining her arms out for a hug. "Can we go to the lake tomorrow?"

William hugged her. "Not tomorrow. Remember, you're in first grade now. You have school every weekday. But this Saturday, I promise."

"Thank you, daddy," she said, falling back into the pillow. She was asleep in moments, twirling at her hair while she was slumbering.

William wished he experienced such a carefree moment, awake or asleep. But finances plagued his waking hours.

He walked back to the den and found the lamp was lit again. His wife standing by the desk, shuffling through the

6

papers. "I can't follow all of this," Joan said. "But I can tell you're right. We're not going to keep our home. Unless."

William sat as a pain shot up his right leg. He did not show any discomfort. Enough problems right now for his wife to worry about. "Unless." Neither of them needed to fill in the other words. He reached for the jewelry box.

"Don't look, dear. It will only make it worse."

"We will have to see them when we sell them," William answered, and he opened the lid.

Inside were five jewels, each attached to a one-of-a-kind necklace. William knew it was one-of-a-kind because he had cut it, as he had cut the jewels himself. The world had been different five years ago. At least their world had been.

The company he had worked for had been booming. Bonuses and raises were commonplace. And, in honor of twenty-five years of quality service, William had been allowed to craft his treasure for his then two-year-old daughter.

He stared at the treasure in the box. The center jewel was a five-karat diamond, circular on top with eight facets that met in a point at the bottom. It rested in a gold, circular setting. The four gems surrounding the diamond were shaped differently, but the same as each other. The sapphire, emerald, ruby and the onyx were each one inch long, a half-inch wide and a quarter-inch deep in the middle. Each of those four were in a silver setting.

William had cut each gem himself, from the original stones that his grandparents had brought with them from Germany. Even then, the stones were already considered family heirlooms. William could not remember if the stones themselves originated with the German line of the family, or with the other offshoot of the Davis family tree, but he hardly cared. The jewels came from his ancestors, and would be his gift to his only child. Every detail was special. Even the settings that the jewels laid in were made by William, each designed with a special hook, curly like a corkscrew, that would fit the necklace, but would be unlikely to attach to any other item.

This necklace, and each jewel on it, was to be Grace's wedding gift. She had come so late into their lives William was unsure if he would be alive to give her away when she married. Considering his age, along with his pains and forgetfulness, he was not sure he would live long enough to attend her high school graduation.

Grace was a blessing, but William doubted he would live to see how she would bless so many others.

The necklace and the five jewels were to be his way of staying with her forever. For him to be present at her wedding. For her to always remember he loved her.

But it was more important to make sure Grace had a home today.

"We have to do it," Joan said. She was not criticizing or correcting, he realized. If anything, she was encouraging him to do what they felt was right.

Two years after the necklace and jewels were finished, the company fell apart. Recession in the economy and scandal in the executives' offices ruined the business. William found work elsewhere, but without the same pay. His wife worked a part-time job as a waitress, but the extra income did not make up the deficit. Bills piled up beyond their ability to cover. Loans backfired.

Money was running out, which meant time was running out. Their home was not large, but soon they would not be able to keep it.

It was a burdensome thing to do. But the gemstones were valuable, more so than most that would be found in a quality jewelry store. The gems should give them the money and time they needed.

William looked at his wife and nodded. But he did not say a word until he walked back into Grace's room. He sat next to her and stroked her cheek.

"I'm so sorry," he whispered. "Please, never forget me."

* * *

In a month, four of the five jewels were gone. Disconnected from the necklace and each other, the emerald, sapphire, ruby and onyx were sold to different buyers.

"Finance is so hard," Joan said, flipping through papers on the desk. Now the files covered the whole desktop. "It doesn't help when you can't keep any of this organized. I'm pretty sure some accounts are still missing. I can't keep track of everything, but I believe, if we are careful, we can still give Grace a future."

"Barely," William added.

"Yes, barely," his wife echoed.

It would be a paycheck-to-paycheck lifestyle. But they would keep a roof over their heads and three meals a day on the dinner table. Grace could go to school in clothes that were not the latest style, but would not show how tight her family's finances were.

William opened a closet and reached into a small safe. After dialing in the combination, he pulled out the jewelry box. Opening that, he saw the one remaining jewel.

The diamond remained on the center clasp of the necklace. It was more valuable than the other four gems combined, William knew. But he could not bring himself to sell this one. That was why he had sold the other four individually. It was impossible to keep all five together, so why keep any of them together?

"What are you going to do?" Joan asked.

William had spent the last week pondering that question when he finally tracked down a buyer for the onyx. Odd fellow, that one. But he was already forgetting about who bought the jewels. The ones that were gone did not matter anymore. What should become of the diamond? He could not bear to sell it. At least, not today.

"I know it would give us the financial freedom we had years ago," he said, more to himself than his wife. "But I also would regret letting all five jewels leave the family."

"Then save it for Grace," she answered. "She will treasure it on her wedding day. She won't judge you for selling the others when you needed to."

"I know that. But any day a large bill arrives in the mail, any day when our accounts dwindle a little, I'll be tempted to sell it."

"But someday you might need the extra money."

William looked back at her. "Whose side are you on here?"

She stood up and rubbed his shoulders. "Yours, and hers."

William loved both his wife and daughter so much, he had to make sure they were cared for. But he could not sell his entire legacy.

"Maybe someone you worked with?" Joan asked.

William shook his head. "I've lost track of most of the guys. And part of the reason we closed down was because I was working with people who couldn't be trusted."

Then he remembered a name.

"Orson."

The massaging stopped. "What about Orson?"

"He retired early from the army recently. Orson is the most dependable relative I have. He's the most reliable person I know, family or otherwise."

"Do you want his advice?"

"I want him to keep the diamond for me. I can trust him. If we are desperate, or if we live to see Grace's wedding, he will give it back to us. But with him holding on to it, I won't be able to trade it in haste."

Joan brought a hand to her chin. "Orson is a distant relative, and older than us," she said. "He is here in Pennsylvania for part of the year. He spends more than half his time in North Carolina."

"Don't be-," William stopped as he felt a stinging pain in his side. It passed, and he continued. "Don't be a pessimist. We are talking about Orson."

"Okay, we can trust him. And he's the picture of health, at least he was the last time we saw him. And if he is okay with this, he'll make sure we have the diamond back when we need it. Even if. . ." She stopped and tried to hold back a shudder.

Even if neither of us makes it to Grace's wedding, William added in his mind.

"I will call Orson this evening," William said. He hugged his wife. "We will be okay. And so will Grace."

"She will grow into a wonderful woman, no matter what happens," she said.

"I know. But maybe we should go check on the girl she is today."

They walked to Grace's bedroom where she had several dolls on the floor. They were not strewn randomly on the floor, but lined up with two boy dolls and two girl dolls in the front.

"What are you doing?" William asked. "What's the occasion?"

Grace picked up the boy and girl dolls in the center. "It's their wedding!" She put them between the other two, standing in front of the other dolls. "He is the husband, and she is the bride. And their best friends are the Best Man and the Maid of Honor." Grace picked up the other two dolls. "Next, these two get married."

The entire scene, narrated by Grace's voice, broke William. He squeezed Grace and started bawling.

"What's wrong, daddy?" Grace asked, sounding confused.

"Nothing, Grace, nothing. Just remember, I will always love you, even if you can't see me."

Part I

The Love of Grace

Chapter 1

Blue. The word did no justice to Grace's eyes.

At least, that was what Adam thought.

Azure. Cobalt. Sapphire. None of these words, nor any other, quite captured the look of her eyes.

Over six years, Adam had looked into her eyes on every significant occasion. When they first met. Their first date. First kiss. First day of college. Graduation. Engagement.

And now becoming one.

"I do," Adam said, not having listened to the official, but in awe of how the woman standing in front of him would be his forever. That he would be hers forever. That all those moments had led to Adam having Grace in his life.

Grace. Just as blue did not capture the shade of her eyes, the name Grace did not ensnare her uniqueness. Her physical motions were always graceful, and her demeanor was as well. More than that, she had embodied grace to Adam from the beginning. Before they dated in high school, he had spilled dye on Grace's senior science report. After they dated for two years, he still blew off many of Grace's interests. Both times, and all the others, Grace always forgave him without effort.

Adam tried to emulate that forgiveness but knew he would never be able to pardon others so easily as Grace did naturally. He knew, in his heart, this was not a marriage between equals. Grace would truly be his better half.

He remained focused on her eyes, but her mouth finally moved as the official finished his questions.

"I do."

There were more words Adam never heard. He did not need to listen to know when the time was right. At the right moment, they tilted their heads towards each other and shared another countless kiss, but their first as husband and wife.

Adam could hear no one or anything else at the ceremony. Nothing else mattered, because now everything was different.

He and Grace finally belonged to each other.

* * *

Same eyes, but now, everything was different.

Adam and Grace were dancing, alone, in the center of the reception hall. No one cared if it was a simple place for their celebration, which it was. No one cared if Grace's gown, though radiant, was simple, which it was. No one cared if neither Adam nor Grace had learned how to dance formally, though they marginally could. Six years of anticipation had finally led to marriage, and that was the only truth Adam could think of as he looked into Grace's eyes.

Blue. One day, they would reach their fiftieth anniversary and Adam still would never figure out the perfect word for her eyes.

"What are you thinking?" Grace whispered.

"Too much to say," Adam whispered back. "But all of it good."

Grace smiled. "I'm thinking of how perfectly we fit."

It was true, physically they appeared to be designed for each other. Grace had chosen not to wear heels because she and Adam were the same height, a wisp over five-foot-

eight. Adam's hair was almost as blonde as Grace's, though
he kept his buzzed short while hers normally reached to her
shoulders. Right now, though, it was styled upwards for their
special day.

They were both in shape, enough so anyone could tell
they worked out, but not so much anyone mistook them for
models or professional athletes. No amount of exercise,
however, would cover for not knowing any dance moves, so
they swayed with each other to the deejay's music.

"I only have one wish," Adam said.

Grace raised her eyebrows. "Your father?"

Adam shook his head. He refused to think about him
now. "That I can make you this happy for our entire lives
together."

Grace smiled and kissed him. The kiss seemed to last
for hours, but it was only moments later when she
whispered, "We will have our ups and downs. But I know you
and I will share so much more than only an amazing
beginning."

They held each other in silence through the song.
When the second number played, their best man and maid
of honor also took the floor. Michael and Rylee had been the
obvious choices. They had been Adam and Grace's best
friends since all four of them had been freshmen at
Shippensburg University. It would be hard to imagine them
holding out against marrying each other for too much longer.

But we made it first, Adam thought.

Other couples glided onto the floor as more songs
played. Bridesmaids, groomsmen, and other guests. Most of
those in attendance were other Shippensburg grads and a
few from Annville-Cleona High School. Most of the school

buddies were acquaintances. Also, there was a co-worker of Adam's, Nate, and a co-worker of Grace's, Michelle.

Adam hardly cared that anyone else was there. The world belonged to Grace and him.

Later, as Grace and Adam slowly made their way off the dance floor, Adam noticed two particular guests had taken their place in the middle of the hall. His mother and step-father danced together. Actually, dancing better than Grace and Adam had, but he would not say it out loud.

Grace was looking at them, too. Adam took her hand again. "You okay?"

She nodded, but Adam was sure a tear was coming free. "I wish they were here."

Before Adam could comfort her, Rylee came running away from the dance floor to her. "No, no, no," she was saying. "I am not letting my best friend cry on her wedding day. Come on here." She started pulling Grace away.

"Even at my wedding, Rylee has to get in her girl talk," Grace called back as Rylee pulled her to where the single women had gathered.

"Especially at your wedding," Rylee called out.

The only thing that mattered to Adam was Grace was smiling again. The memories of the stroke that took her mother, and first dementia and then Alzheimer's taking her father, would return another day. No need to dwell on the past.

Also, no need to dwell on how Adam's father was not here. Not for the reason Grace believed. One day, he would have to tell the full story of his father to her, but a day long after this one.

Michael stepped up from behind Adam. "I hope you approved of my speech," he said, sipping his drink.

"Oh, yes," Adam said. "I kept waiting for the dreaded inappropriate story or offensive joke, but you controlled yourself."

"I might say something inappropriate when it's only the four of us, but Rylee is the one who will shout it in front of everyone." Michael gestured to the edge of the dance floor, where Grace, Rylee and the other bridesmaids huddled together. Rylee, who stood at least two inches taller than the others and was the only one with auburn hair, nodded her head and waved her arms. "See that? I don't know what she's talking about, but I can guarantee it's inappropriate."

All the women, Grace included, started laughing out loud, the joyous sound spreading through the whole reception hall.

"Maybe," Adam admitted. "But I still appreciate your restraint."

"Besides, I don't know if there were any inappropriate stories to tell about you. Or Grace. Four years at Shippensburg together, and I couldn't decide on anything that could embarrass you. Unless failing to make the college golf team is considered embarrassing."

"Grace kept me on the straight and narrow," Adam said.

"Yeah, about that," Michael said, looking around and lowering his tone. "Since no one can hear us, I have to ask an inappropriate question in private."

"Won't be your first. Go ahead."

"Tonight. Is it really going to be...the big night?"

18

Adam was sure Michael knew the answer. He was probably trying to make Adam's face red at his wedding reception without doing it during his speech, nothing more. Michael succeeded.

"Grace kept me on the straight and narrow," Adam repeated.

Michael patted him on the shoulder. "Yeah, I was pretty sure that was the case. No reason to be ashamed of it. Living that way helped you marry an amazing woman."

"Speaking of," Adam said, pointing to Grace, who had her back turned to the bridesmaids and the other unmarried women, holding her bouquet. "Let's see if you're going to be marrying your amazing woman."

"I doubt it."

Grace threw the bouquet without a glance at the other women. The women gave a fair effort to catch it, but there was none of the pushing and shoving that accompanied stories about these moments. Rylee, with her height advantage, put her fingers on it first, but then it slipped away for a moment. The flowers skittered on the hands of others who could not quite grab it before it rolled off of one bridesmaid's hands and back to Rylee.

"The die is cast, my friend," Adam said, putting his arm around Michael. "You and Rylee are next."

"Living with her for two years should prove my commitment enough," Michael said, shaking his head. "It appears Grace is coming back to claim you."

She walked over, the smile that had been there since the wedding ceremony began still brightening her face. Adam understood this high would not last forever. There would be challenges, money troubles, arguments and a hundred things he could not imagine now. But he did not care.

Now, all he wanted was to share everything with Grace.

"I'll leave you two alone," Michael said. "But not before I give you your wedding day advice."

Adam waited.

"Tonight will be awkward, but it will be wonderful."

"I kinda guessed that," Adam said as Michael wandered away. A moment later, Grace had pulled him back onto the dance floor.

There was a slow number playing. Grace and Adam swayed together, her head on his shoulder.

"Always us," Grace whispered. "Always us."

"Always us," Adam echoed.

* * *

Adam gazed into Grace's eyes one last time that night. Again, everything was different.

He stroked her flaxen hair, now unkempt, the ends reaching the bedsheets. She caressed his scruffy cheek, the one not on the pillow.

It had been awkward, but it had been wonderful.

Chapter 2

Adam and Grace sat in their seats at the round table, and Michael and Rylee sat across from them. Adam could have told them their meals during their honeymoon had been mostly seafood and suggested somewhere else. But he did not know when they would see their best friends again. So they made themselves comfortable at the seafood restaurant in the middle of Hershey. The food did not matter. Having one last meal together with Michael and Rylee before they flew back to Chicago did.

"So, did you have a good time while we were gone?" Grace asked after ordering her meal.

"Excellent," Rylee answered. "I was embarrassed to admit I had never been to the park, even after four years of college not too far away."

"Now she has one of those 'I survived' t-shirts," Michael said.

"Please tell me you were more courageous than getting on the old, looping roller coaster and calling it a day," Adam said. "It doesn't sound like you, Rylee."

"I rode on six coasters, thank you very much," Rylee said. "But don't be trying to shift the spotlight. We're not here to talk about what we did. I want to hear all about your honeymoon. And spare no details."

Adam hoped they would spare at least a few details. But Grace dove right into the subject.

"It was amazing. Virginia Beach is lovely, but not as crowded or crazy as other beaches I've been to, even in May. We walked along the shore every day and night, the weather was perfect and we ate like royalty."

"So, no honeymoon nightmare stories?" Rylee asked.

"None," Adam said, putting his arm around Grace. "It was as close to perfect as it could be."

"Well, I'll drink to that." Rylee started waving her hand, and a waiter came to the table carrying two bottles of wine. "Consider this one last wedding gift. I ordered it before you two arrived."

Grace put her hands up to her mouth in surprise. "Oh, you didn't need to do anything else." Then she read the labels. "Those are. . .never mind."

"Expensive?" Michael finished for her. "Yeah."

"But I get what I want," Rylee said.

"That is true," Michael confirmed.

"And I get what I want for myself and my friends. I'm thankful you had a great honeymoon, and one last gift is my way of wishing you a blessed marriage."

The waiter set the bottles on the table. One was red wine, the other white. Adam kept his mouth shut to be polite, but he and Grace did not drink white wine. Still, the way he moved his eyes must have given away his thoughts.

"Oh, sorry, buddy," Michael said, grabbing the white. "The red is the gift, the white is for us."

"You get what you want," Adam said with a grin, gesturing to Rylee.

"Exactly," Rylee answered as Michael opened their bottle.

Grace stood up from her seat and hugged Rylee. "Thank you so much. You've always done more than I could have asked."

"You always have, too," Rylee said. "Makes you wish the guys would keep up the pace."

Adam and Michael both spread their arms out in a questioning gesture, but Grace stood up for her man. "Leave my husband go in the first week of marriage." She turned to Adam. "I will tolerate laziness for another couple days."

That elicited laughs from the other side of the table, but Adam made his plaintive expression more exaggerated. Then Grace sat and leaned into him. "Seriously, guys, Adam has been working so hard at his job. He earned his first raise last month."

"So you work harder at the actual accounting firm than you did in your accounting classes?" Michael asked.

"I don't mean to contradict you, so I won't," Adam answered, sliding his arm around Grace's shoulders again. "Shippensburg did not see my best effort. But Ms. Douglas will."

Grace cleared her throat.

"And Grace will see my best effort, squared," Adam corrected with a smile. They kissed, just long enough to be slightly inappropriate in a public setting.

"Newlyweds," Michael said. "What are you going to do?"

Rylee leaned back in her chair. "You two seem destined for outstanding things. I just hope that Hotel and Restraint Management degree pays off for you, Grace. I don't want you at a front desk forever."

"I have bigger plans," Grace answered with a grin.

"I wish we could be around more," Rylee continued. "Especially if you move out of Grace's little apartment and need help to get a bigger home."

"There's plenty of time for that," Grace said. "It will be an adjustment, like everything now. But we will be content there, just the two of us. And it's not my place, it's our place now."

Adam was not sure he would have said that they will be content, but with their plans for future years, the apartment in Palmyra was their best option for now.

"But I wish you guys lived closer," Grace finished. "I guess life happens to all of us."

"Both of us getting job offers in Chicago after graduation?" Rylee asked rhetorically. "I think we both intended to stay in Pennsylvania." Michael nodded but let her continue. "But full-time employment so quickly for both of us was a temptation we couldn't resist. I already feel like that's where we belong."

"Speaking of cross-country travel, has your mother permanently moved down to Florida?" Michael asked.

Adam nodded. "I had hoped she would decide to spend only winters down there, and summers here, but my step-dad did not want to handle two properties. I don't blame them, but that means no family nearby." He hoped no one would bring up the whereabouts of his father, which might force him to lie, or the death of Grace's parents, which might force her to cry.

But their friends knew better than to touch either of those subjects on a joyful occasion. "Well, if you guys ever need us, our place isn't too far from O'Hare, just five minutes if you take the el."

"Whenever you can come back here, you are welcome," Grace said. She picked up the red wine bottle. "But in case that isn't for a while, we'll save this for our first anniversary. We'll always have a little of you guys around our home."

A waiter served their dinners, and the couples spent the next hour talking about everything that happened during the last week. Grace described each of the new swimsuits she wore at Virginia Beach. Adam talked about the aquarium they visited. Rylee mentioned she was closer to her goal of getting a new job that included international travel. Michael bragged he picked up tickets for both Chicago baseball teams in the next month.

"Please," Adam pleaded. "Don't start about that. I have a co-worker who is always talking about baseball. Can we talk about a different subject?"

"Well, you asked for it," Rylee said, setting her dessert fork down on her empty plate. She stared at Grace. "You're big on telling important things face-to-face when you can look into someone's eyes. You know what I'm going to ask."

Adam's eyes shifted back and forth between the two women. He was not sure what this was about. At first, it seemed Grace didn't either. But then she started laughing. "I'm shocked it took you this long to mention it."

Rylee chuckled. "I know I should be more discreet, but why bother? How's it feel to be in the club, finally?"

Adam was pretty sure he understood Rylee's meaning, but she was not being direct. Michael saved him from any more embarrassment by asking, "'The club?'"

Rylee turned to the men, and with a lower voice than before, explained, "Some nights, Grace would come back to the dorm late, after seeing Adam. I'd always ask. . ."

"If we were 'in the club' yet," Grace finished. "Well, I wasn't ashamed to say we weren't then, and I will not be ashamed to say now we are ecstatic to be full-fledged members." She put her arm back around and Adam and leaning into him.

Adam was not ashamed, though he was a little shocked the topic had sprung up now. But Michael and Rylee had talked about their sex life in front of them before, so he was not surprised this happened now.

"Oh, thank goodness," Rylee said. "After you waited so long I was worried for you, that you wouldn't be able to make that transition."

Adam could not decide if the more mature thing was to keep going with this conversation or to redirect it. He stumbled over the words, "It was kind of natural," before Michael cut in again.

"You don't have to say anything," Michael said. "Rylee has always been the nosier one of us. But some men and women like to talk about it. Goodness, you heard the two of us say very personal things back at Ship."

"Usually, one of you was drunk when that happened," Grace pointed out. "No, usually, both of you were drunk when you'd tell us the details we really didn't need to hear."

"True," Rylee admitted. "But I expected a couple of double-entrees to come up today, and when you didn't say anything suggestive, well, I didn't know what to think. We are your friends, and you can say anything around us. If you want to keep it quiet, I'll never bring it up–in your lives or ours–again. But if you're comfortable sharing those details we don't need to hear-"

"Rylee," Grace interrupted her. "Let me use an example from Adam's financial world. We will have a joint bank account. No surprise to anyone I said that, right? That's what wives and husbands do. But I wouldn't show anyone but Adam the details of our finances. That's personal. This is the same way. I'd never be ashamed to say we do what husbands and wives are supposed to do. But, even my best friends don't hear any more detail than that."

Adam felt his cheeks warm. He was not embarrassed he and Grace had waited for marriage, nor that they were enjoying each other after marriage. Grace was right that those statements alone were nothing that had to be hidden–marriage was for, among other things, physical intimacy. But it would take some getting used to when Grace said it out loud.

Rylee nodded, not offended by Grace's reluctance to give out any further details. The bridesmaid of their wedding took the white wine bottle and poured into the four glasses on the table. "I know you two don't drink white, but at least join us in this last toast to you before we fly out."

Each of them grabbed their glasses and raised them. "To your love," Rylee said. "To a love, which I know will endure everything."

They all drank, though Adam and Grace merely sipped. Then Michael added, "It will even endure friends who put their noses where they don't belong."

Rylee smacked his shoulder but laughed along with the others.

* * *

"Did I embarrass you?" Grace asked, now that Rylee and Michael had left for the airport and only she and Adam were at the table.

"A little, but I guess I'll adjust to it," Adam answered, draining his glass of the last of the white wine. It would never replace red. "At least you embarrassed me with the truth. And it was only our best friends who heard it. It's not as if they avoided saying private things to us over the years."

"Such as Michael's wedding day advice?"

"And plenty of other things, back in college," Adam answered. "Do you expect them to get married?"

"I don't know, but I hope they do. I think those two need each other. I know Rylee better, and I'd worry she'd make some rash decisions without Michael to make her slow down." Then Grace put on her mischievous smile. "And you should be glad I didn't tell her the one disappointing thing about our honeymoon."

Adam froze. The last discouraging words from Grace were from the wedding rehearsal, the mix of nerves and missing her parents leading to some sadness. This was the first he heard anything from her that their honeymoon had not been perfect.

She must have sensed his apprehension. "Fireplace?" she purred.

Adam sighed. "We agreed on that months ago. The places we could afford to take a week-long honeymoon..."

"Didn't have one in the room. I said I was disappointed. I didn't say it was your fault. But someday, on an anniversary or some other occasion...," she leaned forward and kissed him, gently and slowly, "you owe me a fireplace."

Chapter 3

Adam opened the sliding glass door to their first-floor apartment. He and Grace had just walked around their apartment complex in Palmyra. They had strolled the path several times when Grace lived alone, but this was the first time they had walked among the maples since their wedding.

"I suppose all good things do end," Adam said, arm around Grace and hand on her right shoulder.

"This is only the beginning," Grace answered, laying her head on his left shoulder.

After Adam closed the door, they walked into their living room. It was a compact space in a tiny apartment. There was a kitchen and a dining room next to the living room. Their modest bedroom was at the back of the apartment. They could enter or exit by the front door if they came through the complex's lobby, or they could go through the sliding door in the living room.

Adam kept trying not to tell himself it wasn't much–but it wasn't much. The home he had grown up in had not been much larger, but the living quarters here were cramped. Grace had lived in a much larger home, but it needed to be sold to pay her father's medical bills and other debts when he passed away a few years ago.

However, his disappointment right now had nothing to do with the size of their home. Being in close quarters with Grace had its advantages.

"I meant that the honeymoon is over now," Adam said. With his free hand, he pulled out his phone and set an alarm. "Work in the morning."

"For both of us," Grace said, sighing. "But we have a lifetime of adventures ahead."

There was knocking at the front door. Adam turned to answer it. "Expecting anyone?" Grace shook her head.

He opened the door and saw Brandi, their neighbor. "Oh, hi there, Adam. I take it Grace is in?"

Grace came up to the doorway. "Hi. How are you?"

"Oh, I'm fine," Brandi said, smiling. "I just got back from the shelter. It looks like you set this down in the lobby. Again."

She held out a phone in a pink case. Grace gave an exaggerated shrug of her shoulders and took it. "I'm glad I didn't misplace it while we were at the beach. That would have caused so many headaches. Thanks."

"No problem. And, I need to say again, I'm sorry I couldn't stay for the reception last week."

"It's perfectly fine," Grace said. "You do important work at the shelter. We completely understand."

Adam nodded. Brandi had been at the wedding and had also helped in the week leading up to the ceremony with moving Adam's belongings into Grace's apartment. Neither of them questioned her friendship or support.

"It's not exactly work," Brandi said. "I'm just a volunteer."

"No such thing as 'just' a volunteer," Grace said. "Whenever you need anything...,"

"I'm okay. Actually, I have to go for a second shift at the shelter. That's why I saw your phone, I was heading out now. I hope you had a great honeymoon. I'll see you soon."

As Brandi walked away, Adam shut the door. "It seems like she is at the shelter as much as she is at her job."

"I think she is," Grace said, walking into the living room and falling onto the sofa. "I hope I can be as dedicated to helping those in need as she is."

"You will be," Adam said. "And more inventive." He reached for the television remote.

"Don't you dare put golf on during the last hours of our honeymoon." Adam pulled his arm back. "Next weekend, it's free game again."

Adam turned to look at her, and Grace's eyes were welling up with tears. Adam knew why. It had almost burst out at their reception. There was too much joy during their honeymoon for sadness then.

Now, Grace realized she would enter this new phase of life with Adam, but without her parents to share her joy.

"You can let it out," Adam whispered.

Grace embraced him and sobbed for minutes. "They should have been here. They should have lived longer," she said when the fit had ended.

Adam only nodded. Six years of dating had taught him when no words were enough.

Now composed, Grace stood. "Tonight will be a night for sleep, you know. Only sleep."

"I understand. I'm realistic, mostly."

Grace laughed. "Could you make me my tea?" she asked as she walked back into the bedroom.

Adam walked into the kitchen and looked in the tea basket to find fifteen flavors. "What kind?"

"You don't know what flavor my bedtime tea is?"

"A side effect of you keeping me on the straight and narrow all those years."

Grace burst out in hysterical laughter. "Lemon chamomile. With half a teaspoon of honey."

After pouring Grace's drink, he took it back to her in the bedroom. She had already changed into her sleep outfit. Adam set the hot drink on the nightstand on her side of the bed and changed as well.

"What did you say a bit ago? About how all good things end?" Grace said.

Adam nodded. "What about it? I didn't mean that married life wouldn't be good."

"I know what you meant. It's just, it made me remember something my mother said to me. She told me, whenever and whoever I married, we would need to be sure we had the marriage routine down."

"Marriage routine?"

"Understanding the details of what it will be like to be together every day. Making sure we are ready to attend to each other's needs, no matter what else is happening in life. Not to let other goals, even wonderful ones, interfere."

"We won't. Or, if I do, let me know. Say it to my face. I'll try to keep my work in perspective."

"And golf."

"You know you like it when I put it on television. One day I will buy a full set of clubs and be a country club member."

Grace smiled and shook her head, making her golden hair bounce. "Before we both go back to the real world, tonight is the time to say it out loud."

"Say what out loud?"

"Some of our dreams will wait. The other dreams. The bed-and-breakfast for lower-income couples? I want to make that happen. I want to help people who are struggling to have that romantic trip they don't always have the opportunity to take."

"And I'll help you, every step of the way."

"I will need your help with understanding and managing the finances to make that possible. But it has to wait, other than saving some seed money for the future. I guess we have to be on board with that."

Ah, the other reason we are in a small apartment, Adam thought. But he let Grace continue.

"But it cannot be the focus of our lives right now. We need to make sure we work together. We connect. It won't be the same as dating or getting engaged. The business goals wait until we know we have our marriage clicking."

"I agree. We wait on that until our marriage is perfect."

Grace tapped him on the shoulder. "Now you're being unrealistic." She giggled and sat down on the bed, her blond hair bouncing on her shoulders. She began sipping her tea. "The same thing goes for the jewels."

Adam laid down next to her. "Do you at least want to tell me more about them?"

Grace sipped more, then took a deep breath. "Not yet. I'm sorry, I know I shouldn't be shutting you out about them. But I don't want us to be distracted. And any time I think about them it makes me miss dad even more."

"But finding them is still important to you?"

"Not as important as making our marriage rock-solid," Grace said. "But, yes. Dad crafted them for me. He's gone now. It is important to me to hold them, to remember him by."

"Then we will find them. Every one."

"We will," Grace nodded. She kissed him. "But later."

Adam turned out the lights and as Grace had said, tonight was meant for sleeping. Guessing that meant the honeymoon was officially over, Adam laid next to Grace, slipping his arms around her as she slept.

He did not sleep at first and pondered many things. Adam wondered what challenges married life would have, apart from balancing the home budget, the one thing he knew he possessed a gift for doing. He wondered if Grace's car, as old as his, would start in the morning after sitting motionless since before their wedding. He wondered how hard it would be to work at the accounting office tomorrow, where his financial mind would be at ease, but his heart would long for Grace.

Adam even wondered if he would ever persuade Grace to enjoy golf, at least a little.

But what Adam thought of most was how Grace was still hiding the details about the jewels her father had cut for her. Even after six years, he knew only a few facts. He wanted to know the complete story behind them, not because he hoped for wealth, but because they were important to Grace.

He could not blame Grace for still keeping a few secrets, though. Adam was still keeping a secret from her about his father.

Chapter 4

Adam scanned his security badge and walked in the back door to the accounting office. He had startled himself at how early he woke, and now he was five minutes early to work.

He was also surprised at how hard it was for him and Grace to part that morning as he drove here and she drove to the Spartan Hotel, both businesses located in Hershey. Something in the back of his mind reminded him they were still young lovers. One day this would be routine. Adam was not sure if that was a wonderful or horrible truth.

When he spotted his work station, Adam was sure his dozen co-workers were having fun at his expense. Two silver balloons were floating over his desk, and paper covering his computer screen. Adam took his chair and saw "Congratulations!" written in large, black letters on the paper, with fancy designs drawn around the word.

Adam pulled the paper away, only to be greeted with another one. "Welcome back!"

Removing that message received a third one. "Now do some work!"

Adam spun his chair around, and called out to the other accountants, "Who did this?"

Two hands raised, and Adam realized he should have guessed. Nate and Tessa, the two who knew him best, walked over from the opposite side of the office to him. "I only picked up the balloons," Nate said. "She's responsible for the messages."

"Aww, you didn't look at them all," Tessa said as she strode up to Adam. She pulled the paper off to show the last message, in smaller letters than the others, "Seriously, we're excited for you, but we're drowning in here."

Tessa pulled that sign off as well, revealing Adam's blank computer screen. He booted up his machine but noticed something as he waited to log into the system. "Those real tattoos?"

She turned so Adam had a better view of the ink on her right bicep. There was a dollar sign there, matching the mark on her other arm. "Everyone else saw them last week. I figure that's what we're here to work with and for."

"I find any tattoos to be a little unsettling," Nate said. "I keep picturing a needle scraping and scratching at my bones."

"That's not how it works," Tessa said. "And you don't seem to mind getting hit in the head by a baseball."

"Don't give him any reason to tell another story," Adam warned as he typed in his password. "I've only been here five minutes. I'm not ready for that yet."

"We heard them all week."

"I still had quite an audience here," Nate said. "Even with you away, the stories don't stop."

"You could find something other than your one great season to talk about," Adam said, opening his first case file for the day.

Someone cleared her throat. There was no reason for Adam to turn. He had heard Ms. Douglas enough to know when a reprimand was coming.

"Nate, Tessa, I see the new husband is back at his station on time," she said from the door to her separate office, in the corner closest to Adam's desk.

Both Tessa and Nate whispered, "good to have you back," to Adam before walking back to their desks. Adam gave them a silent nod and focused on his screen.

Ms. Douglas walked over to him. "I hope you had a wonderful honeymoon."

Adam nodded. He had worked for Ms. Douglas for over a year, but still was cautious about what he said around her.

"I'm happy for you. But Tessa's messages to you were correct. We actually are drowning here. It's excellent news. We picked up two more contracts while you were out. But more businesses outsourcing to us means less chatter time for us here."

Adam did not remember Ms. Douglas ever allowing much chatter during work hours. She was not mean, but determined. She expected the same determination from everyone in the office.

"It's quite a load for a dozen accountants to keep up with," she said. "So you need to be focused all day. Now, hopefully, that means fewer sports stories from Nate."

"Good," Adam said. "More business and less baseball should make things better in the long run. We aren't going to be forced into overtime, are we?"

"I don't plan on it. You still leave here at four every day until I say otherwise. Now, chop-chop."

Adam focused on the cases in front of him for most of the day. He found the work comforting. It was more than his natural comfort with mathematics and finances. It was a reminder some things would continue, even through married life. The truth was, Adam was nervous over what Grace had said the night before, that they need to adjust to life as a married couple. There would be changes, large and small.

The numbers in the office did not change. This would be one area of consistency. The office could never be as comforting a place as home, but there was always a certain sense of belonging here.

Near the end of the day, Adam's phone buzzed. He saw a text message from Grace. She had to stay at the hotel later than usual.

He looked up, deciding if he should head home or somewhere else when Nate passed by his desk.

"I'm out for the day," Nate said. "Are we still on for Thursdays, or does Grace not want you hanging with the guys anymore?"

"You're the only guy I hang with unless you've started inviting more people along for lunch."

Nate shook his head. "It was only me last Thursday. The barista started making a cold brew for you out of habit."

"I'll be there this Thursday. I'll tell you stories about our honeymoon."

Nate raised an eyebrow.

"Clean ones."

Nate laughed as he walked out, but Tessa came up right behind him. As Adam shut down his computer, she stared at him, hands on her hips.

Adam stood, gave her a questioning glance, and grabbed his jacket off a hanger.

"You didn't notice either, did you?" Tessa asked.

"What?"

"Everyone says something about my tattoos. No one comments on my hair."

Only then did it register with Adam. Her black hair was now cut back to ears. "I'm sorry. It looks nice."

Tessa smiled and waved a hand. "I'm kidding. Well, not about how guys don't notice."

"Please tell me I'm still on the free food list."

"Everyone always is," Tessa said. "I plan on bringing in doughnut holes tomorrow."

"You know, most of us here are willing to chip in on your little snack runs. You're always getting stuff for everyone."

Tessa might have blushed, but Adam could not tell. "Don't worry over it. By the way, will we be seeing Grace around here again anytime soon? I'd like to congratulate her, too."

"I doubt it. Her shift at the hotel changed months ago. Usually, if we aren't heading home, I have to go to her after I'm done here. Not the other way around anymore."

"Give her my best," Tessa said as she turned to the exit. "I don't get to see Grace often, but I always look forward to the times I do."

When she walked out, Adam stopped thinking of his work, co-workers, or boss for even a moment.

Adam could not wait for his new bride to come home. Meeting up with her sounded like a magnificent idea.

* * *

Adam stepped through the sliding doors at the front of the Spartan Hotel. As he often did, the mixture of happiness and jealousy hit him harder than the air conditioning in the entryway. He valued how Grace worked in a five-star hotel, since this was the industry she hoped to work in later in life, too. But he also knew many of the rooms here were bigger and nicer than their apartment.

He walked to the desk and saw a youthful woman working behind it, but the brunette with curly hair scrunched atop her head was not Grace. Michelle looked up from a computer screen. "Hello, welcome to... Sorry, Adam, I didn't realize it was you. I'll try to track her down."

Michelle looked around for a second, probably to see if anyone else was near to the check-in desk, and walked away. There were a handful of guests around, most of them wearing clothes from the nearby amusement park, but no other employees of the hotel visible.

"Hey, Grace, there's some guy with a scruffy beard out here for you!" she called out as she walked toward the hotel's restaurant and disappeared.

Adam only knew a little about Michelle, and what he did came from Grace. But Michelle's work ethic impressed Grace, as did her willingness to listen to any of her problems, and so Grace had invited her to the wedding. Grace's approval was the only thing Adam needed to trust someone.

Moments later, Grace and Michelle came back. "I texted you," Grace said. "I had to fill in on the restaurant cash register for an hour."

"I know," Adam said. "I thought I'd catch you here. Maybe we could go somewhere now that you're done."

Grace shook her head. "No, today was a little hard. Getting back into the work routine, you know. I'd rather drive back home and relax tonight."

"Hey!" a voice boomed from somewhere behind the front counter. "They ain't kissing with her in uniform, are they?"

"No," Michelle called back.

"But she is away from her post during work hours!"

"Actually, my real shift ended an hour ago, and my spur-of-the-moment-shift ended two minutes ago," Grace said. "And my real post is supposed to be the front desk, anyway."

Adam turned around but could not spot to whom they were talking.

"Who are you speaking to?" Adam whispered to Grace.

"My boss. His office is back there," she explained, jerking her head towards a hallway behind the front desk.

"And he just shouts like that? Where customers would hear him?"

"Look around."

Adam glanced around. The tourists were no longer present, only Michelle, Grace and himself.

"He has a monitor in his office. Calls out to us when no one is near the front desk."

"Well, okay, but can you talk to him like that? Mouthing off about what your real post is?"

"If we do what we are asked to do, he's fine with it," Grace said. "He understands we have to vent sometimes."

"I would never talk to Ms. Douglas that way. Especially if customers were within earshot."

"Are they whispering sweet nothings to each other?" the voice boomed again. "Tell them they need to be quieter for me not to notice."

Michelle started laughing. "I bet they're telling each other you should have let them reserve the honeymoon suite for free."

"It was already booked!"

"When we're not busy, this goes on all day," Grace said. "He thinks it makes him mysterious, but I think it just makes him our hotel's comic relief. C'mon, let's go home."

They said goodbye to Michelle and walked out together. "You sure you want to go home?" Adam asked.

"We have to adjust to real life, honey."

"I know. I'm just trying to avoid making dinner. I don't want to cook."

"I'm sure you don't, and I'm sure don't want to eat it." Grace smirked. "Small steps. We'll microwave something tonight."

Adam walked with Grace away from his car but over to hers, parked behind the hotel. "Did you want to use the Honeymoon Suite here?" he asked as he slipped his hand inside hers. "I didn't expect you wanted to go right back to where you worked after our wedding, and I don't remember you mentioning it."

"Once we picked our wedding date, I checked on it. Somebody had booked the suite more than a month earlier. I didn't think there was any reason to mention it."

"But you were happy to go to Virginia Beach, right?"

"I loved every minute of our honeymoon," Grace said, reassuring Adam with her tone and the kiss that followed. "It's not as if we went to a dumpy motel, like that less-than-savory place south of town. But I will admit, the suite has one special thing that our hotel room, and our apartment, didn't."

She looked at him with a determined stare that told Adam he should be able to figure out what the missing item was. It took him three seconds, which he hoped was quick enough.

"A fireplace."

Grace gave a coy smile. "I promise I won't keep throwing it in your face, but you do owe me something. On the other hand, I shouldn't be greedy. Do I owe anything to you?"

"Not exactly like that."

"I meant 'anything' literally."

"A full set of golf clubs. And a membership at a course."

"'Any-thing', honey. One."

Adam's face fell. Had he asked her for too much?

Grace laughed. "Oh, I hope no one saw that." She kissed him on both cheeks and his mouth. "I'd never be that angry with you. One day you'll get to punch the ground."

"Hit the links," Adam corrected.

"But these dreams, including the bed-and-breakfast and the jewels, will have to wait. We both have to be patient."

"Can we not be patient about heading home? I'm feeling awkward talking through these things out here."

"Okay. I'll see you at home." Grace opened her car door, but before she entered, she called back, "Just remember. We have our entire lives to live out our dreams."

Chapter 5

Grace's hair laid over Adam's left shoulder and flowed down his arm. She had not trimmed it since long before the wedding, so it hung nearly to her waist when she was standing, exactly the way Adam liked it.

She was not standing now, though. Grace rested her head on Adam, arms around him, on the living room sofa. He held her around her waist. It was an almost perfect position, one they had taken countless times since dating: half embraced, half watching golf on television.

The golfer on the screen took his stance over the ball, eyeing a putt for an eagle on the seventeenth hole in day three of this four-day tournament. To Adam, it was drama. To Grace, it was an opportunity to nap on her husband's shoulder.

Adam would not have it any other way.

The golfer tapped the ball, and, since he had already known the lay of the greens, angled it to the left. It arced to the right and fell into the hole.

"I never figured out how to do that quite right," Adam said.

"I wish I had seen you play in high school," Grace mumbled. "Maybe I'd understand this sport better."

It was only a fifty-fifty proposition Grace would fall asleep during a golf show, and it seemed this might be one day where she stayed half-awake. "You should have asked me out a month sooner," Adam said. "By the time we were together, I had to sell my clubs to make sure I had enough money for college. Well, enough for college without too overwhelming of a loan." Curse those payments, he thought.

"There seems to be a theme about selling things that are important to us in our family," Grace said. Adam assumed she was referring to the gemstones her father had crafted, but he did not want to change the subject. So far, that topic was still avoided.

"I'm not sure what you find so confusing," Adam said instead. "I mean, I can see how understanding what club to pick for each type of shot you are taking is a little difficult for an outsider. The game itself is straight forward. Put the ball in the hole in fewer strokes than the other guys. Or girls, depending on who's playing."

"That's not what I mean," Grace said, lifting her head from his shoulder, her hair rippling back behind her shoulder. "I've dozed off to enough of your golf shows to understand that much. I mean, why?"

"Why what? Why do basketball players keep dunking the ball over and over? It's what the game is."

"But going through it alone seems unnatural."

"It's an individual sport, honey."

"Then that's why it's not for me," Grace said, laying her head back on Adam's shoulder, hair again draping over him. "I think as much of our lives as possible should happen in unison, in community, in relationships. Even in teams, if you're talking about sports. Not that I have any sport I am particularly excited about. Speaking of, how many times did Nate try to tell you old baseball stories this week?"

"Four," Adam said. "Two of them about games from that summer when his team was so outstanding. One was focused on a celebration they had after they won one of their tournaments. The other was about what his team was learning off the field that year from that life coach they met."

"See? That's what I'm talking about," Grace said. "The athlete who competes alone won't have those group experiences. I think I'd find the team aspect of a sport much easier to connect to than a solo effort. I couldn't imagine working alone in a job. I'm much happier with Michelle there, and even my loud-mouthed boss." She squeezed Adam gently. "And I'm much happier with you here than when I was living in this apartment alone."

Adam squeezed back. "And I'm much happier here than in my old place. But for life all around, we face those moments alone. Like the golfers do." He gestured to the television with his free hand. "Look at him, about to tee off on number eighteen." A different golfer hit the ball, driving it over three hundred yards, but well to the right of the fairway. "Sometimes in life, you're almost in the right place, but to arrive where you need to be, you face the challenges on your own. Only he can put himself back onto the green and save par. Sometimes, only you can place yourself where you belong."

Grace snuggled and pressed in on him. "If that's what you need to tell yourself. Truth is, you and I both need each other for everything, and you know it. We'd both fall apart if we were away from each other for a week. Even a shorter time, and we'd be a mess."

Adam did not argue. She was probably right. Grace usually was.

"And that's why you need to find a better sport for my nap time."

Adam could not let that statement go. He stood, almost making Grace fall into the sofa. "That's it. We're going."

Grace snapped back to full alertness. "Where?"

"To Lebanon. I'll show you golf is the best sport in the world. And part of what makes it the best is you're on your own."

* * *

"Focus. Keep your swing straight. It's better to hit it too light than too hard."

Grace looked up from her putter and her yellow ball. "I realize I don't know much about this sport, but I'm pretty sure the strategy is different when a pirate is standing between me and the hole."

Adam laughed. "Okay, then whack it off of the starboard bow."

Grace did exactly that, and the ball ricocheted off of the faux wood and rolled within a foot of the hole.

"See? That's a solid stroke for someone who hasn't been on a mini-golf course since junior high."

Adam lined himself up for his second shot on the eighth hole, the one after the cannon but before the helm on the pirate-themed golf course in Lebanon. The sun was setting, but this mini-golf course was lighted, and only a fifteen-minute drive from their apartment. Adam had decided Grace could never understand why he loved this sport so much unless she picked up the clubs herself.

If one considered mini-golf the same sport as golf, he corrected himself. Carrying one putter around thirty yards from a highway was not the same as carrying a full golf bag on a well-manicured course, but it would have to do.

"Now, this is a twenty-three-foot putt," Adam said. "Like you saw on television this afternoon."

"Actually, I don't remember any of that," Grace said, her long hair now scrunched up into a bun. "But again, I'm sure there wasn't a pirate in the way then."

"From my angle, I can putt between his feet for a straight-on shot," Adam said. He steadied his hands and pushed the ball from the center of his putter. His purple ball rolled between the pirate's feet, but nicked the left heel, causing it to veer wide of the hole by three feet.

"Looks like you're still a while away from the professional tour," Grace teased.

"But you are having fun," Adam pointed out.

"Of course. We're playing together."

"Yes, but we are playing against each other."

"No, we're not," Grace said, lining up her next putt.

"Yes, we are. When you play golf, you try to take fewer strokes than the other player. Even if it's a friendly competition, it's a competition. Every player for himself. Herself. You know what I mean."

"I know what you mean," Grace said, setting her putter next to the yellow ball. "But you're wrong."

"How?"

"Look at our scorecard."

The scorecard. Adam had picked it up when they paid and picked the putters. But he had forgotten it almost right away. Neither one of them had been keeping score.

As he realized this, Grace took her swing and hit the ball much too hard. It hit the cup, but spun out and rolled farther away than it had been when it started.

"Just as well no one is recording this," Grace said with a shrug. "But admit it. Golf, life, whatever—everything is experienced better together."

Adam walked over, not willing to argue any further but not willing to admit he had lost, at least this time. "Here, let me help you." He helped Grace to square up over her ball, holding her from behind and putting his hands over hers to grip the club. "A gentle force," he whispered into her ear.

"Is there anyone playing behind us?" Grace asked before the swing.

"No."

She turned her head to him and kissed him. And kept on kissing him. Adam felt their hands move, but more than that he sensed something where their skin met, like a fire that had no connection to the June air. He did not expect simple kisses to still carry so much passion after marriage, but Grace always provided warmth no matter what they were doing.

When their embrace ended, Grace kept her eyes on him. "Missed by a long shot, didn't we?" She asked.

"Bounced out of bounds," Adam confirmed. "But I don't think we missed at all." Glancing to make sure no one was approaching this hole, they kissed again. "I think we play well together."

Chapter 6

Thursdays used to be the worst day of the workweek, Adam decided. Monday was not as stressful as others made it sound like, because he felt refreshed by the time he turned on his computer that morning. On Friday, he anticipated an evening and two days with which he and Grace could do anything they wished.

But the days between were a slow descent from energized and engaged to drained and bored, bottoming out on Thursday. That is why, soon after Adam had been hired and connected with a few of his coworkers, he and Nate decided Thursdays should be a guys' lunch day. No one else joined them, but Adam and Nate would walk to a cafe two blocks from the office and spend the hour drinking coffee and talking.

Often, they talked about issues at work. Sometimes they talked about trucks neither of them could afford. Sometimes, Adam talked about golf courses he still hoped to play on, especially the Country Club in Lebanon, which was the only private course in the county. Many times, Nate brought up the baseball season he found so memorable.

Today, for example.

"When Pete scored on John's bunt, we all knew we had the game wrapped up," Nate said as they finished their sandwiches. "We had several other games we won later on, but that regional title was the last championship we would win. I'm grateful we finished on top there. If we had let the region slip away, I don't think anyone would have walked away from that summer satisfied."

Adam grabbed his half-finished cold brew, tossed his trash into the bin and walked out with Nate. He always tolerated the baseball stories. Some were more interesting than others, even if the sport itself was dull to him. Adam would take eighteen tee shots over nine innings any day.

But it was important to Nate, and Nate listened to Adam's golf stories. Give and take. Of course, Adam did not include magical characters in his golf tales.

"And this life coach of yours, he predicted what would happen in all these games?" Adam asked as they walked down Chocolate Avenue. He wanted to give Nate a chance to redeem himself.

"Oh, yes," Nate said, ruining his opportunity. "I guess he didn't tell us every play, but he knew everything we had to do to win each game. He predicted all the winners in each tournament game, not only the games we played. Those bunts I told you about? He even mentioned them two games before they happened."

"Hmmm," Adam said, sipping on his drink to avoid pointing out how ridiculous it was. Predicting several games correctly? Possible. Individual moments in the game? Over the top.

"That's not why we were so attached to Jonas, though," Nate continued. "He made us see life differently. I'm not sure where I'd be now if he hadn't helped me see the errors in my ways back then."

"He sounds unbelievable," Adam said as he walked up to the front door of the office and swiped his ID. He wondered if Nate picked up on the literal meaning of the word. "Out of curiosity, and against my better judgment, I want to ask what you did in these stories."

"I was on the winning team. That was the only thing that mattered, on the field, anyway."

"But do any of your baseball stories include you making a big catch in right field?"

Nate walked into the office with him but hesitated as Adam asked his question.

"You played in right field, correct?" Adam asked, wondering if was mixing up baseball terminology and positions.

"Yes," Nate said, his eyes losing their focus. "Actually, in a way, I made what I thought was a big catch that season. Now, looking back, it was nothing to brag about."

"Maybe a baseball fan would understand what you mean. A little too vague for me."

"It's a story for another time," Nate said. "I'll see you after work."

They walked to their work stations. As Adam worked through the various accounts, spreadsheets and files, he kept thinking of Nate's words. Not the odd response to making a big catch, but what he said about his baseball team winning the regional championship.

"We took advantage of that opportunity when we had the chance."

Adam mulled over those words. He could not care less about a chance to win a sports title. Those are forgotten in a moment. But what if he and Grace were allowing an opportunity to pass?

They had been married only six months, but each day that passed might make finding the jewels that should have belonged to her more difficult.

Adam had remained silent over it since the end of their honeymoon. They were Grace's jewels, so he meant to let her decide when to begin looking for the gemstones. After speaking with Nate, he wondered if now was the time for action.

Tonight, it was time to find out.

* * *

Grace had been home long before Adam opened the door. A traffic jam had held him up on the western edge of town, between Palmyra and Hershey. Cooked carrot, broccoli and cauliflower scents reached him the moment he stepped into the apartment.

"I'm trying a new dinner, hope you enjoy it," Grace called over from the kitchen.

Adam walked to her. She was out of her work clothes and now in a t-shirt and shorts, stirring her vegetable mixture on the stove with a wooden spoon. Adam placed a hand on her shoulder and glanced in the pot. Besides the ones he could smell, there were vegetables in the pan he did not recognize.

"Yeah, it looks horrible," Grace admitted. "But it's healthy, and we've been microwaving too much stuff. We both need to try cooking more."

"More?"

"Okay, in your case, at all," Grace said, lifting some food out with the spoon for Adam to sample. He hesitated but took it.

"It's a solid mix. Don't care for the zucchini, though."

"Live with it tonight," Grace said, turning off the burner. She looked at him in silence for a few seconds.

"What?" Adam asked.

"Something's distracting you. No hug, no kiss. No, 'Hi, honey, how was work?'"

"Sorry."

"No, I'm not upset, but I want to know what's on your mind. We both still need to work on opening up more ."

Adam pulled two bowls from the cupboard and explained himself. "I've been thinking about some long-term things."

"Here or at work?"

"Mostly here. I've been wondering, when are you going to be ready to start going after the jewels?"

Grace served the food onto the dishes while shaking her head. "Maybe soon, but not quite yet."

"How about telling me more of what you know about them? The things your father told you."

They walked to the dining table and sat. "Again, not yet. It's not that I don't trust you. We need to focus on other priorities first before we look for my father's jewels."

"Your jewels. You said they were supposed to be a wedding gift for you," Adam said, taking a forkful of the meal. "What priorities? The bed-and-breakfast? It will be years before we have the seed money and the credit scores to receive a decent loan..."

"Not that," Grace said. "I told you before, that waits, too. I mean us. Our relationship. We still need to work on it."

"We have been. We haven't had any fights. Unless... are you upset about something?"

"No," she answered after consuming a carrot. "Though I admit, I'm not thrilled with this meal. But you have to realize, things between us need to be different now. Better, but different."

"Why?"

"We are still adjusting to being married. We both still want to eat fast food every time we are together, stay up late, and do everything as if we were still in college. We've gotten better in the last few months, but we have to shift some things in how we live."

"I can learn how to cook and look for the jewels at the same time."

"Yes, but I need to know you will remember the jewels will never be as important the bond between us. The bed-and-breakfast will never be as important as you and me being one."

"I know that."

"But it's such a simple thing to forget. Before I tell you everything I know about the jewels, you need to understand marriage was not the last item to check off the list of our relationship. It was a commitment for both of us to always place each other first, no matter what other goals we chase."

Adam leaned back in his chair and thought while Grace pecked at her food. "Are you saying I'm not mature enough to do both?"

"Never," Grace said. "But I don't think anyone adjusts to married life that quickly. I haven't. We both want to be open. but be honest: you and I still haven't allowed ourselves to be vulnerable. There are things we aren't willing to say, even to each other. Growth in a marriage requires sharing everything, even if it scares us to be that honest."

Adam remembered his father, everything he had told Grace about him, and everything he had not. But she was still speaking.

"I'm not ready to take on these other goals yet either. We're close to it, but I don't want us to burden ourselves with those dreams until we know our most important dream is secure."

Adam nodded. "I believe we are ready. But, if you think we need more time, I accept that." Then he gestured to his plate. "But I don't know if I can accept this."

"I know," Grace said, pushing her plate back. "I guess you can't mix every vegetable into a hodgepodge." She sighed. "Burgers?"

Adam nodded and smiled. "Burgers."

Grace slid out of her seat and onto Adam's lap. She caressed his face and kissed him. "One day, you will put the five gems around my neck. One day, we will run a bed-and-breakfast that gives relief to struggling couples. But what we have right here will always be most important to me."

"It always will be to me, too," Adam said, kissing her in return.

After more embracing, Grace whispered, "Honey, dinner can wait."

Chapter 7

The scent of popcorn in a movie theater lobby. One of life's simple pleasures.

Date nights were few and far between so far in Adam and Grace's marriage. Well, ones that cost money were rare. A picnic at Lebanon's Memorial Lake or a walk at Harrisburg's Wildwood were common, and enjoyable when the weather was nice. But they were also free, and sometimes Adam became jealous of couples who could go out for dinner and a movie on a whim.

He and Grace could go out more than they did, Adam admitted to himself, but so far they had stayed true to their goal of saving money for future endeavors while still paying the rent and Adam's college loan. Grace would soothe him with, "delayed gratification," when he worried over their humble lifestyle.

But Grace did not live to be all work and no play, and tonight became a play night. After their Friday work shifts, they ate leftovers at home. But following that, it was a night out at the multiplex on the opposite end of Palmyra.

To his left, Grace breathed in the delicious air. "Brings back a lot of memories, huh?"

Adam nodded. "I think there were weekends our junior year where popcorn was the only thing we ate."

"With butter dripping everywhere," Grace added. "And a box of chocolate raisins for each of us. You miss those movie dates, don't you?"

"Well, we're here now."

"I know your code for 'yes, but I don't want to argue about spending money.' Don't worry. Give it time and we'll be able to do this more often. I have to stop at the ladies' room. Would you buy our tickets?"

Adam walked over to the ticket counter, hoping Grace was right about being able to enjoy life more. Yes, they were saving money. But operating a bed-and-breakfast would be an enormous burden, both on their schedule and their finances. If Grace ever opened up about the jewels which had belonged to her father, trying to find them could be an expensive adventure as well.

Life's joys were not only about how much money they spent, but Adam sometimes wondered if they would ever have the choice.

His thoughts were cut off the same moment he was cut off by four teenage girls rushing by him to jump in line. They talked over each other, even while ordering their tickets. None of them even seemed to see Adam had been standing in line in front of them. He suppressed a giggle when he noticed each of the girls had their hair dyed a bright color–blue, pink, platinum and orange. Nothing wrong with that, he reminded himself, but they looked like a box of crayons.

It made Adam appreciate how much confidence Grace held in her appearance. She rarely used makeup, and only in modest amounts when she did. And she never dyed her golden hair.

The girls took their tickets and snacks and strode down the hallway leading to the individual screens. At last, Adam made it to the cash register and ordered two tickets to the romantic movie showing that evening, along with a large popcorn and soda. He was hungry and would have considered eating the whole popcorn himself, but both the food and drink would be split between him and Grace. Adam was ready to pay for everything when Grace called out behind him.

"Wait, don't tap your card yet," she said, hurrying over to him. When she made it to the register, she added, "Add six tickets for the movie in theater...," she scanned the board. "Three. Six tickets, theater three. Four of them for children."

"What are you...," Adam started, but Grace never stopped speaking.

"Add on a couple large of popcorns, too. Now pay for it, honey."

Adam looked around himself to figure out what was going on, and when he spotted two adults and four children together, he had his answer.

He did not want to argue in the lobby, so Adam felt cornered into paying the bill that was three-quarters for someone else. But he needed to talk to Grace later.

Adam grabbed the tickets and snacks that were for Grace and him, while she took the items for the other family. They walked over, and Adam saw the mother of the family was almost in tears.

"Thank you," she said. "Kids, everyone, say thank you to our new friend."

"Grace. My name is Grace."

The children, none of whom appeared to be ten years old, echoed their mother's gratitude, if somewhat robotically. But they were quick to run down the hallway a moment later to the theater showing a family movie.

Adam carried the empty cup to the soda machine, filling it with cola and using the time as an excuse to figure out how he wanted to speak to Grace now. They still had not had a big argument, only forgotten little snips that ended with self-depreciating humor and kisses, but he knew money was one thing that could lead to those nasty fights.

Grace made it easier for him. "You're upset with me. Or at least confused."

Adam nodded as he capped the soda, and they walked down the hallway to their theater. "I thought we agreed about saving money. Deferred gratification and all that."

"We are. We live simply now so we can pursue our goals in the years ahead."

"So, buying those extra tickets for strangers was, what?"

"It was helping the same people I mean to help with the bed-and-breakfast someday," Grace answered as they reached the door for their theater. "That mom and dad told their kids they had to leave without seeing their movie because they misunderstood how high the prices were. They thought the matinee prices were good now."

"That's not your fault."

"No, but a difference of two dollars a ticket made the difference between having a night out with their kids or going home. How could I do nothing? How could I say I want to help a couple like them have a romantic weekend someday later if I didn't help them out when they were right in front of me?"

Adam was about to answer but stopped himself. A voice spoke in his mind.

Trust her. People are more important than the money she spent.

Sometimes his conscience agitated Adam, but often it was because his conscience agreed with Grace. Her goals with her business plans were altruistic. If her goal was not to make money for herself but to help struggling couples have a romantic vacation, then Grace's actions made complete sense.

"I'm sorry," Adam said. "I know why you do that. But we can't make a habit out of putting money in strangers' hands."

"I understand. And I also understand you probably would have rather gone out for dinner than having random leftovers in the crock-pot."

"Actually, the carrots came out nicely."

Grace smiled. "I know it will be a challenge, trying to save money for big goals, have a little fun together now, and help others when we have the chance."

"And don't forget the other challenge, one that will be expensive."

"How could I?" Grace winked. "We'll figure it out how to make it work. But now, we're here and the movie starts in a few minutes. Let's enjoy the moment and worry about everything else later."

Adam nodded, kissed her, and then they walked into the theater arm-in-arm. The screen was still showing the repeating commercials which ran before the trailers began. They found their seats and started munching on the popcorn.

"Honey?" Adam whispered.

"Yes?"

"Never stop being compassionate. Even if I become a scrooge about the money."

Grace smiled again. "You're not a scrooge. You have financial concerns, and I'm glad you do. Just remember our priorities. A chance to help a family in a tough spot is more important than holding on to a few dollars." Adam considered pointing out the extra tickets and popcorns were more than a few dollars, but he let her continue. "It's the same between us. We aren't searching for the gems yet because..."

Grace was interrupted by a shout two rows behind them and then had to duck as pieces of candy flew over her head. Adam turned and saw the same four girls who had cut him off in the ticket line sitting there, laughing and shouting in response to each other's jokes. Hence, the candy flying. Adam was sure it was not intentional, but none of the reckless women offered an apology.

"Shouldn't they be home doing schoolwork or something?" Adam whispered. "Labor Day was last week. All the kids should be in classes."

"Yeah, right, honey. I don't remember either of us staying home, especially on Friday nights."

"I don't want to berate a bunch of teenage girls," Adam continued. "But if there were one guy over there with them, I'd get them in line."

"Oh yeah, tough guy," Grace said, shaking her head. "When's the last time you were in a fight?"

"Sixth grade. But that's not what I meant. I'd intend to have a, how shall I say, good talking to them."

"Oh, I can do that," Grace said, and she stood up and walked two rows back. The lights dimmed, and the movie trailers started. Adam could not hear what was said behind him and focused on the previews. He hoped one of them

62

would be an action movie, but they were either romantic comedies or dramatic romances.

He was grateful for the time with Grace, but this was becoming a long two hours.

When the trailers ended and the feature film just began, Grace slid back into her seat. "The situation has been taken care of," she whispered.

Adam slid his arm in behind her, then reached for the popcorn bag. It was gone.

"Oh, I forgot," Grace said. "They lost so much candy being silly while talking about boys, I gave them our popcorn."

"Why did I tell you to be compassionate again?"

"Because," Grace said, "you love my heart, and I love yours."

They kissed, and Adam resigned himself to watching a romantic film on a not-quite full stomach.

* * *

Adam knew Grace would want to sit through the credits. She always had, ever since the first movie they watched together during their senior year at high school. Grace never said it, but Adam sensed she tried to appreciate each individual involved in the film and the contribution each one made.

His hand in hers, Adam patiently waited for the names to finish rolling up the screen. He did not focus on the words himself, but the thought occurred to him: that's why she wants to have the bed-and-breakfast for struggling couples.

It was her way of saying she saw the difference each person made, even if the world did not.

Adam turned to Grace and reminded himself how he had shot an ace on the eighteenth hole when he married her.

The moment the credits ended, a young woman came up to them. The theater lights were back on, and his eyes adjusted. Adam recognized her as the blue-haired girl who had cut him off and made a ruckus in the theater earlier that evening with her friends.

"Hey," she said, turning toward Grace. "Look, I just wanted to say I'm sorry, and my friends are sorry, too. We were being really jerky before the movie, and you were great to us." She held out two boxes of candy. "I felt bad that you gave up your snacks for us when we were being so rude, so I grabbed these and thought maybe this could help make us even."

Adam, stomach now growling, had to fight the urge to grab both boxes. But Grace stood and walked in front of the girl.

"What's your name?"

"Avery."

"Avery, I appreciate this. You didn't have to, but that was very sweet." Grace took the boxes and handed them to Adam. "Here you go, hungry boy." Then she turned back to Avery. "But if you truly appreciated how I treated you, treat the next person who does something wrong to you the same way."

"Give them a snack?"

"Forgive them, even before they say they're sorry."

Avery gave a quick nod, as if she only now felt awkward getting that kind of life advice from a stranger. But she smiled, blurted out, "Well, thanks, um, goodbye," before walking toward the exit.

Adam and Grace walked out of out of the theater as well. He turned the car out of the parking lot. Grace was going on about how impressed she was by the movie.

And on and on.

"...and what made it so sweet was you knew the most important thing wasn't that they had more money at the end, but that they had each other," she continued. "People don't realize that most of the time, but it's relationships that give you comfort, not the stuff you have."

When Adam could focus on what Grace was saying, he thought her observations on life were right, but her thoughts on the movie itself were a little off center.

"It was sad in the middle of the film when the man was so frustrated with his actions he couldn't forgive himself. I would hate to be in any depression, where I couldn't let the guilt go."

"That was actually why I didn't care for the movie," Adam said, turning the car onto Route 322 on their way home.

"You didn't like how he kept punishing himself?" Grace said, reaching over and caressing the back of his neck with her fingertips. "I love that little sweet spot in you."

"That's not what I mean. I didn't like that the woman forgave him. That's not how the story should end."

"Everyone needs forgiveness, honey. Think of those girls at the theater. If I would have ignored them or shouted at them, they probably would have acted worse, or saved their misbehavior for someone else. But by showing them kindness, it led to them showing kindness to others later."

"Of course, though, I think you were a little quick to forgive them. But the man in the movie had a completely different situation. He was feeling guilty because he cheated on his wife. The movie should have ended with her separating from him. Not necessarily getting revenge, but freeing herself from him. Cheating can't be swept under the rug and forgotten."

The caress on his neck stopped, though Grace's hand still touched him. "Forgiveness isn't sweeping something under the rug. Forgiveness means you know you've been wronged, but you choose not to treat the other person as if that wrong happened. You don't change what is right or wrong, you simply show mercy despite the wrongs."

Adam kept driving, pondering Grace's words. For a lie, for taking money, even for punching someone, he understood. But truths could be explained, debts could be paid, and wounds could heal. Once you've been with someone else, there was no erasing it. There was no way to go back and make it right.

"Well, I'll never put you in that situation," he promised.

"You better not," Grace said, not with a shout but with enough emphasis to show her passion. "I'm never going to be the wife who gives you a free pass. But forgiveness is a different action from a pass. If you strayed, and you came back, I would forgive you."

"I know. But it's irrelevant. There is no circumstance that I would ever be with another woman. Never." They were stopped at a red light, and Adam turned to her. "You're everything to me. It's not only I wouldn't let another woman come between you and me, but I also wouldn't let anything in life come between us."

Grace surprised him. They had not kissed at the movie theater, but now she cupped his face in her hands and kissed him as if they had been separated for a year. Adam started to kiss back, but then realized the light had turned green when he heard horns honking behind them.

"Sorry, forgot myself there," Grace said as he drove them home.

"Don't apologize," Adam answered with a smirk.

They were quiet for a few minutes. Then Grace broke the silence a mile from home.

"It's time. You're ready now."

"Ready for what?"

"It's getting late tonight, but tomorrow, we start."

It took Adam two seconds to make the connection. "The jewels?"

Grace nodded. "I've always told you what is between you and me has to come first. I knew you understood it, and I think now we are ready to chase after that goal, and can do it without losing any part of our relationship."

Adam tingled with adrenaline. He could finally learn all the details behind the jewels Grace's father had lost, and hopefully information on where to find them. They had been meant as his gift to Grace, but now, they would be the best gift Adam could ever give to her.

"But don't be too excited," Grace warned. "This will be anything but easy."

Chapter 8

Christmas morning, it was not.

Still, sitting on the living room floor, still in his sleep clothes, Adam sensed some of that holiday anticipation he had experienced as a child. All the mysteries behind the jewels would be revealed, or as much of it as Grace knew.

Grace, also in her pajamas, pulled the two briefcases out of the closet by the front door. Adam was ready to grab them, but then he remembered they were not merely the briefcases that held the information concerning the jewels. They had belonged to her father. Maybe it was important to her to do each step today.

She sat on the floor next to Adam but left the cases unopened. "When I was a child or in middle school, I can't remember which, my dad told me bits and pieces about the gems. I think he meant to tell me more when I was a teenager, but by then, I noticed the first signs of dementia. What he told me later on, some of it contradicted previous stories. Even with the stuff that was consistent, I'm not sure what details he gave me later on that I could trust."

She stopped and wept. Adam pulled her close but said nothing. They held each other for a few minutes, letting their touch express everything that needed to be said.

"Anyway," Grace finally spoke, "when I was younger, he would sit on the floor with me in my bedroom, while I was playing, and tell me about the jewels. That's why I asked you to sit on the floor, not at the table. It somehow seems that's how we should do this. It's the way he would talk to me about them. He always regretted selling them, but always felt he did not have a choice. Even years after selling them, I saw how conflicted he was over it."

"It was important to him that you have them," Adam said, setting his hand on her knee. "But he had to care for you, too. And your mother. Now we can fulfill his wish, your wish too, by finding them."

"Not everyone gets to have a tangible reminder of their parents once they're gone," Grace said. "I should be grateful I do, or will, hopefully. But please, I need you to remember something, whether we find any or all the gems." She put her left hand up in front of Adam. "These rings will always be the most important jewelry I have. The gems from my father matter, but not more than this."

Adam had no idea how to respond to that and kept quiet.

"I know you want to charge into our dreams. The bed-and-breakfast. These jewels. But they will take time. And in that time, our marriage has to come first, no matter how long and frustrating the rest of life is."

"You will always be first to me," Adam assured her.

"And, to be honest, the bed-and-breakfast is more important. Other people will enjoy that. The gems are for us alone, and my father's memory. But the jewels might not take as long to track down as it will take to start our own business. Or, it may go on forever without ever finding any of them."

"Why are you being so pessimistic? We have the information here," Adam gestured to the two briefcases. "Finding all five jewels may be hard, but I have to think a couple will turn up somewhere. I'm sure we can find a way to buy them once we locate them."

Grace sighed. "I'm sorry. I should have told you how hard this would be. But I didn't want to put this ahead of our relationship, and I didn't...Well, it makes me remember how sick dad was when he moved into the home for Alzheimer's patients."

She turned silent again. Adam held her more tightly, and now Grace sobbed. He had been there enough times before when Grace mourned for her father to know words were useless now. The only thing to be done was to cry it out.

If Adam could ever bring himself to tell Grace the complete story about his father, he would appreciate the time to cry it out, too.

When the grief had passed, Grace recovered her usual poise. "The day I moved dad to the home, I finally searched inside the closet where mom had told me he kept the papers associated with the jewels. When they were sold, who to, the prices, everything was supposed to be here."

Now Adam became nervous. There should have been plenty of room in one briefcase.

"This is what I found," Grace said, opening the first briefcase.

Adam's fears were confirmed. Hundreds of papers, possibly even a thousand, stuffed the case. Many of them slid over the floor. He reached inside the case and suddenly a year's worth of pressure weighed on his heart. Many papers had yellowed. Others had some ink fade or smear. A few had writing scribbled over the original document.

"My dad was always disorganized, even before dementia started," Grace said, opening the second briefcase. Adam saw more of the same. He only flipped through about fifty of the pages, but it was clear there were no solid leads.

"Every one of these documents are about the jewels?" Adam asked.

Grace was already shaking her head, both in answer to his question and out of frustration. "No. I tried to go through this one time, shortly after you proposed. I had hoped to find the gemstones for our wedding like he had intended from the beginning. But I had trouble reading half of the papers, and most of the ones I could read had no obvious connection to the jewels. Receipts from restaurants. Heating bills. Old letters from people I've never heard of, then or now. Even a couple old Harrisburg baseball ticket stubs. But I'm afraid to throw any of them away, in case there is a connection I didn't notice."

Adam pulled more papers out, but they were in the same condition as the others. He did not want to say it out loud, but there was a chance none of these papers were connected to the jewelry. Any paper trail might have been disposed of years before Grace's father had to move to the home.

No, he decided. He would not doubt on the first day of his new mission.

"Oh, there was one thing I found that will help," Grace said, reaching into the second briefcase. On top of another pile of sloppy papers sat a thin oblong box. She grabbed and opened it, and at first, Adam thought it was empty. But then he spotted a black necklace. "My dad specially designed this to hold the five gemstones he had cut. Each of the jewels was in a setting that had a unique, corkscrew hook. If we ever find one, and its still in the original setting, the hook would snap into any of the five clasps. A perfect fit," she said, pulling the necklace out and dangling it from her fingers.

"Well, it's a start," Adam said.

"We have weeks, even months of work ahead of us looking through this. I'm not sure how much worthwhile info is here, or how long it will take to find it."

"When your dad told you about the jewels when you were younger, do you remember anything he said you feel you can trust?"

"The jewels are a diamond, an emerald, a sapphire, a ruby and an onyx. All five were cut from stones that my great-great-grandparents. . .or was it three greats? Whatever the case, a long time ago, my ancestors came from Germany to the United States and brought some valuable, rough stones as heirlooms. The jewels my father cut came from those stones. Each was one inch long and a half-inch wide. A quarter-inch deep in the center. The settings were silver. Except for the diamond. That setting was golden, and the diamond itself was circular."

"How large?"

"Five karats. Though I'm not one-hundred percent sure of that, to be honest."

"You're sure of the other details?"

"He repeated them many times. So did mom. There was not much else that was consistent in each story, but those facts remained the same."

"Yet he never told you to whom he sold the jewels."

"I don't think he ever expected me to try to find them. As a child, I didn't understand, but now it seems dad was trying to tell me he crafted those jewels out of love. He would tell me the details of how beautiful they were as a way of expressing how beautiful I was to him." Grace picked up a faded paper, glanced at it, and set it back on the pile. "He loved me and mom, but I think he loved those five jewels more than any other person he met. It broke his heart when he had to sell them when I was about seven years old. Well, not the diamond."

Adam froze. "Wait, the diamond? What happened to that?"

"My parents said it was given to a relative. For safekeeping. I don't know all the circumstances, but I think it was to avoid the temptation to sell the diamond, too."

"Maybe he still had hopes of holding on to one jewel as a wedding gift. It was probably the most valuable of the jewels."

"It's possible the sapphire would be more valuable to an appraiser, especially if I'm wrong about the diamond being five karats. But, more importantly, I barely had any extended family, and the few I knew about are long dead. They never told me who the relative was that they gave the diamond to, or I have no memory of it now. I didn't care when I was young, and when I was older, mom had already passed, and dad could not tell me anymore." She shook her head again. "And I don't know who bought the other four jewels. It may have been four unconnected people, or one person, or an organization, or someone still living nearby or in another state..."

Adam put his hands on her shoulders and massaged her. "Easy, honey. We won't solve this in one day. But now we can take steps forward."

Grace smiled again. It was always a charming expression, but more so after she was frustrated or grieving her father. "Thank you. For taking on this challenge. For being eager to help with all this. It wasn't meant to be this way."

"But it is. And I will do this for you."

He drew her in to kiss her, and as he did, Adam heard that small voice in his mind.

"Do it for her. But always keep her first."

Chapter 9

"That is quite the collection," Grace said. Adam looked at the front of the refrigerator, several cards scattered over it.

"And here I thought everyone sent text messages and memes," he said. There were cards from Adam's mother, Nate, Brandi, Michelle and several members of their wedding party. One important couple was not represented, though.

"Rylee and Michael are too busy with their jobs to bother with real mail," Grace said. She adjusted her top and then spread her arms out. "Do I look good?"

"Always."

"You know what I mean," she said. "I don't worry about appearances that much, but I want us to stand out like a couple on our first anniversary."

"You're gorgeous. I'll have to fight off any guys in the restaurant."

"You're ridiculous."

Adam stroked his hand through her hair. It may as well have been gold, as far as he was concerned. "You underestimate yourself. I can't imagine a man who wouldn't want to be with you."

Grace tilted her head, meeting his. "I can't imagine being with another man."

They started kissing, but Grace pulled back. "We better save that for later. Reservations."

Adam glanced at the microwave clock. "Whoops."

"I have to grab my shoes," Grace said as she hurried to the bedroom. "Give me a minute."

"Are you going to wear heels?" Adam said, following her.

"No, I never picked them up from the store."

"What? We agreed you could buy a pair of new shoes. Even two pairs. The budget is looking better."

"I know. But I didn't want to tower over you on our anniversary date. I mean, I didn't at our wedding, so why now?" Grace slipped the black flats on and stood in front of the full-length mirror in the bedroom. Adam glanced at her shoes but took more time looking at everything above them. A midi and loose, turquoise blouse looked good on her. But she made anything beautiful.

Grace was looking at her reflection. "Well, I don't mean to be vain, but I do look good. Don't I, or am I being arrogant?"

"It's not vanity when it's true. But how's this outfit for me?" he asked. A moment ago he was confident in his appearance. Now he felt inadequate next to Grace's radiance. "This is almost what I wear to work. Maybe I should upgrade for tonight."

"This is actually the perfect outfit," Grace said, pulling him towards her by his tie. She kissed him. "It even comes with a husband handle, to keep you away from all the ladies I'll be fighting off."

"I don't think that's the case with me."

"Okay, a handle to keep you from wandering to the bar to watch some random golf match."

"They don't have an alcohol bar yet. They only applied for a liquor license last week. Those things take time. Oh, that reminds me," Adam said, walking back to the kitchen. He opened a cupboard and pulled out the wine bottle

Michael and Rylee had given them a year ago. "This is the night we intended to drink this, and I'm pretty sure the restaurant is BYOB for now."

"Glad you remembered. Let's go. I don't want to lose our table."

They strode from their apartment to Adam's car. He kept his free hand on her lower back the whole way. She smiled in return. When he opened the door for her, she said, "You know how to treat a lady. At least once a year."

"I hope that was a joke."

"Of course. You've been romantic three or four times since our honeymoon." The smile in her eyes told Adam she was kidding. Marriage had been good for them.

Adam drove them to an Italian restaurant in Hershey. Along the way, Grace's phone buzzed.

"Two things before dinner," Grace said before she answered it. "In the restaurant, no talking about jewels, gems, stones, none of them. And no talking about bed-and-breakfast either, and we turn off our phones before we walk in the door."

Adam nodded, sensing of peace within, knowing they should have a night during which they would mention none of those subjects. The search for the jewels had barely started in earnest, with most of their efforts put into posts on social media, which so far had been fruitless. The bed-and-breakfast was still no more than a percentage of savings in their bank account. Still, both had been on Adam's mind, and he agreed with Grace to clear his head of these things.

We only had our wedding once, he realized, and we will also have our first anniversary only once. But he hoped for fifty more.

Adam thought back on the memories of the past year: their first holiday season as a married couple and candle-lit dinners at home. He was pulled out of his reverie when Grace mentioned who had buzzed her. "It's a text from Rylee. She's congratulating us, and she sent a picture of the wedding ceremony. Didn't we already have a message from her and Michael?"

"We did," Adam said. "Michael texted me this morning. He said it was from both of them."

"Rylee says this message is their 'congratulations'." Grace chuckled. "Sometimes they don't communicate."

"I hope that's never a problem for us," Adam said as they pulled into the parking lot.

"I think we're almost there."

"Um, yeah, that's the restaurant right in front of us."

"No, I mean where we truly bear our souls to each other. No secrets, ever. Not even silly ones."

"Well, I am keeping at least one secret from you," Adam admitted as he parked.

"What?"

Adam stepped out of the car, then ran around to open Grace's door. "After dinner, we aren't going straight home. We are heading somewhere special."

* * *

"I should have known," Grace said. Her smile was wider than when they drank the wine or when they ate the special dessert cake with "Happy First Anniversary" scripted in caramel on it. "I was a bit afraid we would wind up at a golf course, knowing you."

"Big events can be at a country club," Adam said, parking the car. "But I thought this would be more meaningful for us."

The sun, setting late since it was deep into May, was obscured by the tops of the trees at the Annville Nature Park. It had been a twenty-minute drive from the restaurant, past their own home. Adam did not give away where they were going, but Grace had realized it now.

"You brought us back to where...," Grace stopped. Somehow, silence filled the moment better than words or music could have.

They stepped out of the car and walked hand-in-hand on the pathway, covered in softwood shavings. Through the trees, they spotted a bridge, spanning a large creek, the Quittie. Grace took Adam's hand, smiled, and pulled him there while running.

Adam felt eighteen again.

They ran onto the wooden bridge and made their way to the center. Adam did not notice anyone else near the bridge but was unconcerned if they were alone or not. It was their first anniversary, and if their public affection were to offend anyone, the passersby would have to complain later.

Once at the center of the bridge, Grace stopped pulling and turned to Adam. He had no time to react before she started kissing him passionately. The rushing water, the songs of birds, the wind through the leaves, it all was silent to Adam. All that existed to him was Grace, the heat between their bodies, and the love between their souls.

When their lips parted, Grace broke the silence. "Where everything started."

Adam caressed her cheek. "Because of you."

"I played it pretty cool." Grace gave a sly grin. "I was sure you'd say yes. But I couldn't bear watching you being alone, or of anyone else taking you away."

"That was never an issue, and never will be."

They kissed again, a tender touch this time. Adam was dimly aware of someone jogging by them on the bridge. While he embraced his wife, Adam did not care if they had an entire gallery following them as the world's top golfers did at a major golf tournament. He was proud to be married to the most beautiful and compassionate woman in the world. Let everyone know.

He risked a glance around the nature park. It was only the jogger who already ran to the path along the creek bank. Oh well, Adam would have bragged about it to more people if given the chance.

"We haven't been here since high school," Grace said, arms still around him.

"I thought this was a good opportunity to return. I wonder where we will be for our next anniversary."

"Together," Grace said. "As long as we're together, that's all that matters."

Their passionate silence resumed and remained until the sun set.

Chapter 10

"I saw the blood from across the field," Nate said.

"Gross," Tessa scowled. "Why do guys have to turn every story nasty?"

"There's not much of this in baseball, but occasionally someone loses their cool and sticks his spikes or cleats into the other guy. In this case, the third baseman's thigh. That's part of the reason this story sticks out," Nate said.

"As opposed to the ninety-seven other stories you've told us about that Central team?" Adam asked.

It was two minutes before the end of lunch break at the accounting office, and when it seemed everyone was about to refocus on work, Nate began another baseball story. But this tale was not about getting a game-winning hit or advice from a life coach. This one had a bit of violence, and a dozen accountants had gathered around Nate's workstation.

"There was a reason Phil spiked their third baseman," Nate explained. "Phil was seeing this girl from another town, completely in secret. One time he drove over for a surprise visit and caught her making out with this other guy, the boy playing third base."

"Now I like this story," Tessa said, perking up to this juicy detail. "Did they fight? Knock each other out?"

"When you've been spiked in the thigh, hard enough to draw blood, you're not able to do much fighting or anything else. We never heard from that guy again, and before the season ended, Phil was seeing a girl from our school, Jo."

"What did that life coach, the one you go on about, think of all this?" Adam asked. "People sneaking around and deep wounds don't sound like the sort of things he would have approved of."

"This happened before the playoffs, so we hadn't met him yet. But the crazy thing is, he was aware of this. Phil's girlfriend, him catching her and the other guy, Phil's revenge. He knew about it before anyone had a chance to tell him."

Adam tried to not roll his eyes. Sometimes the baseball stories became a little trying, but the mystical qualities Nate attributed to this mentor were more tiring. He tried to remember his name, but forgot if Nate had ever mentioned it. But before he interjected another question, Tessa tried to pull more saucy details from Nate.

"Go back to the sexy stuff. Did your teammate see that girl again? Did she slap him? Try to get back with him?"

Adam hoped not. Infidelity, whether it was among teenagers or married couples, was inexcusable. If someone chose that lifestyle, he or she did not even deserve to speak to their ex again. And being the "other" in the relationship warranted at least having spikes drilled into your leg.

"Not that I know of," Nate answered, and Adam felt like the story had an acceptable ending. "As I said, he wound up with Jo, a member of the softball team who came to all our games. They're engaged to marry later this year, and I believe they plan on moving south to North Carolina. Actually, a few of my teammates have moved down..."

Someone cleared her throat. The accountants turned their heads to the corner office, where Ms. Douglas stood in the doorway. She was still smiling but had her eyebrows upraised. Translation: she was not annoyed yet, but expected story time to end and work to resume.

Adam dropped into his chair and opened the case he had started before lunch. After glancing at the two photos at his workstation-one from his and Grace's wedding and one from their honeymoon-he started typing. But before he got too far, he remembered to show gratitude to a coworker.

"Hey, Tessa," he said as she walked by toward her station. "Thanks again for the Chinese food."

"No problem."

"You sure you won't take any..."

Tessa shook her head before he finished. "It's my way of showing appreciation to everyone who chips in here. I'm not taking any money for it."

She walked back to her desk, and Adam began punching numbers into his file. Numbers. In some ways, they were comforting to him. Numbers were stable, easy to understand. Numbers did not create mystery or tension. Things in life that raised questions were the things digits could not quantify.

Like people, he thought. Nate and Tessa were excellent examples. Nate was so level-headed, so reasonable, almost always. But then, he talked about the life coach from that successful baseball season and attributed miraculous events to him. How would anyone put that inconsistency into a formula?

Tessa might be easier to figure out, though it was still a mystery how she bought food and gifts for a dozen people so often. She never mentioned another job. Maybe she built up debt and was not concerned over it.

But Grace, she was dependable. Trustworthy. As much as he trusted in mathematics, Adam could not reduce the most important person in the world to him down to numbers and cold facts. Someone that good was also beyond his ability to explain.

The afternoon hours slogged on, dragging slower than the morning hours, as they often did. But Adam kept pushing through his spreadsheets and reports. Thirty minutes before his shift ended, Adam sensed his phone buzz in his pocket. He pulled it out and read the text from Grace.

"No need to reply, don't want your boss to catch you texting. I just really wanted to let you know I have exciting news when you get home. Could tell you now, but this is one of those look-into-your-eyes moments. Love and kisses."

Adam smiled. The last thirty minutes zoomed by until quitting time.

* * *

Adam hopped out of his car and jogged to the apartment. He was not sure what Grace's text message meant, but he knew it must be something good.

He rushed through the vestibule and hurried down the hallway. The door opened as Adam was reaching for his key. Adam saw Grace, her blue eyes wide. "Come inside quick," she said, flailing her arms.

Adam nearly leaped into their place. Grace quickly shut the door, then turned back to Adam and stared at him out of breath. Her face shown with excitement. Not the romantic excitement he had seen at their wedding or during their first-anniversary date, but an intensity of spirit lay behind them.

Even so, she grabbed and kissed him, hard and fast.

"What's going on?" Adam asked when they parted.

She smiled. "I found it."

Adam looked around the apartment. There was nothing new near him. He double-checked Grace's outfit for any new apparel, but she was still wearing her outfit from her job at the hotel. "What?"

Grace reached down and grabbed one of her father's briefcases. "It took time, as we expected it would. But I found one."

"You found a gem? How?"

Grace nodded. "One of these papers made sense, at last. And I found a picture to confirm it online. I know exactly where the ruby is, and we can see it tomorrow morning."

Adam was at a loss for words. He had almost lost hope of finding any jewels so soon. He gave up thinking of the right words to say when Grace started kissing him again.

Chapter 11

Adam and Grace rushed out the door of their apartment and sprinted out of the building. They took a second to say hello to Brandi, who was waiting for a friend to go to the shelter. Under normal circumstances, they would have stopped to talk for a few minutes, but nothing felt normal this morning.

They both prayed that today would unlike any day before it.

As Adam started the car, he asked, "The website did not mention if the ruby is for sale?"

Grace shook her head as she snapped her buckle. "No. But there was nothing on the website that said the items were not available for sale. Either way, we have to go and see it."

Adam nodded and tried not to speed on his way to Lebanon. Grace had explained her finding last night. One paper in her father's briefcase, a document with two coffee stains on it, mentioned a historical society in Lebanon. Most of the rest of the ink had faded or was obscured by the stains, but Grace checked the society's website. After a few minutes of clicking through pages, she found a photo of what appeared to be the ruby her dad had crafted and sold.

Adam looked at the picture, too, after Grace filled him in with the details of her research. Based on the description Grace had provided, he agreed the ruby was probably the same one her father had crafted. But the society's website did not describe most items, including the ruby. The society had closed by late Friday afternoon, so there was no reason to call for information then.

86

They decided it would be better to be on the road to the historical society's building, hoping to arrive there as it opened. Maybe, by the end of today, the first of Grace's jewels would be theirs.

* * *

They arrived fifteen minutes after the society's display area opened. There were three rooms open to public viewing, the entry hall and an additional room on either side. After taking a quick look through the hallway, Grace chose the room on their right.

On the far wall, there was a wide, wooden display case. Grace practically sprinted to it.

"Easy, honey," Adam said, trying to keep up and hoping the security guard by the case did not mind her rushing. "If the ruby is here, it's not going anywhere."

The display case had more than thirty different valuables in it. Not every one of them could be fairly described as jewelry, but each looked valuable in a historical context. A piece of Native American artwork, pearl earrings from revolutionary times, and a sword owned by a Union officer were in the display.

Grace, smiling, stared at only one of them. The ruby sat on the right side of the case, Adam realized, because it was a more recent item. Not as long on history, perhaps, but someone at the historical society must have realized its value.

Adam could see Grace felt a connection to the ruby already. It was not the smile alone, but also a glimmer in her eyes. She was remembering her father, not the memories that brought sorrow over missing him, but the memories that brought joy by bringing him a little closer.

"'The Timland Jewelry Company was founded and run in eastern Lebanon County for over fifty years'," Grace read from the plaque next to the ruby. She skipped on ahead. "'This ruby was crafted by one of their longtime jewelers, William Davis, as a unique piece for a personal collection."

"That's it," Adam said. "We found one."

Indeed, it looked exactly the way Grace had described the gemstones. One inch by one-half inch on the front facet, with the silver setting around it. Since it was in the case, the depth was hard to judge, but a quarter-inch seemed to be a reasonable guess. Protruding from the setting was an odd, corkscrew latch, which Adam surmised would attach to the necklace.

"Do you think there's any way we can buy it?" Adam asked, but Grace was already on the move. She walked back the way they had entered and returned moments later with a middle-aged woman they had seen and had rushed by when they entered.

The historical society employee–or volunteer, Adam was not sure–stood on the other side of the display case. Her pin read, "Hannah," as she hovered over the ruby. "I can't say I know much more about this piece than any other," she said. "But I'm afraid the only time any of our items are up for sale is at the annual auction and fundraiser."

"When will that be?" Adam asked, probably interrupting her.

"Oh, not for another eight months. And even then, I don't know if this item will be put up for bidding."

Adam glanced over to Grace. The smile vanished, a frown in its place. The light in her eyes had disappeared as well. There were no tears, but Adam could sense the pain.

"Please, we need to speak to someone," Adam said. "This ruby was cut by her father."

Hannah glanced back and forth between the two of them as if trying to figure out if they could be trusted.

"I already told her that," Grace whispered to Adam. Then louder, she said, "I can prove William was my father. And I can prove the ruby came from my family." She pulled the necklace out of her purse. "This necklace was specially designed to hold this gem and four others. A circular diamond, but the other four gems were cut into rectangular prisms and held in settings that would connect with the special clasps..."

Hannah shook her head and waved her hands before Grace finished. "Look, as I said, I know little about the history behind it. Maybe everything you are saying is true, but I don't have the authority to release any of our items. Steve?"

Adam looked over his shoulder at whoever Steve was. Steve turned out to be the security guard.

"Please watch everything while I find Mr. Lindor."

Hannah walked out of the room again. Steve kept a steady eye on Adam and Grace. This was not the way Adam had pictured today going.

But only a minute passed before another man, with bronze features and a lean appearance, walked into the room. "Don't worry, Steve, all is well."

The gentleman, presumably Mr. Lindor, walked in behind the display case. He reached out his hand to Adam first, and then Grace. As they shook, he said, "Hello, my name is Juan Lindor. I am the president of the historical society. Hannah tells me you are interested in acquiring one of these items."

"Yes, this ruby belongs to my family," Grace said.

"Careful," Adam whispered. "Technically, they own it now."

"Sometimes I have to be bold," Grace hissed back.

Juan chuckled. "Don't worry, sir. The items here at the society are not for sale, but the ruby is a unique piece of our collection. Years ago, the society took an interest in it because of its connection to a once-successful business here in Lebanon County. Owning a valuable from Timland was an honor, especially to the ladies. But this gem is unique because the society needed to agree to an odd contract to keep it."

Adam raised an eyebrow but said nothing.

"I'll do what I what I need to do to buy it," Grace said.

"First, some identification, please."

Grace reached into her purse again and pulled out two driver's licenses. "This one is current, and this one is from before our wedding."

Juan looked at the two cards but focused on the older one. "Grace Davis. Very good. You're halfway there."

He handed the driver's licenses back to Grace, and only then did Adam realize Juan never actually spoke the name he was intending to see. He may have been making this process up, but it was more likely he did not want to tip his hand to potential scammers.

"What else do you need?" Adam asked. "Anything from me?"

"No. When William Davis sold the ruby to the historical society, there was an agreement made beyond paying him. For the society, a guarantee we would have possession of the ruby for at least fifteen years. For him, if he or his daughter returned after those ten years with proof of their identification and the special necklace, we had to give it back. We could not demand payment in return after that date."

Juan focused on Grace. "It has been seventeen years, I believe. And I have no reason to doubt you are or were Grace Davis. The necklace?"

Grace pulled it out of her purse again. Adam realized it had always been that–a necklace, and nothing more. Now, it had the potential to begin making Grace's dream come true.

Juan looked at the necklace but did not take it. "Five clasps," he muttered. Then he called out, "Steve, turn off the case's alarm."

The guard walked to what appeared to be an electric box in the opposite corner of the room, opened it, and typed in a code. He nodded back to Juan, who opened the case and slid the ruby out of the back.

Juan held the gemstone out. "Grace, I believe this ruby is yours, or at least should be. But I need to see you attach it to the clasp first."

Adam was amazed Juan was letting Grace do this, and even glanced at the security guard to make sure this was still permitted. In theory, if they were thieves, they could have tried to make a break for it. But the guard did not move.

Grace took the jewel and connected it to the second clasp. It was a perfect fit.

"Daddy," Grace whispered. The light had returned to highlight her azure eyes.

Adam forgot his surroundings and hugged his wife. "We did it. We found one of his jewels."

They held each other for a moment longer, and when they separated, it looked like even Juan had a tear in his eye. "I became president of the historical society seven years ago, the same year the ruby became available to your family. After this much time had passed, I assumed it had been forgotten. I'm disappointed to lose it, but at the same time, I am content to know you have it back."

"Put the necklace on," Adam encouraged.

"Not yet," Grace said, smiling and focusing on the ruby. "I won't put it on until I have all five of the jewels. For today, holding one is enough."

"I need you to fill out some paperwork before you walk out of here with it," Juan said. He stepped away. "Nothing serious or complicated, and no charges, just old-fashioned rigamarole."

"Mr. Lindor, we will mail a donation first thing Monday morning to your historical society. I doubt it will be as much as the ruby is worth, but I wish to show our appreciation in some way."

Adam would not have minded walking out with the ruby for nothing and putting the money on his college loan– or a nice 5-iron–but Grace was right. They should give something in return. They could decide how much later. Obtaining the ruby now was the most important thing.

Wait, maybe it wasn't.

"Sir," Adam called after Mr. Lindor, before he exited the room to get the forms. "You wouldn't happen to have any files on the other jewels Mr. Davis cut, would you?"

"I can double-check, but the only thing I remember about the others was they were meant to be on that necklace along with the ruby. I doubt we have any information on the other four here."

A hint of disappointment crept into Adam's heart. He did not expect to locate all the jewels in one day, but there had been a chance of getting leads on the other gems. It was like scoring a birdie on the seventeenth hole when you had a chance at an eagle–impressive, but a missed opportunity at something special.

Grace put her hand on Adam's shoulder, and he turned back to her. "Don't worry about the others yet," she said. "We have one of my father's jewels now. Today is a blessed day." She kissed him. "Thank you for being with me through this journey."

"I'll be with you wherever this journey takes us," Adam answered with a more passionate kiss.

A grunt from Steve, rearming the alarm, reminded them this was not the place to become more amorous.

* * *

"We have the entire day in front of us," Grace said, spreading her arms out as if she was trying to hold time between her and the windshield. "And it's a gorgeous day. We should celebrate."

"Well, it's your jewel," Adam said. "You should choose the celebration."

Grace turned to him. "I'd let you pick a few things, too."

Adam thought for a moment but shook his head. "Not this time. Today is for you. Don't worry about time or money. Anything you want."

Even with his eyes on the road, Adam could see Grace's smile widen. There were things he would do with a free Saturday if the choice belonged to him, but he desired for Grace to enjoy every second of today. There was no way of knowing if they would ever find the other four jewels, so it was important for her to take pleasure in the ruby. Her happiness was enough to give him joy today.

"Well, if you're willing to be such a gentleman about it," Grace teased, "Then let's drive to Hershey and walk through the gardens."

Adam nodded. Not the most exciting activity, at least for him, but if that was what Grace wanted, Grace would do it.

"And then we will come back to Palmyra and go to the movie theater for a late afternoon showing of-," Grace hesitated. "It doesn't matter to me. I want to see a movie, I don't care what the story is. Anything. Afterwards, we can hit the Italian restaurant in town and eat dinner with a glass or two of red wine. And maybe a bottle to save for our next anniversary."

I told her not to worry about time or money, Adam reminded himself as he turned the car onto 422. But the movie and dinner would be fun for both of them, and he decided he would not concern himself with cash either. He had to allow himself to enjoy each moment of today, too.

He pulled the car up to a red light at the edge of Lebanon and stopped. "Sounds like quite the celebration we will be having. I like it."

"Oh," Grace answered, lowering her voice and putting her arm around his shoulders. "That's only in the daylight when we are celebrating the ruby." She leaned in, kissed his neck, and then gave the slightest nibble on his right ear. "Tonight, I'll celebrate you."

* * *

"C'mon, you can say it," Grace said, smirking. "We both know it's true."

Adam did not want to say what Grace was hinting at, and he did not want to say what he was thinking: Grace was trying to trap him. It was not like her to fool him into saying something that would make her upset. Other men told Adam about girlfriends and wives who played games. Never Grace. But she seemed to be now.

"I've never said it out loud either," Grace continued. "But it won't hurt my feelings. It's a natural thing."

They had done all the celebrating Grace had planned. After stopping at their apartment to put the necklace and ruby in the jewelry case, they walked through the gardens in Hershey for more than an hour. That was more than enough flowers and butterflies for Adam, though he had kept his silence as stoically as he was now. Grace knew he was getting bored with flora and chose an action movie for the next fun event. It was not a wonderful picture, but having one arm around Grace and the other reaching into an extra-large popcorn was a much better experience. Grace had tolerated it, even cheered when the heroes succeeded in the ending scene.

Dinner was different. They both enjoyed it. That was partially the ambiance of the restaurant and partially the effect of multiple glasses of red wine with the meal. They even gave themselves something to look forward to, purchasing a valuable bottle of wine to be saved for their second anniversary. But their joy came from being together. Knowing they had found the ruby, and they did not need to concern themselves with money or time, was all they needed today.

Then they came home and celebrated each other.

Even after that, though, both Adam and Grace stayed wide awake. Adam had finished brewing Grace her favorite lemon chamomile tea and was about to give it to her while she lay in bed. That was when she asked him to say the words he was certain would incriminate him.

Grace sighed, then laughed. "Fine. I'll be the one to say it first. We started awkwardly, then we became comfortable, and now-," she lifted herself from the bed and kissed Adam. She lowered her voice. "Now, we're amazing."

Adam laughed as Grace took the teacup from him and sat again on the bed. She patted the sheets with her free hand. "But I don't just mean this. I'm talking about everything. We understood each other in those years of dating, but not in this way. Now, we truly understand each other."

"That's how marriage is supposed to work," Adam said, sitting next to Grace. "We will be getting closer for the rest of our lives."

"I didn't even ask for this," Grace said, tilting the teacup. "The first few months, I had to ask. You know now."

"Half a teaspoon of honey," Adam said.

"You see? No one else would know that, and no one else would brew it for me without saying a word." Her face tightened a bit. "But it's more than the big and little shows of affection. We can talk about anything now."

With a shrug, Adam leaned in closer. "Not anything. I wasn't able to say what you said to me. The whole awkward, comfortable, amazing bit."

"That's not the same thing," Grace corrected, sipping the tea again. "You were afraid it would hurt my feelings, saying our nights together were awkward at first. What I mean is, we can discuss any of our hopes, any of our fears, any of our dreams, any of our nightmares. We thought we could before, but now we honestly can trust each other with everything."

Adam wondered if Grace was trying to lead into something. "Do you need to talk about one of those dreams? Or one of those nightmares?"

Grace hesitated for a moment. She sipped more tea and then set the cup by her phone on the bed stand. "A fear. It scared me to tell you even after we were married because I thought it might hurt your feelings. Now I can say it."

"I know you'll never hurt me," Adam said, resting his hand on her shoulder. "Tell me."

"It will seem irrational," Grace started, then stopped. She took a deep breath. "There is nothing more important in my life than you. Never take this any other way. But I know I have you for life. So my greatest fear is not about you."

Adam nodded and waited for her to continue. Whatever this was, he would let Grace tell him at her own pace.

"I want to run that bed-and-breakfast one day. Several of them, if possible, but at least one. I want to help the people who are on hard times be able to travel, to have those romantic getaways. But if that does not happen, I could still have another meaningful purpose in my life. I want to find the other four jewels, but if I don't, I will always have the memories of my dad to treasure. But what I truly fear is never having children of our own."

Adam felt a smirk coming to his lips, but he fought it down to a neutral expression. This was serious to Grace. Still, he had to point out, "We agreed when we were engaged we would have at least one child, maybe more, and we have years for that to happen. We're only twenty-four."

Grace smiled again, but Adam could see the strain behind the expression. "As I said, it's a little irrational right now. On the other hand, every fifty-year-old couple who wished they had a child was twenty-four once."

Adam grazed his hand over Grace's back. "We will have a child together. But whether that is soon or years away, you will do wonderful things."

"And so will you," she answered, and the smile became genuine again, the strain gone. "But I believe the two most important things anyone can do are being a great spouse and being a great parent. You've already been a wonderful husband, and you will continue to be."

"You've been the wife of my dreams," Adam said, though his mind cringed at how unoriginal it sounded.

Grace did not seem to notice. "But I want both of us to fulfill the second half of that goal. I want us to be the best father and mother that we can be."

She leaned into him, resting her head on his shoulder. He held her for a few moments, her hair covering his arm. Then she pulled back.

"Your turn."

Adam tilted his head. "My turn?"

"Tell me something you couldn't bring yourself to say before our wedding day."

In the months since their wedding, Adam had never considered any of his fears or concerns this way. But now he realized he had filed away a few thoughts in a corner of his mind he wanted to keep away from Grace. He was not trusting her as a husband should.

No longer.

"Since you bring up the subject of fathers-," he stopped. He wanted to tell Grace, but even with her unconditional acceptance, this was difficult.

Grace made it easier. "Your dad. You still have scars from never meeting him."

"Well, yes, sort of," Adam mumbled. He kept talking but felt himself pulling away from Grace. "You see, I never told you, but I found him."

The words hung there. Grace simply reached over for her tea and sipped again. She was not being dismissive, Adam realized. She was giving back to him the time to collect himself he had given her earlier.

"One night, mom and my step-dad drank a little too much," Adam said when his courage built up again. "Mom started sharing embarrassing stories from when she was married to my dad, telling mean jokes about him. And then she said something about him wasting his life in Jonestown. I never remembered her mentioning where my dad lived. Now I had a name."

"Jonestown is a small community," Grace thought out loud. "So you tracked him down to his home?"

"Yes, in a way. I knew his name and what town to look in. A little searching and I found his address. I had passed my drivers' license test a couple of weeks before, and Jonestown is not a lengthy trip from Annville."

"But you told me you never met your father."

Adam swallowed. "I didn't lie to you. But I hid this one part of the truth. I shouldn't have. This is too important."

"You weren't ready before," Grace encouraged. "Tell me now. For your own sake."

Another deep breath. "I found the house. Small, but clean and well-kept on the outside. For a moment I was sure my dad had it all together and was as scared as I was to meet. I knocked on the door. I didn't want to call or send a message. I guess I was looking for the same thing you do. I wanted to see his eyes."

Grace smiled and nodded. "That's so important."

"But I never had the chance to see his eyes. His widow answered the door."

Adam stopped. He rarely saw Grace shocked, but she did not hide her amazement.

"I know I always made it sound as if my dad was still alive, but the woman told me he died nine months before I figured out where he lived. After I drove home, I did an obituary search online. That woman was telling me the truth."

For the first time in the conversation, Adam's eyes left Grace. He stared at the bedsheets. "I didn't tell you because I had difficulty understanding what this meant. As a teenager, I knew my father had robbed me of any chance of knowing him. I would never have anything with him, good or bad. But now, I realize, I do have one thing from him. Rejection. The only piece of my father I still carry with me is his rejection."

It took an effort of will, but he looked into Grace's eyes again. "I'm not trying to compare what happened with our fathers. You also lost your dad too soon."

"Yes, and it still hurts like hell," Grace said. "But I know he loved me. There's nothing I can do about what happened between you and your dad. But I can promise you this: you will always be loved."

Grace set the tea back on the bed stand, then reached out to Adam, putting her arms around him. "No matter what happened before or what happens now, you have my love. No matter if I am close or something takes me farther away, you have my love. Nothing, no circumstance or any amount of time, will change that."

Adam returned her embrace. The only thing he could do was whisper "I know" as Grace comforted him.

Then Grace pulled back a little, enough for Adam to focus on her face. Only enough for him to see a smile that excited him. "You know, I'm still not tired, and I don't think the man I love is either," Grace purred. "Let me celebrate you again."

Chapter 12

Adam called out for Grace, but only heard the echo of his voice. He checked each room of the apartment–not a lengthy task–but she was nowhere to be seen.

Usually, Grace would make it home minutes before Adam, but there were always exceptions. Something must have come up at the hotel. It had happened other times. While Adam had been looking forward to relaxing after getting back from the office, he decided at first to work out for twenty minutes. After a set of crunches and pushups, he worked up an appetite. Thinking to surprise Grace, he looked through the cupboards and refrigerator to prepare dinner.

After Adam gave up on cooking the chicken tenders that had been stored in the freezer, his phone buzz from the dining table. Leaving two salad bowls behind for a moment, he glanced at the message.

"On my way home now. So excited. Marvelous news. Well, mostly great. Another time I want to look in your eyes. Wonderful things are starting. Love you so much!"

That was followed by several kissing images and winking faces. Adam was not sure what had happened at the hotel, but it put Grace into an excellent mood.

He had prepared the salads and heated a dish of mashed potatoes in plenty of time. Adam was questioning if his choice of mozzarella cheese sticks for the main course was well thought out when Grace opened the front door.

"Honey!" She ran over to Adam and collided into him over with her hug. The ranch dressing bottle in his hand, closed, flew across the dining room. Adam did not care.

Grace peppered his face with quick kisses. She was in a pleasant mood, indeed.

When she stopped kissing, Grace kept the tip of her nose on his. "It's starting," she said.

"What?"

"Our journey to having our bed-and-breakfast. One that can be designed for bringing in lower-income couples."

Adam leaned back a little. "How? What actually happened?"

Grace let go. "After my shift was over, my manager called me back to his office."

"And he's an actual person, not just a voice?"

Grace nodded. "I've seen him plenty of times. But I haven't seen the owner too often. He was there, too."

"Really? For something good?"

"It's short notice, but a conference is coming up next week for hotel managers, motel managers and anyone else with 'manager' in their title. It's a leadership event, helping anyone try to advance to the next level in the business. But mostly, they only expect people already somewhere in management to be there."

"Which you're not."

"No, but my manager told the owner about my, sorry, our dream of running a bed-and-breakfast for lower-income families. He likes it, but he also likes how I'm doing a good job at his hotel..."

"He's sending you to the conference,"

"Yes, but not only that. He said he has a long-term plan. I'm almost up to two years of experience. When I am, he will find a management position for me, so I can get more experience in the actual running of a hotel. Then, I would be qualified to transition someday to running my, did it again, our place."

Adam's first thought was running the bed-and-breakfast would still be a financial challenge, but he knew better than to slow Grace's momentum.

"Now, the owner might hope I become comfortable at the hotel and stay there," Grace continued. "But this is a big break, regardless. They see me as management material, honey!"

She embraced him again, this time with one long kiss, which lasted until a beeper buzzed.

"Oh," Adam said. "Dinner."

He ran over to the oven, turned off the heat and pulled out a pan.

"I didn't even notice," Grace was saying back in the dining room. "Salad, potatoes, what a nice..."

Adam brought plates over to the table with his main course on them.

"Cheese sticks," Grace finished. Then she laughed. "You made cheese sticks the main course."

Adam grinned as he set the plates on the table. "Sorry."

Grace cupped her hands on his burning cheeks. "I love you. Your heart is in the right place." She kissed him again. "But you are going to the financial side of our business."

* * *

Adam and Grace had finished dinner. They had talked about Grace's upcoming trip again and even fit in the time to jog the outside trail for today's workout. As evening fell, Adam and Grace were lying under their comforter, talking about more details to Grace's upcoming conference.

"Have you ever been down there before?" Adam asked.

"No, I've never been to North Carolina," Grace said. "Unless my parents took me there when I was young, before all the financial problems and selling the jewels."

"I guess you haven't come up with any more information on the other four jewels."

Grace shook her head. "We need to be grateful we found the ruby and wait for the others. Taking this next step towards our own business is the priority right now."

"That's not what you were saying when we brought the ruby home."

"Some priorities are allowed to change from time to time," Grace said, sliding in closer to Adam. He raised her left hand and showed her engagement and wedding rings. "But this priority never does."

"I hope it's not too crazy there. Schools are out by now. If there's a bunch of families at the beach..."

"Paradise is not that close to the coast," Grace's phone buzzed. She groaned and turned to it, lying on the nightstand. "Looks like Rylee is calling. Do you mind?"

"Go ahead. Make sharing the good news the priority tonight," Adam said, letting her go.

Grace grabbed the phone, but before accepting the video call, she winked. "Afterwards, you're my only priority."

Then she brought up the call. Adam could see Rylee's face and realized she had no positive news to share with them. Her face was red, her hair was unkempt. Rylee's camera was far enough back he saw her shoulders slouched. Before she said a word, Adam sensed defeat coming from their friend.

Adam never remembered Rylee looking defeated.

"Rylee," Grace started, her shaken voice revealing she noticed everything Adam had. "What's wrong?"

"It's over," Rylee answered, forcing back a cry.

"What?"

"Everything. Everything is over."

"You mean, you and Michael?"

Rylee nodded and started to wipe tears away. There was an awkward pause. "I guess he hasn't told you. I thought he might text Adam."

Adam shook his head. "I haven't heard from him for a while."

"Well, it's been horrible for the last few months," Rylee said. "I'm a go-getter. He was getting comfortable with how we were already living. We worked in Chicago, and he thought that was enough. But I wanted to run a big business in the big city. We had an adequate apartment on the north side, and he thought that's where we should start planning to stay permanently. But I saw us moving into a big house in the suburbs. Enormous yard..." Her voice faded.

"You don't need to explain," Grace said. "We're here for you, no matter what."

"Yeah, she speaks for both of us, Rylee," Adam added. "Whatever you want or need, you can get it from us."

"Thank you. I know I can trust you," Rylee said, padding at her tears with a tissue.

106

"If you want to talk about anything now, or another day, we're listening," Grace said. "But please understand, from the start, if Michael opens up to us, he..."

"I know, he's your friend, too. I don't want to ask you to pick sides. It's only...we always had these conflicts, ever since college. But now, those conflicts stopped being different ways to look at life. They've become fights. Nasty fights. A lot of, well, words I don't think I've ever heard you use, Grace."

"Where are you now?"

"Still on the north side of Chicago. I found a different apartment, but I hope to be somewhere else by the end of the year."

"I will fly over to you as soon as I can," Grace said. Adam turned his head in surprise, hoping his motion was not visible to Rylee. "I have a work trip coming up and I can't cancel, but right after that I'll come over the next weekend."

"You don't have to rearrange your life for me. It's too far."

"No distance is too far for someone you love," Grace said. "Even if it takes me longer than we'd like, I'll be right there next to you when you need me."

Adam wished Grace had consulted with him before promising a trip to Chicago, but this was Rylee. They would support her. And he had to reach out to Michael, to see how he was taking this situation.

"I'll leave you two alone to talk," Adam said, leaving the bedroom and sitting on the sofa in the living room. He pulled out his phone and sent Michael a simple text, asking him if he was okay. Grace and Rylee's voices drifted into the living room, but not clearly enough to eavesdrop, which was for the best. Rylee was a friend, but not close enough to Adam for him to listen to the most personal details of her life. She could let out any of those details that needed to be released to Grace, Adam hoped.

Moments later, a message came over Adam's phone. "Not doing great. But I'm getting through it. Not ready to talk yet. You'll be the first one I'll call."

Adam left it at that and respected Michael's privacy. The women's voices continued to drift in from the bedroom and became a background sound as Adam began to doze.

Before sleep overtook Adam, Grace roused him. "Come to bed," she said. "Rylee was exhausted. We'll probably talk more tomorrow."

Adam forced himself to drag his feet over to his side of the bed. "I'm almost sick now. They had differences, no news there. But I always expected they'd compromise. They did back in college."

"Rylee made it sound as if meeting in the middle is too difficult now. But I know what you mean. The entire conference trip...I almost feel guilty for having any good news and having you here, and things getting better for us while they...fall apart."

With the lights off, they laid next to each other. "I always looked forward to returning the favor for them," Adam said.

Grace squinted to question him.

"I was looking forward to being Michael's best man. And you know you would have been Rylee's Maid, um, Matron of Honor."

Grace nodded. "It's important to mourn with those who mourn. But it is a pain no less real than when something terrible has happened to us." She did not add any more, but Adam was sure she meant their parents, who had been gone for years.

There was silence, then Grace confirmed his thought. "I know you don't want to think about it, but when your mother passes, put your burden on me. As much as possible. Never feel as if you have to mourn alone."

Adam kissed her forehead. "As long as you're here, I'll be able to handle anything, no matter how depressing. You could handle everything even without me."

"I hope to never find out. But even if I could, I would never want to face life without you."

Chapter 13

Adam rolled over to put his arm around Grace, but there was no skin next to his own.

He sat up in bed and looked at the sheets. This was getting old quickly. Adam grabbed his phone off the nightstand to see if he had missed any messages.

"Woke up late. Heading to the first session. I will call soon. Love you!"

It was no surprise Grace needed the extra sleep. Their video-chat conversation lasted until two in the morning. Their first time apart since their wedding was difficult for both of them.

Then Adam looked at his phone's clock. He had slept in, too. He needed to hurry to make it to the office on time. The one positive from rushing through his morning routine is that it gave him no time to think of how Grace remained several hours away.

* * *

"Cutting it mighty close, Mr. Thompson," Ms. Douglas said as Adam sat at his workstation. He turned to where his boss looked in from her office. Her expression was neutral. Adam straddled the line by coming in when he did, but he was not in any trouble.

"His wife isn't around to dress him," Nate hissed from the other side of the office to the snickers from Adam's other coworkers. He took the joke in fun but inspected himself and made sure his tie and outfit were proper.

The day, to any outside observer, progressed as any other day at the office. Adam processed various cases for companies outsourcing their accounting needs. He spent the minutes and hours balancing figures. Or, occasionally, noting when figures were not balanced.

But on the inside, it felt different to Adam. It had been different every day this week. Even though Grace never set foot in the office, and had only met a few of of his coworkers, knowing she was away affected Adam here. During a normal week, they would be apart anyway while he worked here and she worked at the hotel. But it was never far from his mind. No matter what task appeared on his screen, Grace was in another state. He would be alone in the apartment again tonight.

Maybe this was part of being married, he thought. They had been apart while they were dating. Even once, during their engagement, Adam had spent three days with his mother and step-father in Florida. He missed Grace during those times, but the separation did not hang over every minute of the day.

It did now. When Grace first told him about her business trip, he thought it might be a chance for him to do some things on his own that were hard to do while she was near. Buying golf clubs came to mind. More working out, possibly. But now that Grace was actually in Paradise, it was hard to think about anything else.

Even Adam did not realize how distracted he was until one o'clock, the start of his lunch break. As he stood up from his desk, he saw two doughnuts sitting on the side of his workstation.

Must have been Tessa, Adam thought.

He walked over to the opposite end of the office, where Tessa was getting ready to head out for her lunch. "Hey, I'm sorry I didn't even notice when you dropped off my brunch. Thanks."

"I only gave you one doughnut the first time," Tessa said, smirking. "You had no idea I was there. I brought a second one over and said something rude. Again, nothing."

"I am so sorry...,"

"Don't worry over it. You're missing your sweetheart. I'm kind of jealous you have someone like that to miss so much."

Tessa turned towards the exit and left. Nate was still there, pulling his lunch out of a bag. "Count me as jealous, too."

Somehow, knowing everyone else wanted what he and Grace already possessed gave Adam some comfort.

* * *

"Today's seminar was on giving hotel rooms personality, but keeping them universally appealing," Grace said. "It ran long, so I never got around to calling you during your lunch break."

"Not a problem," Adam said, looking at her on his phone screen. No matter how advanced a phone was, it would never capture the blueness of her eyes. "We have all night to talk if you want."

"Oh, I do. I miss you terribly. Especially at night."

They each smiled and chuckled knowingly.

"Learn anything else today?" Adam asked, leaning back into the sofa.

"Not much that I think you'd find interesting."

"I have to admit, the personalities-of-hotel-rooms talk did not sound like it provided a rock-concert atmosphere."

"Okay, even most of us here don't find the actual information interesting. But I've made a few connections with the other guest services managers. I've even found a handful of people who run bed and breakfasts."

"Bet you want to pick their brains."

"It's hard, though. More than half of the people are here to schmooze. There's a lot of networking for personal gain, but not much networking to improve anybody's company overall. That only comes across in the actual seminars."

"You'll find that in most businesses. Most people, even people with good intentions otherwise, become focused on their bottom line."

"I've noticed. People here seem to understand making places appealing to the middle class. But once I tell them I want to make a bed-and-breakfast affordable to people who are on the financial edge, they blow me off. They either tell me it's not a realistic business model or can't understand why I wouldn't chase a more profitable venture."

"'Business model'? 'Venture?' You're talking like a manager now."

"It's all I've heard for the last three days."

"Well, it will be a difficult thing to accomplish. But it is doable if we are willing to face the challenges. Speaking of being challenged, any seminars on financing a new bed-and-breakfast?"

"There's a financial breakout group on Friday. There's not much on that subject since this conference is focused on middle management, not ownership. But I'll make sure to relay everything back to you. Did you do anything out of the ordinary today?"

Adam sniffed the air in the apartment. "Not out of the ordinary for me."

"Did you burn dinner again?"

"This time I could still eat it."

"Grab something tomorrow. I insist. Order the most unhealthy food in the world and work off the calories the next time you exercise. Double bacon cheeseburger. I don't care. I don't want our home to be on fire when I get back."

"Oh, I just remembered. Have you been asking anyone there about the jewels?"

"Once or twice. But it's not a topic most people care to talk about, and I'm not getting as much time to connect with anyone long enough to work jewelry into a conversation. But I may try walking to the conference during the next couple of days."

"Don't like your rental car? Or public transportation?"

Grace shook her head. "There are people who are walking from the Pine Hotel to the seminars each day, and it would be more of a chance to network and slide in a question about the gems. You know, in case a manager from Moose Lake snatched up the onyx."

"Moose Lake?"

"In Minnesota. Check a map."

"It would be nice if there were a way to inform more people. I'd like to think the other four jewels are nearby, but they could be anywhere in the country."

"Possibly the entire world. There are people from across the country here, but having people around doesn't make it easy to talk about important things with strangers. Have you discovered anything since I left?"

"No one has reached out to me, and to be honest, I'm not in the mood to do any extra searching right now. It did cross my mind that we could try to find an ex-coworker of your father's, but I'd rather wait until we are together to start that. I just want to be with you. I'm not thinking about anything else."

"Not even golf? I bet you thought about sneaking out and buying some bats."

"Clubs," Adam corrected as he leaned in closer to the image on his phone. "Maybe for a moment. But nothing else lasts. Just you. Man, I've turned into a sappy husband."

"I love my sappy husband," Grace said, tilting her head forward.

"I am grateful you made me focus on us before we started searching for the jewels."

"I'm grateful you made me the center of your world," Grace said. "I can't wait to be home. I want to look you in the eyes again."

"I miss your eyes," Adam said, knowing he was looking into them but over the phone. Grace was right. Seeing each other this way was not the same.

"Always us," Grace whispered.

"Always us," Adam whispered back.

Again, they gazed at each other. Adam anticipated it would be a special time when Grace returned home.

Chapter 14

Adam yawned but forced himself to stay awake as he waited for Grace's late-night call.

Flipping through the stations on television, and settling on golf highlights, he wondered what was taking her so long to return his call.

Adam scrolled through their texts from that morning. All their usual "I love you," and "I miss you" messages. He wished he had thought of something original while she was away.

Then there was one more text in the afternoon. He had missed it while working, but finally saw it when he left the office.

"Big news. Something for when I can be with you. Very good news. Can't wait to see you. Will call tonight."

Adam double-checked the time. It was half-past ten, well past the time he had received her other phone calls. He had tried to reach her over two hours ago but could only leave a message.

She could already be in bed, Adam thought. It was a long conference, and she had one more day tomorrow. Grace must have meant to call him and fell asleep the moment she sat in her room.

Adam missed her. He had known he would miss having dinner with Grace and holding her as they laid in bed each night. But what most dismayed him was how much he missed the quick moments. The quick kiss they would give each other before work, or when they returned home. How she would roll her eyes when he turned golf on television, or sigh when he would ask when he would have his own complete set of golf clubs.

He looked forward to running the bed-and-breakfast. He anticipated finding the other four jewels. Now that they had the ruby as a piece of evidence to prove their story, it might generate interest for local reporters. If they presented information about the jewels on local news sources, their chances of tracking the others down would skyrocket. Then they could grab a hold of the emerald or the sapphire...

Sapphire.

Blue.

He missed Grace's eyes. The only thing that reminded him of her eyes were the photos in their apartment. Nothing else captured the particular hue of her eyes.

Adam turned off the television and walked into the bedroom. He changed into his sleep outfit. He was reaching to turn down the bedspread when he looked at the wedding day photo over the head of their bed. Even the picture, despite the professional quality, did not quite show the blueness of Grace's eyes as they did when she stood in front of him. Adam doubted that her particular shade existed anywhere else in the world.

Then he glared at the empty bed.

This is getting old, Adam thought.

He turned off the lights and laid on top of the sheets. But before he could force himself to sleep, he checked his phone one last time. He decided to text Grace to let him know he was going to bed, and he would call again in the morning.

But as he typed, a phone call came through on the screen. It was not Grace. Adam did not recognize the number. He declined the call and resumed his text.

After sending the text, he received a notification. A voicemail had been left for him. Wondering if this was a credit card scam or someone pretending to be a federal agent, Adam opened the voice mail, already preparing to delete it.

"Mr. Adam Thompson, I am Officer Ritter of the Paradise Police Department in North Carolina. If this is your voice mail, Mr. Thompson, I regret to inform you..."

Adam disconnected.

No. No. No.

He did not want to listen.

Adam sat up in bed for minutes. His skin tingled while his heart pushed against his ribs. He started to sweat even before he paced through the apartment. After several more minutes, he stopped moving, wiped his brow and took in a deep breath.

He knew he had to listen. The truth would not change with time. He deliberately tapped the buttons, as if being gentler might make the message less painful.

Maybe it was not the worst-case scenario.

Adam started the voice mail again.

"Mr. Adam Thompson, I am Officer Ritter of the Paradise Police Department in North Carolina. If this is your voice mail, Mr. Thompson, I regret to inform you that there has been a fire at the Pine Hotel. We have not been able to find your wife..."

Part II

The Company of a Friend

Chapter 15

"There was a gas leak..."

Adam tried to focus on the officer's words. It was important. It mattered. But nothing he said could change the truth.

"They evacuated everyone else in the hotel..."

"But not Grace," Adam said. "You told me this when I drove to North Carolina after...after everything."

"We aren't sure..."

"You can just say it," Adam said.

The officer hesitated. "Security cameras show her leaving the building, presumably for the conference, that morning. The footage from the ninety minutes before the fire was damaged and unreliable. But we do not know when she returned. However, in her room, we found what was left of her phone and burned-out credit cards from her purse. And your wife's rental car was outside, in the hotel parking lot."

"You can say it," Adam said, wanting to beg, not desiring to hear the details that had already been burned into his brain.

Grace.

Dead.

No reason to avoid it. "By now she would have called me. Or one of our friends would have. You can say it."

The officer paused again. "Technically, she's still a missing person."

"Officer..."

"And it has been two months."

Two months? Had so much time passed? Adam felt as if his heart stopped. How had he endured all those days and nights without Grace? What would life mean without her?

He also realized how much the fog of sorrow overwhelmed him if two months had passed without him being aware of it.

"I'm sorry," the officer said.

Adam had no memory of what happened after he hung up, but he was sure wherever he went, he spent the night crying.

* * *

The sorrow, Adam expected. Time collapsing around him, he did not.

There was a fog over everything Adam did for months after that phone call. His subconscious forced him to keep going, to eat, to drink, to work. But there was neither happiness nor sadness in any of his days. Only emptiness.

Grace was dead.

Minutes, hours, sometimes days passed, but he did not recall them. Maybe his memory failed. He was not sure he cared. Adam did not know if it mattered to him. His thoughts had become so fractured, he did not even know if any part of his life should matter anymore.

Snippets between the fog would resurface. A couple high points, more low points. Another raise at work. The car breaking down and needing repairs. But one feeling enveloped Adam through the months. Sorrow. A few times, he would try to fill in the gaps between the memories, but all he could remember was the same sorrow overwhelming him.

When his memory went blank, he would find himself back in the bedroom, as if he had sleepwalked there.

He only lied on the left side of their bed. The right side was Grace's. He thought how only half of the bed was his, and the other half belonged to her, every time. A dozen times? Forty times? A hundred? He had no clue.

Then sleep would take him. Sometimes, Grace would walk next to Adam in a dream. Sometimes not. But either way, sorrow followed him through the night.

Even when he saw her in his dreams, he was always aware of the truth.

Grace was dead.

* * *

They called it a vigil. Adam knew better. It was a memorial.

Roughly forty people showed up, holding candles in the square in Palmyra. Around the intersection of Main and Railroad Streets, they sang songs Adam did not recognize.

Nate was there, and Michelle. Brandi was not. She had said something to Adam earlier, apologizing and giving Adam a card. What was the reason? He did not recall. Something else lost to the fog. Maybe she was helping at the shelter. That was better than being here. At least she spent her time helping the living.

You need to keep on living yourself.

Adam ignored the voice. He ignored most of the surrounding people. They meant well, but gatherings would do nothing to bring Grace back.

The memorial brought two other friends back, though. Michael and Rylee were there. Each had hugged him. Each had cried with him. Each had said they could not believe Grace was gone.

But they had told him separately. Even afterward, Michael stood on the southeast corner of the square, by Adam's shoulder. Rylee stood on the northwest corner, as far from Michael as possible. Adam realized the breakup between his friends was depressing, but with Grace gone, it was hard for him to acknowledge sadness elsewhere.

Other acquaintances and friends stayed outside for an hour before returning home. Michael and Rylee left soon after going their separate ways. Adam stayed in the square, alone, for another fifteen minutes. The air was chilly, but otherwise, the evening felt like another lonely night in his apartment.

Empty.

* * *

Adam continued working at the accounting office. He found no happiness there, but it muted the sorrow. He could work with numbers. Numbers had no emotions, no feelings. Simple calculations. On a spreadsheet or report, no reminders of Grace haunted him.

His coworkers meant well. They usually kept a respectful distance and were gentle in speech when they talked to him. Even Ms. Douglas was softer when she found an error, and less likely to mention when Adam came in a few minutes late.

Thursday lunches with Nate continued, but Adam never remembered the conversations. Nate probably talked about baseball. It did not matter. Adam appreciated the support.

He also appreciated Tessa continuing to give him the extra snacks, drinks and trinkets each week or so. She bought those things for each one of her coworkers, but Adam's often came with a hug now. Did she kiss him on the cheek once? Did Adam imagine that? Maybe the fog was causing him to create memories.

As he finished each case and each assignment, Adam forgot them. He found he was forgetting almost everything he did. His mind still worked. He simply believed nothing was worth remembering any more.

Adam opened a new assignment, and lost himself in the numbers again, for as long as possible.

* * *

We never had our first fight, Adam realized.

He was walking outside the apartment complex, along the same path he and Grace had walked and had run so many times in their first year of marriage. Adam did not remember coming outside or why he did it. Maybe he had thought walking the path would help dim the pain.

It did not.

But it gave him a moment to realize that he and Grace never had that scream-at-the-top-of-your-lungs fight that all couples eventually hashed out. They said none of the words that they would wish they could unsay.

They had disagreed. Adam had felt restricted by Grace's goals, keeping them from enjoying certain simple pleasures in the present moment. There were days she was frustrated with him watching golf instead of spending time outside together. But Grace never let these disagreements escalate. She always calmed him, no matter what decisions they came to, or if they decided nothing at all.

Adam missed her even more.

He fell back into the fog before he made it back to the apartment.

* * *

Adam's mother had called several times. Adam was not sure exactly how many calls he received from her. Some conversations were brief. Others lasted longer. They all ended with the same question.

"Wouldn't you like to move here?"

She meant well. She loved him. But every time she asked, it seemed wrong to Adam. Somehow, leaving Palmyra, leaving the apartment, made him feel as if he was betraying Grace. Here they had started their lives together. Somehow, moving on without her, in Florida or anywhere else, felt unfaithful.

So he stayed. Adam had grown used to the size of the apartment, but the emptiness was difficult to accept. Over time, the apartment changed. Adam ignored the dishes. Clothes were strewn across the bedroom. Such tasks seemed pointless. He rarely checked on the budget or bank accounts. He did almost nothing anymore, so he was not spending. What did it matter how much he possessed?

But the emptiness of the apartment still stung him. The quiet sounded loud. Adam tried playing music or putting a golf match on television. Both sounded hollow and he would turn them off quickly.

Sometimes, he remembered holding a bottle of red wine in his hands, while standing in the cluttered kitchen. He considered drinking his sorrows away. But he could not bring himself to open the bottle. He drank red wine with Grace, and this was the bottle meant for their second anniversary. He refused to drink it without her. Adam had no memory of how that night ended.

Another evening, he walked back into the kitchen, even more cluttered now, and checked the cupboard. The bottle remained on the top shelf. This time, he refused to even touch it.

Do you think Grace would want you to torture yourself?

Adam told the voice to go away.

You are right to miss and mourn her. But you don't need to deny yourself every enjoyment.

Adam shook his head, hoping to clear the fog and to keep the unwanted thoughts from returning. It was a restless night. All nights were tough now, but some became unbearable. How often he experienced these lows, he was not sure. The fog of mourning prevented him from knowing. But he knew when they occurred, and when they did, he could not force himself to enter the bedroom.

The worst moments of Adam's suffering came when he would lie in the bed. On nights when he was at his weakest, he needed to stay away. He realized if he would lie down, he would instinctively reach over to Grace's side of the bed to hold her. He knew when he woke up, for a second, the pain would be fresh again.

It had been...how many months? The fog. He was not sure. Many. An important date was coming up, Adam sensed, but what it was escaped him.

Adam laid on the sofa that night, as he had for many others. As usual, sleep was a long time coming.

"Grace," he whispered. "Grace."

Silence.

"Grace!"

He only heard the echo of his voice.

* * *

Adam woke well after midnight, but long before the dawn. His phone was lit. He reached over to the nightstand and looked at it. A number he did not recognize was there, showing a voice mail had been recorded for him.

At this hour? Maybe the call involved Grace. Adam did not know how that was possible, but he listened to the message.

It was an offer for car insurance.

Adam wanted to crush the phone, blaming it for giving him so much as a second of false hope. Instead, he opened the voice mail and missed call listings. He had ignored other random numbers, and the unwanted calls and voice mails totaled in the hundreds.

He only answered calls from work or his mother. Michael only ever texted. Rylee may have called once or twice. He included the police stations, both in Lebanon

County and in Paradise, on his phone contacts, but had not heard from them in ages.

No reason to keep all these messages from robocalls and scammers. He deleted the voice mails from the random numbers, leaving the file as empty as the apartment.

He felt the fog, or exhaustion, or both overcoming him again. But before he succumbed to it, Adam threw the phone against the wall.

* * *

My father died before I found him, Adam thought to himself.

Grace died before we could live out any of our dreams.

Her parents died before she graduated from college and before we married.

Adam punched his hand into the dashboard. He hurt two of his fingers, not enough to injure them but enough to sting.

What was the point of life when death had the ultimate word?

Tears form in the corners of his eyes. Adam parked his car behind the office. He rushed to the door. He had to lose himself in numbers again.

* * *

One time Adam drove by the Spartan Hotel. Did it happen in the first weeks after he lost Grace? Or later? The timing, like so much else, lost to the fog.

Not lost to the fog was the anger Adam felt looking at the hotel.

His anger burned toward the people there. Michelle had called him and attended the memorial. Grace's manager had sent a card. They could not have known what would happen when they sent Grace to the conference.

Adam's anger was against something unseen, something beyond his ability to describe. He saw the hotel, and in his mind envisioned the dreams Grace wanted to pursue. The bed-and-breakfast, finding the jewels, having a child.

All gone with her.

He punched the dashboard, feeling pain in each one of his fingers this time. He didn't care.

* * *

It's our anniversary, Adam realized.

Time slammed back into place. The pain remained, but the fog lifted, and time made sense again, even if the rest of his life still did not.

He gazed at the date on his phone, having tapped it to turn off the alarm. He had known for a long time this day, what should have been their second anniversary, was coming. But now it was here, and it awakened his soul.

You must go on, the voice inside of him whispered.

Adam sat up in bed. He still thought of it as their bed and their apartment, even if Grace would never return to them. But he could not let those thoughts continue to dictate his life.

Life still had to be lived. But for what? Now that Grace was gone, and he accepted it, he needed something to keep pushing forward.

He absent-mindedly dressed for work, noting his clothes pinched on him, but focusing on this new question. What should he live for now? He could continue working at the office and continue living in Palmyra, at least for now, but that was merely where he would spend his time. What was there to do that mattered?

His eyes wandered to the wedding photo, still hanging over the head of the bed. After he finished with his tie, he considered it for a moment.

Grace was so radiant that day, he remembered. He remembered being lost in her eyes so many times during the first week of their marriage.

Maybe he could still make his life focused on her.

Adam walked around the bed and found the jewelry case. He unlocked it and pulled out the necklace. The ruby reflected the morning light. But he stared at the remaining empty clasps as if force of will would make the missing gems appear.

He wiped away tears with his empty hand. He and Grace would never have the child she had hoped for. It was unrealistic for him to pursue a dream of running a bed-and-breakfast, for the unfortunate or anyone else.

But Adam might be able to achieve one of Grace's goals if he tried hard enough, he decided. Even though he would never see her again, he would force himself to make Grace a part of his life.

He had to keep her as the center of his existence.

On the outside, Adam smashed his hand into a fist around the necklace, sparing the ruby but pushing as much strength as he possessed into the rest of it. On the inside, he tried to strengthen his own heart. He made two vows to himself.

He would find the other four jewels to honor Grace.

And he would never be with another woman.

Chapter 16

"I knew you were really low, even the last few weeks," Nate said, holding the door open for Adam as they left the sandwich shop.

"Please tell me I wasn't crying in public," Adam replied, walking through with a half-full cup of cold brew in his hand. "I'm serious when I say I can't remember what I did most days."

"I never noticed any crying," Nate said as they walked down the street, back to the office. "But you kept ordering the same thing for our Thursday lunches."

"Did I?"

"A double-bacon cheddar cheeseburger. Every time."

"Well, that explains the extra pounds. I need to do my arm and leg exercises again. I feel as if I have no strength at all. What was I drinking?"

"Oh, what you have there, like always," Nate said, nodding to Adam's cup. Then he added, "Well, not like always. You didn't flavor it with anything, just like today. You always used to put some fancy-sounding flavor in it."

Straight cold brew, Adam realized. Somehow, the bitter taste fit, though he did not remember making any change to his orders. It was for the best he could not recall those lengthy periods. No sense in recalling the bitter taste.

They arrived at the office. Adam opened the door for Nate. "I don't consider vanilla or hazelnut 'fancy'. But thanks for listening to me all those weeks. And for being here at all. I can't remember what we talked about."

"Anything and everything. But I understand if you can't remember it. Nothing important."

"Out of curiosity, were most of these conversations about that baseball team of yours?"

"Only when I knew you had stopped listening but needed the background music of a friendly voice."

"That still didn't stop him from telling the rest of us old sports stories," Tessa said, walking up to them as the door shut behind them. "Here. I hope you two didn't eat dessert over there because I bought these for everyone."

Another source of the extra pounds, Adam thought as he took a warm chocolate chip cookie from her bag. "Thank you. Again. And thanks for these little favors you gave while I was...out of it, if I didn't say it then."

"You always did," Tessa said before walking along the work stations to deliver more of her desserts.

"Hey, what about me?" Nate asked.

"You can have one at the end of the day. That's if you don't refer to suicide squeezes or infield flying rules."

"It's called the infield fly rule!"

"Looks like that cookie is mine."

Nate shook his head and turned back to Adam. "Well, we better get back to work before Ms. Douglas pokes her head out."

"Wait," Adam said. "Before you go, one other thing. If you notice me ever, I don't know how to say, falling back into that fog I was in, tell me you see it. I'll always feel lonely, but I don't want to go through life without realizing the consequences of my actions. Gaining a few pounds isn't an enormous deal, but I might have done something worse."

"I hope you're on the back end of this," Nate said, patting him on the shoulder and smirking. "But certainly, I'll stab you in the face if you need it."

"Thanks," Adam mumbled. He was unsure if opening up to Nate about how overwhelming his depression had been was wise, but facing his problems alone seemed foolish. Other options were limited. He trusted Michael, but he was too far away to help him if he slipped back into the fog.

One thing Adam remembered from those difficult months was how working with numbers helped numb the pain for an afternoon. Things were different now, at least in his heart. Still, the best part of his day remained typing into spreadsheets and reports in the sterile office. He had finished two reports when he heard his name called from the corner of the office.

"Adam, please come in."

He turned his head and saw Ms. Douglas standing in the doorway of her office. "Sure," he called back, and then made sure his files were saved.

As he stood and walked over, he wondered why she summoned him. The only reason he was in his boss's office before was for his semi-annual reviews. The experiences were not stressful, but nothing to look forward to, either.

Adam walked in, and Ms. Douglas closed the door behind him. "Don't look so tense," she said. "This is my corner of the world, not the principal's office."

They sat on opposite sides of her desk. "How are you?" she asked.

"Fine," Adam answered with a slight nod.

"Good. Now, give me a genuine answer."

Blunt. That was what Adam should have expected. "I'm better than I was. In the last few weeks, I've been thinking clearer. I'm sorry if I came across as aloof before that."

"Don't apologize." Ms. Douglas grabbed a picture on her desk. It was turned away from Adam. "I hate to be the person who says, 'I know what you're going through,' but it's somewhat true. It still stings, doesn't it?"

Adam tried to remember if his boss had talked with him about Grace since her passing. He could not remember for sure. It may have been one of the memories lost in the fog. "It does. Has my performance here been less than..."

"That's not what we're here to discuss." She turned the picture around. Adam saw Ms. Douglas in the photo, though she appeared to be at least ten years younger. She stood in a park, with her arms around a tall, black man, who Adam guessed was the same age. "Andre and I were close to your age now when we were married. Crazy how young we were. I remember when Grace came over here a few times to pick you up, when you were dating. You two reminded me of a white version of us. We had so many dreams. One of them was to run our own business." She chuckled. "Back then, we couldn't even decide on what the business would be. All we had was determination."

She set the photo back in place and leaned back. "It took fifteen years before we had our focus, a few extra college classes and experience, but we could finally open our firm here. Small, but we didn't worry over that. It was ours."

Half of Adam's mind wondered why Ms. Douglas opened up to him about this. The other half tried to figure out her age. She must be ten years older than she appeared.

"Andre didn't live too long after that," she continued. "Heart attack. Much too young." She hesitated. Going through his mourning process did not make Adam any more comfortable being around her as she thought of her late husband. But before he figured out if he should say anything, she spoke again. "I've been determined to keep this business running ever since, and it has been succeeding. But I wish I could have taken a break during the hard times."

"You were still working afterward? I mean, right away?"

"No. I mean the anniversaries. When certain dates would come around. Those days were hard, but I had no one else to carry the load for me at the time. But that's not your situation. I have an office full of people who can carry that load for you temporarily if you need to take a little time off."

"I appreciate it," Adam said, astonished at the offer. Adam and his coworkers received a fair amount of time off, but he never heard Ms. Douglas push someone to step away. "But what would have been our second anniversary was last month."

"Am I correct that the anniversary of...when it happened, is this upcoming week?"

"Um, yes."

There was a moment of silence. "Your secret is safe with me. I experienced this, too. Even seeing the date on the calendar coming up is painful."

Adam nodded. "When I realized it was May, our second anniversary...it shook me, even if it helped me get out of my depression."

"Take vacation time next week. On me. You never used your vacation from last year. I'll roll over a week from then and list it as 'grieving–manager's authorization' or something like that."

"Can you do that?"

"Do you remember those union papers you signed when you started here?"

Adam shook his head. "We don't have a union."

"Exactly. Finish out this week. Then stay home week. Mourn. Rest. Go to a country club. Drink. Whatever you need."

Whatever I need, Adam thought. He nodded, shook Ms. Douglas's hand and thanked her. But he pondered those last words.

When Adam returned to his workstation, he looked at the wedding and honeymoon photos there, and was struck at how Grace's eyes did not seem to be the right shade of blue.

What he needed was not sleep, alcohol or anything else Ms. Douglas mentioned. He needed Grace. He needed to see her unique eyes again. But being deprived of her, he needed to make use of this extra time.

Not to mourn any more than he had already. Not to rest, nor to go to a country club. Even golf seemed empty now.

It was time to find the remaining jewels.

Chapter 17

Don't dwell on the date, Adam kept telling himself. This only made him more aware.

This was the anniversary of the fire.

The pain did not sting the way he had expected. Maybe the fog of the past several months dulled it. Maybe this was the natural healing when a widower entered the acceptance phase of the grieving process. Whatever, the pain was not as strong as he had feared.

But it still haunted him.

Adam would not spend another day only mourning. If he was going to honor Grace's memory, the best way was to take a step towards finding the remaining jewels. Today, printing out fliers he could post around the region was that step.

He had considered running off copies at a store but decided he should buy a printer, something else he and Grace had talked about but never did. As it pushed out the posters, he looked over the social media updates he had posted over the last few days. They each mentioned each of the four of the remaining gems: the onyx, the sapphire, the emerald and the diamond. A rough description of their dimensions and a photo of the ruby ran along with the posts.

But looking at the computer screen and pondering why he did any of this only made today's date more prominent in his mind.

He prayed Grace had not suffered. It may have been a year ago, but the anniversary made it feel as if it was happening to her again.

Adam pulled out his phone and texted Michael. "Have a chance to talk? It's been a year since the fire. I'm off from work this week. Need someone to talk to."

He set his phone on the desk as the printer continued to buzz. Too late it occurred to him even if he wanted a printer in his home, Ms. Douglas might have permitted him to run the copies for free in the office. Possibly not, but he did not even ask.

Then he realized he had never updated his bank account in months. He knew his account and transactions were available online, but he had no organization otherwise. What bills were soon to come due or had increased during the past year? He had no idea. He assumed he could afford the printer, but with the disorganization in his home there was no way to be sure.

This was also why he was eating a baloney sandwich with no plate. The dishes sat in the sink, and he did not bother to clean any of them until he found himself eating ice cream from a coffee cup.

The fog might be gone, Adam thought, but I'm a long way from recovering.

As the last of the fliers printed out, Adam's phone buzzed with a reply from Michael. "Sorry. In and out of meetings today. I'll see if I can text you tomorrow or later this week. Hope the time off helps. I didn't realize this was the anniversary. Sad for you, man. I hope you can find the other jewels. Hope that it helps when you find them."

Adam appreciated Michael using "when" instead of "if", though to be honest he possessed no confidence. He had shared about the jewels on social media, but he and Grace had done the same thing over a year ago, and no one replied. The ruby was on the necklace because of Grace's research. Still, something could come up now.

He sent a quick reply to Michael, then put the fliers together in a folder. He planned on heading out the next day to place them anywhere in Palmyra, Annville and Hershey that allowed posters. The fliers were bland, with black print on white paper and little more to them. Grace possessed a better eye for making something artistic to grab someone's attention.

Adam sighed. Another reminder of how unique she was. Another reminder of what he had lost.

The phone buzzed again. Adam set the folder next to the computer and read Michael's next message. "About to go into another meeting. But wanted to say I feel for you. Not saying I've been through what you have, but two years ago I was certain we both found our match. Still haven't connected with anyone since Rylee. It's hard being alone. You need anything, call. I'd be back more often if it was possible. Gotta go."

Adam replied with another thank you. Michael was right, he did not go through what Adam experienced. But loneliness was loneliness, no matter the cause. And Adam appreciated Michael had made the trip from Chicago to be at the so-called vigil. His presence reminded Adam that someone still cared. Michael could not understand what he endured, but traveling so far to support him for one night was more than he ever would have asked. The vigil remained the only time Michael had been back to visit him since the month after he married Grace. But that was the reality of the situation, whether or not he liked it. He lived in Illinois. How much could Adam ask of anyone living in another time zone?

His phone rang. Not expecting anyone to reach out to him, Adam glanced at the caller ID, expecting a random combination of numbers and an unfamiliar town name.

It displayed, "Rylee Bixler."

Perplexed by the coincidence of the ex-lovers contacting him so close together, Adam answered the phone.

"Hey," Rylee said before Adam finished his greeting. "I know you would have told me not to do it, so I did it anyway."

Rylee put Adam off-balance, and he did not respond right away. What was Rylee referring to? Had they said something while he mourned in the fog of depression? He remembered her being at the vigil but had no memory of her telling him any plans.

"Am I supposed to know what you're talking about?" Adam asked.

"Of course not."

"So, what's going on?"

"I saw your posts, about the jewels. I was thinking, the four you still need are probably around where you live, right?"

"Well, I hope so. Grace's family lived in Lebanon County when her father needed to sell them. We found the ruby in Lebanon County. I'm hoping that at least one of the others is nearby."

"That's what I thought, too."

"Wait, do you have a lead on one of them?"

"No. Not yet. But I saw that you're ramping up the search for them again. So, I took a week off, and I'm all in for the next few days."

"All in what?"

"The search. I'm here for you."

She didn't, Adam thought. "Here? You mean, Pennsylvania here?"

"I picked up my rental car at the Harrisburg Airport a few minutes ago. I've reserved a room in the city. Tomorrow morning, we start."

"I'll be happy to see you again. Truly. But you don't have to..."

"You shouldn't do this alone. And don't you dare try to talk me out of this. Grace was my friend, too. I need to do something."

Don't be proud, the voice spoke from within his mind. *You need help.*

"Having a partner will be nice. Especially one I can trust."

Chapter 18

"Honestly, I would not have refused you."

Adam was sitting across from Rylee at a coffeehouse in Palmyra, the morning following her surprising phone call. Her height struck him. She was always two inches taller than him, but she appeared even taller now. Had she grown? Or had time distorted his memory of her?

"I don't take chances like that," Rylee said with a smile. "Especially when I'm doing something for someone else's benefit. So it was flight first and ask questions later. I'll corner you until you let me help."

"Yes, I remember," Adam answered. A waitress came up to them.

"Ecuadorian blend with cream," Rylee ordered.

"Cold brew. Straight," Adam followed.

This cafe differed from the one in which he ate lunch each Thursday with Nate. That was a national chain that served nice food and coffee but lacked the charm of this local business. The light was a little softer and the mood a little cozier. Somehow, that made it a more proper setting to reconnect with an old school friend.

"Straight?" Rylee asked after the waitress walked away. "Yick. Since when did you start drinking cold brew like that?"

"I used to flavor it a little, usually with vanilla. Still do, occasionally. But not much. It may sound crazy, but sweet things aren't the same anymore." Adam paused. He should not have said that. Rylee had arrived yesterday by her own choice. No reason to dump his emotional baggage on her. "Sorry. I shouldn't be overdramatic."

Rylee reached across the table and placed her fingertips over his. "No, don't apologize. You're hurting. That's why I'm here. It won't take away all the pain, but if we can find these gems, it might bring closure for both of us."

"So, do you have any ideas on where to look? I've got two suitcases full of old papers but no real leads from them."

"Sorry, no. But I have some ideas on how."

"Do tell."

Rylee started to speak, but their coffees arrived then. Adam sipped his cold brew. As Rylee said, it was bitter. But, as it had during the year after losing Grace, it fit his mood so well he did not mind.

"I've seen all your posts online. I think they look fine, and they can reach some people. But there are many more people who won't see them, or who see your post and assume it's a scam."

"I'm not asking for anyone's money."

"But what you're saying could be misread as a made-up story to fool others into giving gems to you that are similar what Grace's father made. Some people believe everything on the internet, but others don't trust any of it."

"What have you come up with?"

"The most basic thing. Just walk up and talk to people."

You make it sound so simple, Adam thought. "If people don't trust what they see on the internet, why would that believe a stranger walking up to them in the grocery store begging for jewelry?"

"We need to do it in the right setting. Places where people expect a stranger to come up and start talking."

Adam sipped his drink again and pondered. "Here?"

Rylee shook her head. "Too many people trying to focus or find their motivation for the day. Over there along the wall? A guy so focused on his computer he wouldn't notice if this place caught fire. A woman drinking her third cup of espresso who still looks half-asleep. These people don't want to be bothered. But if you've ever been in a beauty shop..."

"Only when my mother couldn't find a sitter for me."

"You can talk about anything with anyone inside."

"And that might work with a barbershop, too." Adam considered the possibilities. "I don't know if we would be allowed to hang around those places without being paying customers."

"I wouldn't mind having a new 'do to show off to my coworkers when I go back home," Rylee said. "I'm tired of using a straightener, anyway. And a little trim on you would be cute."

Adam ignored the compliment–unless it was a putdown to how he looked now. Either way, he was trying to determine some more possibilities. "A bar?"

"We'd have to read body language well," Rylee said. "Some people are in bars to hide from everyone. But others will be very social."

"And if we found even one person who has seen someone with one of the jewels..."

"Someone who knows someone who knows someone. We can at least track them down."

Adam nodded. For the first time since he lost Grace, he felt excitement within. The pain and loneliness were still there, but something positive was finally mixed with them.

"I'll take a walk-in appointment in town, at the barbershop on Railroad Street," Adam said. "Have my hair snipped and talk to anyone who will listen. I'll aim for a time they're going to be busy. If I can catch the barbers' attention, they might say things to future customers."

"And have a few inches taken off," Rylee said, smirking. "You're scruffier than I ever remember."

So it was a putdown, Adam noted. "It's been a while, but want to barhop tonight? They probably won't be crowded in the middle of the week, but we can find a few people out there."

"Each person willing to listen is a minor victory," Rylee said. "It will be like old times, when it was still the four of us."

"You and Michael had more experience at that. Grace and I waited until we actually were twenty-one."

"She really did keep you on the straight and narrow." Rylee smiled. "We knew where to get fake I.D.s for you."

Adam shook his head. "I was tempted, but I wasn't going to cross Grace."

"She was something special." Rylee's smile faded. "I already missed you guys ever since moving to Chicago. Now, I can't comprehend that she's gone."

"I'm still having trouble with the acceptance part," Adam admitted. He gazed at Rylee. Her eyes were hazel. They could not compare to the blue of Grace's. He had never cared what color any other woman's eyes were, but now, seeing Rylee's eyes made him pine for Grace even more. "To be honest, I was such a mess those months after...the fire. I can only recall snippets between long gaps of lost time."

"You looked horrible at the vigil," Rylee said. "Pale, as if there was no blood in you at all. I wished I could have done something to make you happy again. I hope this is it."

Adam nodded. "The ruby, the one jewel we found, is all I have left of her. Other than the photos, I guess. But those gems were so important to her. That's why they're important to me. I will find those other jewels, even if it takes my lifetime. It won't give me Grace back, I understand that. But maybe, with each one, some degree of happiness can be restored."

"Well, then I guess my mission this week is to make you happy again." Rylee stood up, and this time Adam noticed she was wearing heels. As if she needed them. "I'll hit the closest beauty shop that takes walk-ins and have some quick work done. I usually get a new style by early summer. We may luck out and find a lead quickly."

She left, and Adam paid the bill, as he had promised beforehand. He planned to grab the flier he had printed last night up before he drove to the barbershop. Then he would decide which bars to visit in the evening with Rylee. The plan was a long-shot, but then again, any other approach was also unlikely to succeed.

But what if they found even one jewel from this? He might feel actual happiness again.

* * *

Adam and Rylee walked out of the bar and onto Main Street in Annville.

"That was embarrassing," Adam apologized. "I'm sorry."

"Don't be," Rylee said, smiling. "Nothing like when I go out for a drink in Chicago."

"Still, at least three guys..."

"Were hitting on me, and three more scoping me out silently."

"I should have stayed beside you. People would have thought we were together."

"It comes with the territory, especially once I had my hair put in waves and the highlights on my bangs. Trust me, it happens any time I change my style, even when Michael and I were living together. And I'm giving off the 'rebound' vibe right now, which makes the flirting automatic."

Adam sighed as they walked towards their cars, parked along the street a block east of them. "I wish I could say it was worth it, but no one knew anything about the jewels. Embarrassing ourselves for nothing."

"Not for nothing," Rylee said, running her hand through his hair. "You honestly do look much nicer now. I'm surprised none of the ladies tonight took their shot."

"I think I'm still giving off a depressing vibe."

"You are. Keep moving forward. Be positive. It's not only about the people we meet. It's also about one of them mentioning it to someone else. Word of mouth is powerful. Speaking of which, I had another idea. One we should have figured out before tonight."

Adam stood by his car, parked behind Rylee's rental. He was tired and disappointed. It was time to go back home. But he nodded for Rylee to continue.

"Tomorrow morning, I'll search for any jewelers and jewelry stores in the region. I'll visit as many as I can in the afternoon."

"Places like that usually don't sell second-hand items," Adam said.

"No, but people with an interest in jewelry work and shop in those stores. And people get jewelry fixed at the jewelers. Something might turn up."

Adam tried not to sigh in resignation, but the hopeless breath pushed out of him. He had spent hours of his day talking to people and putting up flyers. There had been no looks of recognition, no phone calls, no texts, no private messages on social media.

"Don't you dare give up after one empty day," Rylee said. "Want to hit a nicer place than this to have a drink?" She shrugged towards the bar. "No questions to anyone. Let's grab a glass of wine and remember the old days."

I'm too young to have "old days," Adam thought. But with Grace gone, it felt like the times when it was him, Grace, Michael and Rylee were decades ago. His body was not old, but his soul was.

"I haven't had any wine since...well, since Grace," Adam said. "At least, I don't think I did. On our first anniversary, we drank the bottle of wine you bought for us when we got married. Then we bought another bottle we were going to open on our second anniversary, and it's still in our cupboard. I'm not sure I can bring myself to drink from it, ever."

Rylee inched closer to him. "Then don't open it. Maybe that can be a way to honor her. But no wine, ever? Seriously? I know you enjoy a glass of red most nights."

Adam shook his head. "It's hard to enjoy anything anymore." Those were the wrong words to say, Adam realized. I overdid it again. He saw the tears in Rylee's eyes, though they had not rolled down her cheeks yet. "This isn't your burden. You don't need to..."

"I'll do whatever I can for my best friend, even if she's gone," Rylee said, releasing the tears. "And I will do whatever I want to do to bring happiness into my other best friend's life, even if he's going to fight me about it."

There's no outlasting her persistence, Adam decided. "Okay. I don't know what I'll do tomorrow afternoon. Maybe I'll check other jewelers. Maybe try to figure out if Grace's father had any co-workers who might still be around. But in the evening, if you want to try another couple of bars together..."

"I'm considering Hershey."

"Fine. Hershey. We will meet up at six."

Rylee nodded. "Rest tonight. We will find something. I promise."

Adam understood, no matter how determined she may be, Rylee was in no position to make a guarantee. But he did not contradict her. They each entered their separate cars. Adam watched her as she drove away.

The new hair style made Rylee appear even prettier than that morning, which was prettier than when she was in college. Adam could not remember the last time he had noticed any woman's beauty. But now, he decided he should not blame the men in the bar for showing an interest. Rylee was striking.

Unfortunately, Rylee's beauty also reminded Adam that Grace had been even more radiant.

Chapter 19

"I could drive you to the airport tomorrow," Adam offered.

Rylee folded her printed-out itinerary and placed it in her purse. "No need. I'm still driving my rental, and I'm most of the way packed already." She grabbed her latte. "Now let's go."

"Go where?" Adam asked, annoyed. "We have no leads to follow, and we've hit nearly every social place the public can walk into for free."

Rylee stopped and fell back into her chair. They were sitting at an outside booth of the same cafe at which they had met the morning after Rylee flew into town. Adam had already finished his cold brew but found he had nothing to do with the caffeine buzz it had granted him. Despite Rylee's gracious help over this week, her time here had yielded no results, and now she was thirty-six hours away from flying back to her home.

"Something will come up," Rylee finally said, though her tone made Adam think she did not believe it. "I will do something for my friend, somehow."

"Do you mean Grace or me?"

"Sorry. Friends. I know it's so much more important to you, but I must do something to honor her memory before I leave."

"I know she would have appreciated it. But this was a harder task than we ever realized. I don't want to give up, but the ruby may be the only jewel we ever find."

"Or maybe we're asking for too much too soon," Rylee said. "This may be a task that takes years, not weeks."

The prospect of an extended search made Adam's stomach turn. That seemed worse than it never happening. He did not want to accept defeat, but if he could, the burden would be lifted. Having the search for the four remaining jewels hang over him into middle age or beyond felt overwhelming.

"But I am convinced," Rylee continued, "if you found one jewel near here, then at least one other is nearby. We need to put the information in front of the right people. Once we do, everything else will fall into place."

As she finished, Adam's phone buzzed. He glanced at the screen. There was no name, but he recognized the number as Michelle's. After answering and greeting her, Adam listened to Michelle go on without a pause between words about a guest they had at the hotel.

After hanging up, he smiled at Rylee. "It looks like the information is in front of the right people. We need to go back to the apartment to pick up Grace's necklace, then to the hotel. Now we have a lead to follow."

* * *

Rylee swallowed the last of her latte before they entered the Spartan Hotel. "So is this woman vacationing here?" she asked.

"Not based on what Michelle said," Adam answered as they walked in the automatic doors. "She told me her name is Kelsey, and she just came into..."

"The restaurant," Michelle said, rushing up to them. She was out of breath. "Sorry to be rushed, but I only have so much time on my break. I never met this person before, but she thought someone here at the Hotel was looking for a sapphire, and I think she has the one that belonged to Grace."

"Where is she now?" Adam asked.

"The table by the northern windows in the restaurant," Michelle said, nodding her head toward the dining area. "Sorry, I don't know much else, or even if she is willing to give the sapphire up or is only curious about its history."

"You've done plenty," Rylee said. "Thank you."

Michelle narrowed her eyes, ever so slightly. "You look familiar. Have we met?"

"I was Grace's Maid of Honor."

Michelle nodded and gave a smile mixed with sadness. "It's so sweet of you to help take care of things. I hope this goes well. But by now...,"

"Time's up!" an unseen voice bellowed from behind the hotel desk.

"What was that?" Rylee asked, but Michelle was already heading back to the desk.

"Don't worry about it," Adam said. "Let's see if Kelsey has the sapphire, and if there is any way we can buy it."

They walked into the restaurant and found a woman sitting on her own by the arch-shaped windows, looking over the amusement park in the distance. She appeared to be in her late thirties. Though well-dressed, Adam only noticed the necklace and the sapphire hanging from it. It was shaped exactly like the ruby. It had to be the one Grace's father had cut.

That will help me honor Grace's memory, Adam thought. I could even feel a little joy if I can hold it. But then Adam realized that the sapphire was hanging from the necklace, which meant it was not hanging from the corkscrew hook. Could he prove it belonged on the necklace without it?

The woman noticed them before they walked to the circular table. She held out her hand. "Hello. Thank you for meeting me. Kelsey Copenhaver."

Adam took her hand briefly. "Adam Thompson. And this is Rylee Bixler, who was my wife's best friend."

Kelsey waved to the seats, and they sat. "I'm waiting for my meal. Feel free to order anything."

Adam shook his head. "I'm afraid I'm in the mood to be all business. Do you know the story behind that sapphire pendant?"

"I think I do," Kelsey said. "I certainly know its story ever since it was given to me. But my jeweler told me that there is more to it."

"Your jeweler?" Rylee repeated.

"Yes, I had gone over yesterday to have a ring resized. I wore this sapphire then, too. He said someone had told him the day before about gemstones cut in this shape. They were supposed to be a wedding gift to a young woman, but he never gave it to her. Now, the same woman has passed on. But her husband was trying to collect the jewels to honor his wife's memory. He did not remember how to contact you, but he said your family had connections to this hotel."

Adam nodded, though hearing the heart-wrenching story told in a matter-of-fact tone was unnerving. "That's the basics of it. There were five jewels. We found the ruby when Grace was still working here. I've been trying to find the other four since she passed away."

"Though I was the one who contacted the local jewelers to be on the lookout," Rylee said.

Adam glanced over at Rylee.

"Hey, give credit where credit's due," Rylee said.

"Let me make a couple of things clear," Kelsey said. "First, I believe you. I don't think anyone would make up this kind of story. I've seen enough awful things happen to people that I can understand how a valuable wedding gift could be lost, and a young life can be lost."

The tone was more sympathetic this time, but the words stung Adam.

"But I also have to say, I have mixed feelings about parting with it."

"How much do you want for it?" Adam asked, regretting how he kept complete accounting records at work but unsure how much he could afford to pay out of his pocket right now.

"It's not an issue of money. It's an issue of memories." Kelsey touched the sapphire again. "Joel was my boyfriend for years. When we moved in together, he gave me sapphire as a gift. Almost as if it was the wedding ring for a couple who had decided not to marry. Joel could be an amazing man." Kelsey paused, and though her eyes still pointed in Adam's direction, he understood she was no longer looking at him. Then she continued. "But as time passed, I saw the amazing less and the disappointing more. Fights. Secrets. Never another woman, but spending money we could not afford and running around with friends who got him in trouble. I couldn't take it anymore. I moved out."

Kelsey stopped, and Adam was not sure what to say next. He glanced at Rylee again, who put her palm up to him. He chose to be patient.

"That was six months ago," Kelsey resumed. "Joel and I split up our stuff. I wasn't sure if he'd ask for the sapphire back, but he never did. Of all the things I have, this reminds me of him most."

Kelsey reached behind her neck and unlatched her necklace. She held it out in front of herself, the sapphire dangling between her and Adam. Now, Adam realized, the sapphire was still in the original silver setting, but upside down. The corkscrew attachment was at the bottom, while a new loop had been added to the top to slide a regular necklace through. Kelsey must have misunderstood the curly design to be a decoration.

"It has nothing to do with money," she repeated. "I've never even had it appraised. I wanted to hold on to it because it carries some of the wonderful memories of our time together. It reminds me of who Joel could be, of the marvelous times we had together."

Adam's sigh was loud enough to draw the attention of diners at the next table. This was not at all like the historical society a year ago. The ruby had no emotional meaning to anyone other than Grace and himself. Kelsey had a right to the sapphire not only because it was a gift to her but because it had a deeper connection to her life.

"If it means that much to you, you should-," Adam almost let out a yelp. He felt a kick from what he assumed was one of Rylee's high heels.

He kept the sound inside and kept some choice words for Rylee in his throat. They had lost. Adam could seek the other three jewels, or he could accept the ruby would be the only one ever found. If Kelsey wanted to surrender the sapphire, that would be fine. But she did not. They had no right to push this any farther.

But Rylee stared daggers at him. She obviously disagreed. Adam's memory flashed back to the college student she had been, who never settled for less than perfect scores or her way.

"Adam, you and Grace were my best friends," she said to him. "I trust you with this." Rylee turned to Kelsey. "And you need to hear what I'm about to say, even though we just met. You need to understand why Adam must have that sapphire."

Kelsey set her hand on the table, but kept a firm grip on the necklace. She took a sip from her water with the other hand. Adam was concerned Rylee was being too forceful, but Kelsey nodded. "I'm listening."

"I went through a nasty breakup," Rylee said, leaning in towards Kelsey but her expression showed sympathy, intimidation. "Michael and I were together for four years, lived together the last two. I thought we could cope through everything. But over time, the fights stopped being a once-a-month problem, and became an everyday struggle."

Kelsey nodded. "Sounds familiar."

"But, like you, I still have memories of my time with Michael. The dates, the jokes, the trips. I wish it could have continued, but I don't regret that we tried."

"I don't regret dating Joel," Kelsey said. "But I don't see what this has to do with the sapphire."

Adam did not see the connection either, and he did not understand why Rylee had said she trusted him with this story. Everything so far he already knew.

"Here is why you need to let Adam have the sapphire. Michael and I can still reconcile. I don't mean dating again. Bringing that romance back to life would be like bringing a person back from the dead. But I haven't given up on us being friends again. There is so much good in him, and I know our breakup was as much my fault as his. I said things no less cruel than he did. He never abused me, he never laid a hand on me in anger, and he never cheated on me. One day, I want to be his friend again. I want to share those jokes again. I want to share those memories with him again, even if we don't make new ones. I've muted him, but actually, I'm still connected to him on every social media channel out there. One day, I'll open them, and see if we can at least talk again."

"And you're assuming Joel and I could become friends again?" Kelsey asked.

"I'm not making any assumptions about your relationship," Rylee said. She took Kelsey's empty hand. "But I can make an assumption about his. No matter how unlikely it may sound, you and I might find some slight part of those lost relationships again." Rylee pointed to Adam. "He can't."

All three of them were silent for the moment. Adam had not known Rylee still had emotional connections to Michael. He had assumed, considering the fighting she talked about, there was a clean break there. That was what she trusted him with–she still held platonic feelings for Michael.

But that could wait. Now he understood the connection between that relationship and the jewel. Rylee spoke it.

"These jewels, crafted by Grace's father, were supposed to be hers. They are all Adam has of her."

Adam could not decide if Rylee was being manipulative or pointing out the truth. Maybe sometimes the truth is manipulative. But when he noticed a single tear on Kelsey's cheek, he realized Rylee's strategy had worked.

She picked up the sapphire again, and this time held it out across the table to Adam. "Take it. And as I said, no money."

Adam reached out but stopped himself. "Are you sure? If it's valuable, I could pay it off over time. We made a donation when we found the ruby. . ."

Kelsey shook her head. "No money to me, then," she repeated. "Honestly, it wouldn't make any difference to how I live my life. Make a donation to a charity as you see fit, if you like. I'm taking your word for it, but if you loved Grace, and you were robbed of her, then this should be yours. You deserve it. You deserve to be happy. But while I'm taking you at your word, I want to hear one promise."

Adam nodded as Kelsey slipped the sapphire into his hand.

"You will never stop looking for the other three, no matter how long it takes. If you and Grace loved each other that much, then you owe a lifetime of devotion to her."

That was a heavy burden for a stranger to ask, but she was freely letting go of the sapphire. And it was exactly what Adam wanted to do, anyway. He clenched his fist around the sapphire. "I give you my word. The rest of my life will still be devoted to Grace, and to finding the jewels, just like when she lived."

Kelsey nodded. "Then that is enough for me."

Adam detached the sapphire from Kelsey's necklace, and then reattached it to Grace's necklace in the fourth clasp. A perfect fit, of course.

"Somehow, it looks right there," Kelsey said.

It did, Adam realized. But without Grace's neck and shoulders to set it on, it also looked so wrong.

* * *

"Thank you, thank you, thank you!"

"You're welcome," Rylee said from the passenger seat, ginning. "Your welcome, how ever many times you've said that since we got in the car."

Adam shook himself for a moment. He needed to refocus on the road. But gratitude was pouring out of him.

"I'm having trouble processing things," he said "But thank you. Again. Thank you for putting yourself out there to talk her into giving it to us."

"I had to convince her," she said. "I couldn't bear to watch you walk away empty-handed. But I don't feel guilty over it. Everything I said was true. If she still would have said no, well, at least we don't need to worry about that."

Adam was uncertain if Rylee meant she would have made up lies or given up, and he did not want to know. It hardly mattered now. He turned onto Route 743. "I do appreciate it. I never even reached out to you and here you are, searching and negotiating."

"I wish I could still be here when you get the sapphire adjusted for the necklace," Rylee said, her hair blown with the wind from her open window. "No reason to keep that extra hook Kelsey added. But I can't stay away from Chicago forever."

"You've already done so much. Maybe you can come back when I've found all five jewels."

"Now that's the optimism I like to hear," Rylee said. As Adam turned the car onto 422, she laughed, reached out and set her hand on his leg. Adam looked over, a little surprised. There had been no physical touch between them all week. Rylee giggled, blushed and pulled back as if she was not sure if she had crossed a line or not. Rylee turned to face the window. She's embarrassed and even confused, Adam thought. But a happy sort of embarrassment. They both were navigating uncharted waters, in more ways than looking for the gems.

When he parked at the apartment complex, though, both the happiness and the embarrassment were replaced. At least for Adam. Rylee was still smiling playfully, but an emptiness was growing inside of Adam, one he recognized.

Yes, he had the sapphire now. He was with one of his best friends. But he could not have what he really wanted. Grace would not be in their apartment. No matter what he did, no matter what successes he had in life, he would never have her back.

Adam stepped out of his car, as did Rylee, but she rushed over to him. She grabbed him by the shoulders. "Hey, what just happened to you?"

Feigning ignorance, Adam tilted his head, but knew his expression must have given him away.

"You look like you just got bad news."

Adam wondered if he should say it out loud. But the voice within him answered that question.

You can trust her with this.

"I still want to see Grace one more time." Adam managed to say it without crying. He was more frustrated than empty now.

"I am so sorry," Rylee said. She looked over her shoulder, towards Adam's apartment. He knew she understood. "Maybe you shouldn't go in there right away. Could a little celebrating could put you in a better mood, somewhere else? I know you don't want to do anything wild, but maybe a sports bar? One with a golf tournament on the big screen? Or grab a glass or two of wine somewhere? We don't even need to talk if you need to think."

Adam shook his head.

"Anything? I understand you're upset, but the odds of us finding any of the gems in one week were astronomical. You should be able to smile afterwards."

"I know you mean well. And I wish I could stay happy. But I can't."

Rylee sighed. "Let me know if you change your mind about having dinner or anything. Remember, I fly back to O'Hare tomorrow night. We might have time to do something in the afternoon, to celebrate a little and say a proper goodbye."

Adam nodded. He would be ready to celebrate tomorrow. He might not want to celebrate, but after a night's sleep, he could at least see his friend off with a smile on his face and more sincere gratitude. "I don't want to promise how I'll be tomorrow. It's complicated for me..."

"Don't explain," Rylee said, cupping his face in her hands. For a moment, he thought she might kiss him. Adam was not sure he wanted her to. Maybe? No. A friendly kiss. More. Less.

She did not lean in and took her hands away. Adam felt mostly relieved, but a little disappointed.

Then the emptiness returned.

"I have to go back to my hotel room, and get some sleep," Rylee said. "Please, whether or not we spend tomorrow together, try to be happy."

After Rylee drove away and the necklace and sapphire were secure in the jewelry case, Adam considered that word.

Happy.

He may find fleeting moments of happiness, as each jewel was found or when he could forget his troubles with a friend. But genuine happiness? That was gone forever.

How would he ever be happy again, when he would never be whole without Grace?

Chapter 20

Adam's face was on the wrong side of the bed again.

He woke, finding himself lying diagonally across the bed, his upper body lying on the side that should have been Grace's. It was as if he needed to caress her, no matter how long she had been gone. He remembered waking near where Grace should have been several times over the past year, though when the last time was, he did not know. Those mornings happened when time blurred, the days and weeks indistinguishable from each other. Now the days contained purpose again. But even with purpose, even with goal accomplished, hopelessness colored each sunrise.

He pushed himself out of bed, remembered the day was Sunday and put on an undershirt and cut-off sweatpants. He was not going anywhere today. No one to impress today.

The days were separate from each other, he thought to himself. Not like the fog that once obscured his days. Yesterday was a big day. The sapphire was in the apartment, a necessary step to completing the collection, to honoring Grace. And yet, as he mindlessly ate a bowl of cereal, Adam found no joy in that accomplishment. He left the bowl and spoon in the sink, along with the other dishes he had not bothered with for a week.

Adam walked to the bedroom closet and opened the jewelry box. He gazed at the sapphire along with the ruby, each attached to the necklace.

One part of his mind acknowledged the accomplishment. Rylee had been right yesterday. The odds were against tracking down any one of the jewels this soon.

But Adam had looked in the jewelry box for happiness. He found none.

This quest was something he wanted to do, something he needed to do. But even as Adam made progress, he felt no real satisfaction. He knew only duty, a duty now closer to being fulfilled, but that sense of responsibility was the only thing he experienced. Emotions, happiness or otherwise, disappeared.

No, he corrected himself. Loneliness still remained.

His phone rang from somewhere. Flipping through the bed sheets trying to find it, Adam realized who it must be. Rylee mentioned something about wanting to meet up before she flew back to Chicago. He thought at the time, he would be ready to celebrate, or at least act happy, but he found himself in the opposite mood.

As he found the phone wrapped up in a pillow case, Adam answered and saw he was right about who made the call, but wrong about her desires.

"I'm checked out of the hotel," Rylee said. "But my flight isn't until eight tonight. Want to hang out in the afternoon?"

Adam almost declined. But then he realized Rylee was the best friend with whom he still connected. Michael may have been his best man, but he made no flights back to Pennsylvania to help. Maybe Nate, but he was more of a co-worker than a buddy. Rylee deserved a personal farewell. Still, he was not in the mood for anything too fancy.

Looking at himself in the mirror, even a fast-food burger would be fancy right now.

"Sure, but, I hope you understand, I'm not up to going out," he said. "You could come over here? I do want to see you."

"Sure, that's fine. And I understand. All this has been hard on you, even on a good day. Could I buy you something for lunch? Want to order. . ."

"No, you've already done so much, don't be spending anything on me. I'll take care of my lunch."

The phone was silent for a moment. Then Rylee spoke up again. "You sure you're alright?"

"I'm down. But nothing to worry about."

"Okay. I'll be over at about two. And you and I are going to be happy. Got it?"

"I'll try."

* * *

Adam passed the time trying to watch a golf tournament on television. It was the final day of a major event, and three golfers contended for the championship. But he was unable to focus. After watching two tee shots, he turned the television off, made himself a small bowl of tomato soup, and pondered on the sofa.

He reminisced about Grace and the jewels. If he was not at work, that was almost all he could think of. Then, he wondered about what he would do if he found all five jewels. Would he be happy then? Would he feel whole? Would there be any other purpose if this mission ever ended?

There were still three more gemstones to be found, he reminded himself. It might be a little early to worry over life afterward.

His phone buzzed. A text from Rylee printed, "I am in the parking lot. Will be there in a minute."

Adam realized he had never changed since this morning. He almost turned back to grab something else, but decided against it. Let Rylee see him this way. It did not matter.

He had looked far more ridiculous some days in college, when Grace, Rylee and Michael would see him at a 2 p.m. class in pajamas. The memory gave Adam a chuckle for a moment.

There was a knock on the sliding glass door. Adam stood and opened it. Rylee waited there, wearing a loose-fitting tangerine top and capris. Adam wondered if she could replace Michael in a heartbeat if she wanted. Probably. The thought disappeared quickly and he let her enter.

She hugged him tightly. "You'll be okay," she said.

"Thank you," he said, though he wondered Rylee's words were true.

They sat on the couch together and chatted for a while, mostly about Rylee's plans back in Illinois. She was considering looking for a different job, and willing to move for it.

"Back here?" Adam asked.

She shook her head. "No. I'm too attached to the Midwest. I want to visit out here, remember our college days. Go down King Street in Shippensburg at least once a year to look back on our wilder times."

She stopped. Rylee seemed to analyze Adam's reaction, or lack of one. "Please tell me you still remember those wild times? Both on and off-campus?"

"Grace and I weren't as wild as you and Michael."

"I guess not. But you enjoyed those times."

Adam nodded.

"Smile," Rylee said.

Now Adam stood. "I'm sorry. I know what you're trying to do, and I do feel better with you around. I appreciate everything you've done, and I'm glad that you wanted to come back here even knowing I'd be-," he waved his arms over himself, "-like this. But please, accept that I am too lonely to be how I was again. I'm not the same guy you knew at Shippensburg anymore."

Rylee rose. "I know you'll always mourn Grace. But if you never smile again, if you're never happy again, her death may as well have killed you too."

"I'm not that depressed."

"That's still not good enough. You're doing something with your life. Working at your office and finding the jewels. You'll discover more to do over the years. But you should enjoy those years. Those days. These days."

Adam looked down, but then looked into Rylee's eyes again. "When I was in that emotional fog for months, I assumed I would never find any kind of joy again. Then, when the fog lifted, there was a part of me that thought I would find glimpses of happiness, if not now, then soon. But as each day passes, I think all the happiness in my life is gone."

"That's ridiculous."

"Then where am I going to find any joy again?"

"There are ways."

It was only the slightest movement, the most minute shift in her pose, but Adam noticed. Any man would have.

Suddenly, he understood why Rylee wanted to say goodbye here and now, and how she wanted to say it.

She opened her mouth, but Adam cut her off. "No," he said. "That's not...not us."

"I know it seems a little sudden," Rylee whispered as if anyone might hear them. She took an inviting stride, closing the gap between them but not touching him. "But I'm sure this is the right thing for us. Especially for you."

No, it isn't, the voice inside Adam's head whispered. *Tell her to leave.*

But the rest of Adam's mind did not want to shove her away, at least not without an explanation. She had shown him friendship in his time of need, and she had helped find and recover the sapphire. Rylee deserved to know why he was spurning her.

"Grace and I-," he started, but then he could not find any more words. How could he describe how wonderful Grace had been? How wonderful she was to him? That he still loved her?

Rylee was now inches from him but did not move to touch Adam. "Grace was my friend. My best friend. I know you still adore her. But she's gone. I hate it almost as much as you do. But if she could have known we would be here and she wouldn't, I think she would understand."

"We never had that conversation," Adam said.

"But you aren't happy," Rylee pleaded. "I haven't been through what you've been through, but I know loneliness, too. You're suffering worse than I am. You can't enjoy watching golf on television or drinking your favorite wine. We even found the sapphire, and you're still depressed."

"A relationship with you wouldn't make me happy," Adam said before he could choose better words. He quickly added, "We aren't a match, even if we wished we were."

"I know," Rylee nodded. "I've always known that. But we are friends. Friends who are suffering from loneliness. I accepted I would be lonely, and was going to fly back home, maybe without seeing you again. But when I woke this morning, I decided I could live with myself being lonely, but not you." She put her arms over his shoulders, a gentle caress that seemed to ask permission to touch without the words. Adam did not return any embrace but did not stop her. "I am asking for no commitments. No promises. Don't you trust me?"

Not with this, the voice spoke in Adam's mind. But his mouth remained silent.

"I swear," Rylee continued, "I'm doing this so you can be happy again."

Her touch did nothing to persuade Adam. Though striking, Rylee's beauty did not match Grace's and was not enough to tempt him. But her words were wearing away at his resolve because there was truth behind them. Loneliness was continuing to push against his heart, and for the first time, his heart was ready to cave into it.

Adam wanted to look back years from now and say Grace was the only one. He forced his heart to push back again.

"My whole life has been about Grace," Adam said. "I don't think I can change."

There was silence between them. Rylee kept her arms draped over him but did nothing more to allure Adam.

"If that is your decision, I will leave. But before you turn me away, I need to remind you of something. Something you know, but need to truly understand."

Adam waited for Rylee to speak again.

"Grace is never coming back."

Adam was stunned. Of course, he already knew that, and he thought he understood it. In fact, he did, but he had refused to think of one simple truth: if he kept waiting for Grace, he would be alone forever.

As much as he loved Grace, Adam could not bear the separation. The weight of loneliness overwhelmed Adam's heart, and he knew he could hold back no longer.

"You're sure?" Adam asked. "You're sure you won't feel guilty about this afterward?"

Rylee nodded, pulled him closer and kissed him. Adam's arms started to encircle her.

No! The voice screamed, but it was too late.

"I just want to make you happy," Rylee purred.

And she did.

Part III

The Help
of a Partner

Chapter 21

Putting looked like the easiest part of golf to an outsider. But Adam was no outsider. Though any aspect of golf had its challenges, putting was what separated the good and great golfers from each other. Though the ball might be closer to the hole for a put than for a drive or a chip, it was while putting that the mental aspect of the sport was most obvious.

A year ago, even a month ago, Adam would not have been able to calm his mind enough to tap in a six-inch putt. But as he lined up this putt on the seventh green from the edge of the fringe, 18-feet away from the hold, he knew he would sink it.

He took a breath, calmed his mind, remembered the lay of the ground in front of him, and tapped the ball with his putter. The ball rolled quickly at first, moving to the right of the hole. It started to trail back, slowed, and fell in.

"I have no idea how you keep doing that," Nate said. "What is that, three 'twos' in a row?"

"Call them birdies," Adam said, reaching into the cup to pull the ball out. "And yes. Though that's not so impressive on a par-3 course."

"It's a lot better than anything I'm doing," Adam said, pulling the scorecard out of his back pocket. "I have so many 'eights' that I look like I have a toll-free number on my card."

"Call those snowmen. And line up your shot. Remember to keep it gentle. You're not trying to hit a fastball."

The moment the words left his tongue, Adam realized that Nate would overcompensate for his earlier mistakes on the greens. He tapped his ball too lightly, and it rolled only half of its distance to the hole. Adam said nothing as Nate finally was able to push the ball in.

"Time to write another snowman," Nate said to himself as he scribbled on the scorecard. "Why do you enjoy spending weekends like this?"

"It gets in your blood," Adam said, beginning his walk to the next tee. "I haven't played a regular 18-hole course in years but I'm still hooked."

"I don't think this ever getting my blood or any other part of my anatomy," Nate said. "Maybe we should try disk golf."

"Disk golf?" Adam looked back over his shoulder at Nate. "Blasphemy."

"What, you can hit a little ball at a target, but you're afraid to throw a frisbee at one? Cheaper sport to play, too."

Adam set his ball on the tee for the eighth hole. "Look, I get that golf isn't for everyone. It's not your blood because baseball is your blood type already."

"It's actually O-negative."

"But once you play golf the right way, the pure way, other versions of the sport are never quite as satisfying. Give me an eighteen-hole, par-72, six-thousand-yard course. After that, this par-3 is fun, but not the real thing. And don't get me started about disk golf."

"Golf on computer?"

Adam was about to line up his tee shot, but reflexively lowered his shoulders in disappointment. "Sport on a computer isn't even a sport anymore."

Because this was a par-3 course, and not a standard golf course, Adam did not need certain clubs to hit the ball.

Which was good, as he still did not have a full set of clubs. Last Monday, he finally grabbed some individual clubs specifically for a shorter course. They were used and cheaper, but they still worked.

Adam lined up his 7-iron to the ball and swung. The ball sailed and landed on the fringe just outside the green. Adam estimated the ball was thirty-five feet from the hole.

Nate did not step up to the tee, though, as Adam walked backwards to give him space. "Don't take this the wrong way," Nate said, "but, don't you try anything new?"

Half of Adam's mind understood the question. Nate, a baseball man through and through, was giving golf a serious try for the first time today. Adam appreciated Nate's interest, but he doubted that he would put on a glove if Nate had offered for him to join a pickup game.

But the other half of Adam's mind raced back six days.

Rylee.

Adam smirked, but only said, "You have no idea."

Of course, Adam would not hint to Nate that he had spent the night-well, afternoon-with her. Nate hardly knew who Rylee was, anyway. There was no question that, after their tryst, he felt renewed. Able to talk more with his co-workers. Able to take a glass of red wine at night. Able to walk a golf course again. If Adam did not exactly feel as happy as he did two years ago, he at least felt renewed.

Nate shook his head and took the 7-iron from Adam. Adam watched him line up and take his swing. Before the iron struck the ball, he could tell Nate's shot would slice seventy feet to the right.

* * *

Adam sipped the last of his wine from the glass. Just one glass a night, enough to make him relax, he reminded himself. Walking the course that afternoon with Nate, even in the sunshine, had not quite worn him down. Nevertheless, Adam was ready to lay down and ease into sleep and, he hoped, a peaceful Sunday morning.

After setting his glass down next to the sink, Adam walked to the bedroom. He sat on his side of the bed and looked to the other side.

He still thought of it as Grace's side. But another woman had been there. Adam realized that all week. But this time, he knew he had made a mistake.

Had Grace been alive, being with Rylee would have been the ultimate betrayal. But even with Grace gone, it was, at best, a poor decision.

Adam could not deny he experienced a new high for a week after his surprising farewell to Rylee. Even after she left for Chicago, he found it easier to treat his home with a little self-respect. The dishes were cleaned and stacked in the cupboards. He finally updated the records for his bank account and found himself in the black. Office banter again filled his work week. His exercise routine became a regular part of his day, focusing primarily on his arms and legs. He even put golf back on the television, even if only as background noise.

For six days, he felt happy, or something that imitated happiness. But the high faded, and now he realized he still was not whole.

He could no longer say Grace was the only one. Not that he would tell anyone else about his last moments with Rylee, but the fact he could not think it to himself was upsetting enough.

Adam tried to rationalize it. Few single men would complain about giving in to a woman. Most single men sought such passionate evenings. And at least he cared about Rylee and knew her for many years.

He would not have caved to anyone, under any circumstances, if Grace were still alive. He should not have been in this situation, under this degree of emotional vulnerability.

The explanations brought comfort with them, but not enough. He and Rylee had crossed a line they should have stayed far behind. If nothing else, he and Grace held back for their wedding night. If ever a second woman would truly win Adam over, would finally make him whole again, he should treat the new relationship the same way.

Adam laid down on his side of the bed with a sigh.

He accepted that sleeping with Rylee had been wrong.

He prayed that experiencing the mistake once had removed it from his system.

* * *

Adam had shared, with as many people as he saw, the news that he had found the sapphire. He hoped the success story would inspire others to keep their eyes open for the remaining jewels.

Over the last week, he had told everyone in the office about the sapphire. Adam intended to tell his neighbor, Brandi, and visit Grace's old co-worker, Michelle, soon. Rylee had been right about one thing. Telling people face-to-face was more valuable than all the social media posts the internet provided. Not only did word-of-mouth lead to finding the sapphire, but there was also something more rewarding about speaking with someone about this victory.

Of course, he considered as he prepared a light Sunday lunch, Rylee only reminded him of the importance of face-to-face conversations. Grace had taught that lesson to him. Since their first date, there was an intensity in their relationship which could only be recreated when they saw each other's eyes. Adam doubted even his memory replicated their unique hue.

If only he could look in Grace's eyes again. An opportunity to let her know he owned the sapphire. One more chance for her to share something that needed to be spoken face-to-face. She had said there was something important for him to know during her last phone call. One more thing to frustrate him—Adam would never know what she would have thought of anything that happened. He suspected she had found some encouragement at the conference, something that would have helped them on the way to running a bed-and-breakfast. It did not matter anymore, Adam supposed.

He took his plate and sat on the sofa. He wondered if he should try to watch a golf tournament, not make it background noise as he did when he organized the apartment. Adam did not remember the last time he observed each stroke as it aired, following every competitor through the course. Though his mood was mildly better, he was not sure if he wanted to focus on sports, even his favorite game.

Before he decided, his phone rang. It was Rylee. Adam was nervous to answer. Since she had flown back to Chicago, Adam and she had texted a few times. Their messages had been friendly, but nothing beyond that, as if their last moments together never happened. But Adam feared talking with her in a way he had never experienced with anyone else. Not fear of harm, but fear there was no longer anything he should do with Rylee. In the last week, the friendly texts still seemed appropriate. Now, realizing they should not have been together, even something as simple as a conversation became impossible.

He overcame his nerves and answered. "Hello, Rylee. How are things?"

"Things are okay," Rylee answered, but with none of the force Adam anticipated. "I just needed to ask you something. It's important."

"Anything," Adam responded.

"It's been exactly a week. I just need to know that you're okay with...You understand that I meant it when I said we're still friends, nothing more."

"I understand."

"There's no reason for you to pursue me. I'm not playing mind games."

She was subdued, Adam thought. She was not making demands, which would have been expected considering their last encounter and her usual forcefulness. "I took everything you said at face value. I don't expect anything out of you. Except that we're still friends if you think we can be."

"We can. Just, please, don't come out here. Let's stick to texting, okay? And no words about last Sunday."

She feels the guilt, too, Adam surmised. "I understand. But if you ever need a friend, I'm here for you."

"Thank you. I pray you'll find the jewels for Grace. Goodbye."

Rylee hung up, but Adam did not pull the phone away from his ear.

Grace was gone forever. He needed to avoid Michael after being with his ex. And now Rylee was distancing.

Soon, the jewels might not only be the last things he had of Grace, but the last things he had to live for.

Chapter 22

"I'll take the tuna salad wrap today," Adam ordered. "And my usual cold brew."

"We're out of vanilla," the barista said.

"Hazelnut?"

The barista shook her head.

"Oh, then I'll live on the wild side and try caramel."

The barista took Adam and Nate's order to the back.

"That's some wild side you have there," Nate said, sitting by Adam at the bar. "Make sure you don't start putting chocolate syrup on your dessert. Or on your pancakes. That might lead to jail time."

"Oh, shut up," Adam said, keeping his tone light. "I was being sarcastic."

"Still, 'wild' doesn't seem to go with you," Nate said. "You won't even sit outside right now because of the heat."

"I like July and August, but only in small doses. Too humid around here. Besides, you don't seem to be one to criticize someone for not being too wild."

Nate looked downward. "Not anymore. I was crazier before I went to college. I Wish I hadn't been."

"Is this going to be a story from baseball?"

Nate hesitated. "No. The craziest thing happened after a game, but that's a story for another time. How about you tell me the wildest thing you ever did?"

"Wow. There's not much to choose from."

"Look, as long as it doesn't include golf, I won't make fun."

The barista came over with their drinks. Adam grabbed his cold brew and thought over Nate's curiosity. He wondered if he had ever done anything others would consider exciting, or even notable. "I didn't have a rebellious streak when I was a teenager," Adam said. "I'm not that much of a risk-taker now." As the words left his mouth, he realized that what had happened between him and Rylee last weekend could be seen as a risk. But he did not want to mention anything about her to Nate. He did not strike Adam as the type of guy who would understand how he had gotten himself into that situation.

"Not every risk is something rebellious," Nate said. "Some of our clients make risky investments to produce more money for investors or employees. Or hope to, anyway."

"Well, if you put it that way, and you really won't joke about it..."

"No golf."

"No golf in this story, I promise. My biggest risk was saying 'yes' to Grace."

"What do you mean? Did she ask you out?"

Adam nodded, but then shook his head. "More like she demanded me out."

"Oh, this sounds good. Keep going."

"You know the Quittie, the creek that runs through Annville? When I was still in high school, sometimes, for a workout, I would jog the path that runs alongside it. I stopped on the bridge one day to get a breather. From the other side, here comes Grace, jogging too. She stopped, talked with me. I thought of her as completely out of my league. Blonde. Amazing eyes. You know, the girl in school who could pick any boy she wanted because every boy wanted her."

"And she chose you."

"I assumed we were having a pleasant conversation and didn't hope for anything else. Then she says, 'so, six at the pizza shop?' I was so shocked I didn't say a word. She started jogging again, yelling something about not being late."

"How early were you?"

"Thirty minutes. I wasn't missing my chance, but the anticipation scared me. You remember how high school was. If you were stood up, rumors flew, and you got labeled. But if you're the one who stands someone else up, you get elevated as a tough guy. Or girl."

"Yeah, we were all kind of stupid in high school."

"If Grace had not come through the doors right on time, I would have been knocked down a peg. It doesn't sound like much of anything now, but how you're seen by others seemed so important then."

"Small price to pay for finding your partner. Especially when you're only in high school."

"She arrived exactly at six. It was awkward, like most first dates. But I could tell right away she had an interest in me. I learned there was something behind her eyes, not only a good mind but a powerful soul. We must have been there for hours, talking about everything and nothing at all."

Adam stopped speaking but continued reminiscing in his mind.

Their senior year of high school.

Prom.

Four years at Shippensburg.

Take classes together.

Romantic dinners.

Movie dates.

Glow-bowling.

Graduation.

Proposing.

It all came back. They had told each other, "Always us." But there was no "us" anymore. He could never have those memories again with anyone.

Adam almost missed Nate's words. "...so, the most important lesson I've learned is that forgiveness is the greatest miracle. But forgiven or not, finding any meaningful connections has not worked out for me."

"Give it time," Adam said, hoping that cliché was appropriate.

The barista gave them their food, and they ate in silence for a few minutes. Adam hoped he did not have to rush his eating. It would be nice to savor something. But even with the minutes to focus on the taste of his wrap, he felt distracted.

The loneliness of missing Grace was still there. But now, it was mixed with guilt over Rylee. Adam tried to force it out of his mind. He would not risk confessing any part of their tryst in front of Nate.

"So, any news on the other jewels?" Nate asked.

"Not yet. I've been updating my social media posts, even paying a little to give the posts a wider audience. I called and e-mailed a few news outlets, but no one has called back. And, following the advice of, um, a friend, I've gone to some places and tried to strike up conversations with people."

"But no results?"

"Not since we grabbed the sapphire."

"Did Grace's parents write out a will? Something in that document might tell you where the other jewels are now. Or, at least, where they were when her parents died."

Adam shook his head. "I was at the reading of the will with Grace. If her dad intended to pass them on that way, it was under a general category of all his earthy possessions going to her. Which was not much by then. Anyway, no mention of any gems."

Nate hesitated before responding. "I don't mean to be negative, but do you know if the jewels are still around? Things get misplaced and lost. Even thrown away by accident."

"Maybe, but I have to keep looking as if each one is out there. There could be one in someone's attic or basement, but my guess is they all still exist. Hopefully, one is still owned by a relative of Grace's. If I could learn more about her family, I might find the diamond without any other research. But everyone I knew is gone, and I never saw a family tree anywhere. If she has any relatives, I'm worried they may be on the other side of the country."

Nate nodded and took a bite out of his sandwich. His eyes appeared pensive.

"What are you thinking of?"

"Am I allowed to mention baseball again?"

"Only if you must."

"Oh, I do. Our life coach's father had been coming to our games for weeks before we met him. But we did not realize the connection ourselves. It was not until he told us who his father was that we figured it out."

"And?"

"Family relations are not always so obvious to the naked eye. Some websites and libraries can help with a family tree search. You might find some branch of her family you or even Grace did not know about. And there's no reason that those relatives of hers must be far away. If you find them, and they have the diamond, they may no longer realize its significance. Years have passed. You'd have to tell them."

"Possibly. But for now, I'll stick with what I've been doing and save genealogy for another time. My schedule is pretty tight already."

As if it heard Adam, his phone started beeping. "Better start walking back to the office," he said, picking up his half-finished cold brew.

While they made their way to work, he said, "The most frustrating part about this search has been when we found the sapphire. We had it, and I found almost no happiness in it."

"Reminds me of when the Central baseball team..."

"Of course."

"...Qualified for the national regionals. That was a monumental accomplishment for us. But things happened off of the field, and we weren't able to appreciate it. On the other hand, after we lost in the national regional, we felt great about the season and having time to volunteer with people in need."

"Do you have a baseball story for every occasion?"

"I'd like to think so."

They made it to the office moments before their lunch break ended. "One other thing," Nate said. "You keep calling your team 'Central', and that you were Lebanon County champions."

"That is one-hundred percent correct."

"But I don't know of a Central in Lebanon County."

"There isn't. The team names weren't always of towns or schools."

"So where did you play?"

"Oh, if you want the name of the town, we were from Ca-."

"Gentlemen," Ms. Douglas called from her office.

"Talk to you later," Nate finished as they walked to their respective workspaces.

Chapter 23

On Saturday morning, Adam knew he was rushing. He did not have to, except he wanted to get out of his apartment. Over the last five days, he had spent most of his time inside his home and office. The apartment may be clean now, but he still had places he wanted to visit.

Michelle had sent him a text shortly after Adam woke. She expected to finish her shift at the hotel early and wondered if they could meet in the hotel restaurant to talk about finding the last three gems. As Adam read between the lines, it appeared Michelle connected with this quest now too, after helping Adam find the sapphire.

Well, Adam and Rylee. But he pushed that thought from his mind.

He stepped out his door, but as he was closing it, he looked down the hallway and spotted Brandi, surrounded by dozens of grocery bags.

"Do you need help?" he called out.

Brandi looked up, only now noticing Adam. "Oh, yes, please," she answered, her relief palatable.

Adam walked over and picked up a few of the plastic bags. There were fifteen bags from the store, plus six reusable ones.

"I am always overwhelming myself," Brandi said as she opened the door to her place.

Adam and Brandi brought all the bags into the apartment. Adam noticed most of the bags were full of the same items. He knew he should not pry, but after spotting the tenth loaf of bread, he had to ask.

"Bread, eggs, milk, over and over. Big French toast party?"

Brandi laughed. "No. The shelter's kitchen was getting low on a few things. They are making a push for donations, but I decided the best thing to do was pick up what I could myself."

She placed most of the bags together in a corner of her kitchen. She put three other bags near the refrigerator, and Adam guessed those were her personal groceries.

"Well, you're going beyond your call of duty," Adam said, hoping it sounded like the compliment he meant for it to be. "The time you volunteer there is a big donation alone."

"Thanks," she said as she started to put her food away. "But, I feel like, if I'm going to help, I should help in each situation I can."

Guilt, different from the guilt he had felt after being with Rylee, shot through Adam's nerves. He realized he had not given any donations to the shelter, not since Grace... "Um, do you need any more help?"

"No, you wouldn't know where anything goes. But have you had lunch yet? Maybe I could make you that French toast."

"I wouldn't want to impose."

"You're being invited. Have a seat. I'll get it started in a moment."

Adam took a chair at her kitchen table. The apartment was arranged like his, so there was not much space in this corner, but it seemed cozier than his place. It must be the difference between men and women taking care of their homes, he decided.

"I thought the bus driver would lose his mind when I brought all those bags on board, and then when I took them back off," Brandi was saying. Adam had forgotten she did not have a car. Of course, he had barely talked to her in the past year. "But he kept quiet since I tried to be quick."

"He didn't help? Or any other passengers?"

"No. And it doesn't surprise me. Many people get so focused on the tasks in front of them they don't recognize a chance to help someone else. Which is actually part of the reason I wanted you to stay a little longer."

"You need extra help at the shelter? I could try to...,"

"You're always welcome to volunteer, but that's not what I meant. Our shifts are full for the next couple of months. I meant I wanted to help you." Brandi paused as she cracked the eggs and started their lunch. "I have seen you only here and there, since, you know."

"You can say it. Since Grace died."

Brandi nodded. "I didn't mean to avoid you for this long, but I wanted to let you mourn whatever way you saw fit."

"I needed time. Space. I don't know if it was good that I isolated myself for a year, but I'm getting out more often now."

"I don't post much on social media, but I saw that you found the second of Grace's jewels," Brandi said. "Congratulations. I'm sure that was important to you."

Adam nodded but said nothing.

By now, Brandi had the bread on her griddle. "But I noticed something in the posts you've put up about the jewels you don't have. They're all so...wordy. You talk about all three jewels and list every place you've looked, and places you want to look, how one might be with a relative, but the others aren't. It's too much."

"I want people to be informed."

"Of course you do. But most people only want their information in small doses. Let me give you an example," she said, holding up a hand to stop Adam from responding. "Our shelter also promotes over the internet. People who are already involved prefer the longer, detailed messages. It motivates them to step up, do more."

"Like clean out a store's egg supply?"

"Yep." Brandi smiled. Adam was glad she took her ribbing in good humor. "But, for someone who is not involved yet, we've found that shorter, to the point messages are more likely to get them to take the first step. If their first encounter is a message with each need, each volunteer position, and each issue the shelter helps with, it overwhelms people. So they do nothing."

"But if they are told the basic facts, they make that first donation and then learn about the rest over time?"

"Exactly," Brandi said, putting a plate with two pieces of French toast in front of Adam. "And longer posts are more likely to be misread. Someone rushes through your posts about the jewels, and he might think the three jewels are being looked for together. Someone might know where one is, but dismiss it because it's not sitting between the other two."

"So even though I say it in the post, not everyone will read those details."

"A few people will read each word, but the longer the post is, the rarer that becomes. You have to make sure the few people out there who know where these jewels are both see these posts and understand them. Orange juice?"

"Sure."

Brandi poured a glass for each of them and then sat down with a plate of her own. "So, it's not that I want to tell you how to do this. I've never gone treasure hunting myself. But you could make your posts about one jewel at a time. It will make more relatable."

"And make it clearer that the jewels are probably in separate places," Adam thought aloud.

"Your food good?"

Adam had taken a bite, but he had been so lost in his thoughts he had not noticed it. Now he ate again. "Excellent. Thank you."

"I should make some bacon or sausage, too."

Adam shook his head. "Don't do that on my account. I have somewhere to go later, anyway."

"Well, before you do, there's one other thing I wanted to say to you. I should have said it a year ago, but then I reconsidered and kept my distance."

"I appreciate that. But say whatever is on your mind."

Brandi hesitated. "At the shelter, people wind up there for various reasons. Everyone seems to think, 'they're poor,' and there's no more to it than that. But usually, there is. Poverty doesn't happen in a vacuum. Many things place a person or a family in a shelter, from bad decisions to abuse. Other times, it's because the breadwinner in the family dies, and there was no life insurance. Or there was, but it wasn't enough. So we have single parents and children in the shelter suffering from more than homelessness. They suffer from losing their loved ones."

Adam chewed his next bite longer than usual, stalling. He was not sure what Brandi was asking.

"What I'm trying to say is, our counselors at the shelter, they have experience in helping people who are mourning, no matter how long it's been. If you need help...," Brandi's voice faded. "There's nothing to be ashamed of. I would connect you with someone, and it would all be private."

Adam finally swallowed. "I don't think I need that right now, but thank you for the offer. There were some dark times," Adam said, realizing his words were such an understatement his statement was almost a lie. "But I think now, I'll be okay."

Brandi nodded and ate as well. After a few moments of silence, Adam said, "I hope this doesn't sound awkward, but there are ways you remind me of Grace."

Her shoulders slouched, but in a way that showed the compliment was a bit too sweet, not inappropriate. "If you find something like that in me, I can only take that as a compliment."

"She was always looking for ways to help others. That's why she was so good at the hotel. She didn't help the visitors because a paycheck depended on it, but because she wanted to comfort anyone who she came across. Whether it was our donations to the shelter or befriending a couple of rude girls at the movie theater, she wanted to lift someone up."

"I can't tell you the number of times she would pass by me here, without time to stop for a chat, and still give me an encouraging word about my volunteering."

"And that was the reason she wanted to run that bed-and-breakfast. Not to be a business person. She wanted to give couples in tough times a chance to get away, to have a romantic vacation they could not afford otherwise." Adam gave the slightest hesitation before saying any more. He did not know if Brandi noticed, but he needed an extra breath. He was tired of remembering dreams destined to never come true.

Adam recovered and continued. "Anyway, I appreciate this. I don't eat much hot food at home."

Brandi shook her head. "Guys," she half-laughed. "But I appreciate you carrying all those bags."

"Need help to get them to the shelter?"

"No, another volunteer will be here in an hour. We'll use his car."

"Well, thank you again," Adam said, getting up from the table. "I must be going."

Adam realized he still had time before meeting with Michelle. But he knew he had to get back into his apartment and donate to the shelter online while Brandi's encouragement still lit a fire within him.

Then Adam remembered that he had never made an extra donation, as Kelsey Copenhaver had requested when she relinquished the sapphire to him. He had forgotten about it after his encounter with Rylee.

Time to correct that oversight, he decided, adding an extra two-hundred dollars to the amount he had already decided to write on his check for the shelter. After that was placed in the outbox, he started posting new announcements about each jewel.

When he uploaded the last post about the diamond, Adam checked the time again. He was now in danger of being late for Michelle.

* * *

"Do you mind if I drink another?" Michelle asked.

"Go ahead. I'm done," Adam said, waving the waiter away. He did not need a third glass of wine.

Michelle handed her glass to the waiter before he left. "I'm so sorry, my mind is going a mile a minute. This is how I cope when things get too crazy."

When Adam arrived at the Spartan Hotel, Michelle had already finished her shift and taken a table in the restaurant. She was still in her work clothes but had her hair down to her shoulders. That was the only thing down, as her anxiety was clearly through the roof. For twenty minutes, she had dominated the conversation, mostly with anecdotes of how tiresome work had become over the past year.

Adam had expected to hear something related to the gems sooner than this, but he allowed Michelle to vent her frustrations. He was under the impression Michelle was single, and he did not know how many friends she had. Maybe this was her one chance to vent some stress to someone instead of her ceiling.

"Even using the computer system has become more complicated than it needs to be," she said. "Supposedly it's based on more efficient programs, but using it is twice as complicated as it was when we used the old system. I bet Grace would have figured it out, though. She always smoothed over any issue. Oh my, I've been so terrible, I'm sorry."

Michelle was speaking so fast Adam almost missed the apology and needed a moment to process it. That was the first time Michelle mentioned Grace.

"You have nothing to apologize for," Adam reassured her.

"Yes, I do. I've been babbling about how my job became harder in the last year when it's nothing compared to what you've gone through."

"It's better to let it out, even if it comes out as complaints about work. I held it in for a year, and that was a mistake. Wait, are you going to get in trouble for complaining about work here?"

"It doesn't matter if anyone hears me. I've been saying all this to my manager face-to-face for months."

"He actually has a face?"

"I get to go in that office, you know. You'll have to settle for those phantom shouts." A waiter brought another glass of white wine over to Michelle. She sipped it. "The point is, he understands. We've never been able to replace Grace with anyone half as efficient, or half as engaging." Michelle sipped again. "Grace rarely shared a drink with me after a shift, but when she did, she always ordered a red."

"It's our favorite," Adam said, his tongue stinging from referring to Grace in the present tense. "It took me a long time to drink it again."

"I'm still willing to pay for your drinks. Especially since I've only wasted your time so far."

Adam shook his head. "Don't worry about that. But if you could tell me what it was..."

"Yes, what I needed to give you." Michelle reached under the table and pulled out a folder. "As I said, the computers here have been an issue, otherwise I would have emailed this to you. But there are so many files to attach...anyway, colossal headache. This was a smaller headache. With my manager's blessing, I was able to get you printouts of contact info for every publication in which this hotel advertises."

Adam took the folder and flipped through the papers within. For a moment, he remembered when Grace first showed him her father's papers, when they began their quest for the five jewels. But this was organized and distinctly printed.

"We promote in some of these places more than others, but everything is here. Online, print, television, radio. All our advertising contacts are in there," Michelle continued.

Adam closed the folder. "I think I know where you're going with this, but I'm not advertising."

"I know. And some of those contacts won't do you any good. They will be too expensive or uninterested in personal promotions. But others will be interested, or at least be able to connect you with a sister publication that would run a PSA on your behalf. And several of those contacts are not local. We need to promote across most of the country to get vacationers to choose us. If one gem is out in Colorado or Arizona, this gives you a new opportunity to reach its owner."

It still felt like a long shot, Adam thought. But it was dozens of long shots. Most would miss, but one will hit. If even one of these contacts could lead to finding a jewel, it was worth the effort.

"I'll start emailing and calling tonight," Adam said. "I appreciate this."

"I had to do more," Michelle said. "I can't imagine what you've been through, but most of the days I come in to work, I still expect to see her. I'll think she'll be coming around the corner, checking a family in, double-checking that the breakfast bar is okay..."

"I didn't know you guys on the front desk were responsible for that."

"We aren't. That's the point. Grace cared about everything, both for us as her coworkers to give anyone a helping hand, and for the visitors to enjoy the best experience. I wish she could have had the chance to run that bed-and-breakfast she talked about. She would have been great at it. And..."

There was an awkward pause. Adam wondered if the alcohol was taking over Michelle's mind for a moment until she resumed.

"I'm a little guilty in this. No one else around here will say it, but many of us feel responsible. Grace was in North Carolina because we told her she should be."

"She wanted to go," Adam said. "This isn't anyone's fault, other than whoever installed a faulty gas line."

They turned silent for a moment, then Michelle spoke again. "I'm sorry. I've let myself get a little drunk. I may be saying too much."

"You haven't. It does me good to hear that you respected her so much. And if you still struggle with guilt, even when you shouldn't, it means you cared about her. That makes it a little easier for me."

"She made it easy to love her and respect her. That much determination and that much heart, I don't know if I've ever seen both in one other person."

Michelle's eyes seemed to lose focus for a moment. "Are you okay?" Adam asked. "Do you need a ride home?"

Michelle refocused and pointed back to the bar. "See the bartender? She's off in an hour and will drive me home. I kinda guessed I was going to guzzle one glass too many."

Adam nodded, wishing he could have had one more glass of wine with Grace. It would never have felt like too many. He would always feel like they had one glass too few.

* * *

Adam laid back on the sofa, grabbed the remote and turned on the television. He flipped through stations until he found a golf tournament being held on the west coast, hoping to relax while watching the end of the event. He wanted to work on the contacts Brandi had given him an hour ago, but after meeting with both Brandi and Michelle, he needed a break.

His muscles did not tire him. More than anything else, it was all the reminders of Grace which made him weary. Not only was he in the apartment they had shared, but Grace had been mentioned so often throughout the day. Even more so, Brandi and Michelle held qualities of Grace in them. Brandi was determined to help others, even at a personal financial loss. Michelle was as hard a worker as Grace, which may be why her frustrations at work became so pronounced.

He considered getting up and pouring a glass of red wine, but decided against it. He already drank two glasses while he talked with Michelle. No need for any more today. He was still vulnerable to moments of depression, and extra alcohol would do him no good if the hole within him began to ache again.

Adam idly wondered if Michelle was okay. He guessed she was safe since he had made sure with the bartender she would drive her home. But she gulped three glasses of white wine. Maybe four. He hoped drunkenness did not make her depressed.

Then a thought occurred to him. He had been in potentially romantic situations with two lovely women today, and neither he nor they responded in that manner.

He had spent the morning alone with Brandi in her apartment. She gave him ideas about how to track down the remaining gemstones, talked about her charity work, and they both shared stories about Grace. She never left a hint of anything beyond friendship, and Adam had never thought to say or do anything which might be misinterpreted.

Then Adam had been with Michelle for more than an hour in the restaurant. Again, after Michelle complained about work, the talk centered on the jewels and the memory of Grace. But neither before they took a sip of their drinks, nor after they had drained their glasses, did Adam feel any attraction to Michelle. She behaved as if Adam were a cousin, not a romantic interest.

Adam knew they were both beautiful. He considered both of them friends and saw qualities in each of them that reminded him of Grace.

None of this awakened any romantic part in him, because no other woman would ever be Grace. A few, like Brandi or Michelle, might possess one or two of her qualities, but no one could be who she was.

The realization should have upset him, but he found it freeing. Rylee was an attractive friend who also shared qualities of Grace, which in itself was a wonderful thing. But it led him to make a mistake with her he could never erase.

Now, in two similar circumstances, Adam did not cross any lines. The desire was out of his heart.

Forgetting the golf on the television, Adam closed his eyes. Knowing Grace would never hear his voice again, he spoke in the empty living room, anyway. "Grace, I still love you. I will honor you one day by bringing all the jewels together. I am sorry I gave myself to Rylee. But having made that one mistake, I know it will never happen again. I promise."

The television stayed on through the night, as Adam fell asleep shortly after his spoken thoughts.

Chapter 24

Adam watched the computer screen. And watched. And watched.

Company policy dictated for Adam to stay by his workspace until the computer completely shut down and finished its updates. This was rarely a time commitment. But today was one of those occasions on which the computer waited as if it wanted to keep Adam in the office.

Not that Adam had anything to do tonight. His social schedule was as barren as ever, hanging out with Nate for lunch on Thursdays but little else. That was something to look forward to tomorrow. Tonight he would likely either flip through channels on his television or scroll through news feeds on his phone, then fall asleep.

He had hoped by now, ten days after updating his social media about the three remaining jewels, he would have found a lead on one of them. But there had been no response anywhere, except for a couple replies of "good luck" and "hope you find them."

Adam tried to console himself with a reminder–he had two of the valuable stones. But somehow, the ruby and sapphire provided no comfort. Each one should. Each jewel found should be an accomplishment. Maybe that would change if he could find another one. Or, possibly, they would never seem to matter unless he found all five.

Or he could be destined to feel as if it never mattered.

Adam pushed that discouraging thought behind him and then began to wonder if waiting by his work computer would matter.

"Yeah, they've been annoying today," Tessa called out from the back door. "My computer froze three times today. You okay to lock the back?"

Adam looked back at her and nodded. "I'll be fine."

Tessa smiled, waved and exited. Adam turned back to the screen, hoping to see only black. But the blue shut down screen stared back at him.

"One more. Get one more," he said into the empty office. He did not care which jewel came next. Diamond, onyx, emerald–he needed to get each of them. But one more would get him more than halfway to his goal. If he could turn that corner, he would lighten the load burdening his soul.

The screen turned black. Adam glanced at the clock on the wall. Another twenty-three minutes of his life gone.

He carried guilt for even thinking of it that way. Grace never had the chance to live out the life that should have been hers. But that was even more reason to use each minute he had left to honor her. He didn't know what to do with those minutes now, at least, not until he received more information.

Adam exited out the back door, swiped his pass on the outside scanner, flipped it open, and punched in the overnight security code. It was a privilege he had received only a month ago, which he was grateful for. Otherwise, Tessa would have been stuck there with him until the computer deactivated. That was not fair to her or him. Though Tessa was quite friendly and generous, Adam was not sure if he wanted to hang out with her for too long. Something about her did not seem to add up. The mystery of how she could always buy lunch or gifts for her coworkers. How did she afford so much excess on a salary like his?

Waiting so long by his computer drained Adam, mentally at least. It left him extra time to dwell on problems he was not in a position to solve. As he walked to his car, he considered skipping the flipping through television stations and news feeds and sleeping. But when he opened the car door, his phone buzzed.

He expected to see someone from work appear on the phone when he pulled it out. But instead, it was a random number from Lemoyne, a town one county over from Hershey. Not recognizing it, Adam set the phone in a cup holder and started the engine.

The phone beeped, showing the missed call. Adam pulled out of his parking space and approached an intersection to turn towards Palmyra and home. But then the phone beeped again, having received a voice mail.

At the intersection, the light turned red. Adam put on his left turn signal and hit the button on the steering wheel to let the voice mail play over the car speakers.

"Hello, I am trying to reach Adam. We saw something in one of our magazines about you looking for an emerald. I think we have it. It looks like it was cut in the dimensions you put in your announcement. I'm not sure if we're willing to sell, but it can't hurt to show it to you and talk about it. Our address is..."

Adrenaline replacing his drowsiness, Adam pressed the callback button and flipped his turn signal to the right.

* * *

Adam shook hands with Mr. and Mrs. Waterson and sat on a chair in their living room. He did not catch their first names. He barely noticed the drive across the bridge over the Susquehanna River on I-83 during rush hour.

This was a chance to tip the scales in his favor. Get the third jewel. Cross the halfway point. Claim the joy which had eluded him for over a year.

He was so focused on his thoughts, he nearly missed what Mr. Waterson was saying, but Adam forced himself to listen.

"We've had this emerald for several years. Beautiful gem. It was a gift from my sister-in-law, but I had no idea of its history before that until we saw it in the one weekly magazine."

"Newspaper, dear," Mrs. Waterson corrected. "The weekly newspaper, from over in Camp Hill."

"Oh yes. I get some of these media outlets confused now. Newspapers have shrunk to the size of magazines by now."

The Watersons looked old enough to remember when newspapers were more influential than the internet. Adam would not have called them elderly, but they must be well past fifty years old. Not that he cared about their ages. If they would be willing to give him the emerald or sell it to him, they would be saints in his view.

"I don't remember exactly which ad I ran in Camp Hill," Adam said. He recalled adding promotions in Cumberland County after talking with Michelle, but no details. He also wrote the ad to focus on only the emerald, following Brandi's advice. His friends had come through for him. "But the quick version is this: the emerald is one of five jewels that were crafted by my late wife's father." Adam hesitated. Things like that were not getting any easier to say. "I'm trying to collect them again, to honor her."

"What about her father?" Mr. Waterson asked.

"Also deceased. Grace wanted to have the gems to remember him. I want the jewels to honor her and her wishes."

"Let me get it," Mrs. Waterson said. She wandered into a hallway.

"While she grabs the gem," Mr. Waterson said, "I'd like to know more about you, young man. Any children?"

Adam shook his head.

"Working?"

"I started a full-time job straight out of college in an accounting firm."

"I hope you're saving money for the future."

Adam thought it odd Mr. Waterson cut him off before he said where he worked, or what his exact position was. "Um, trying to. Grace was big on giving a percentage and saving a percentage before worrying over the bills."

"Well, I hope those college loans don't come back to bite you. I've seen that happen to so many young people. Even a few of my old buddies."

"My wife was at Shippensburg on a scholarship, but I had to come up with some money to keep my loan under control."

"But you can keep up with the payments?"

Odd question, Adam thought, but simply nodded.

Mr. Waterson leaned back in his chair. "Very good, young man. Good head on your shoulders."

Mrs. Waterson entered the room then, her husband still nodding. She walked up to Adam and opened her fist.

There was the emerald. Adam was sure of it. The dimensions looked equal to those of the ruby and sapphire, and it was in a silver setting with the corkscrew hook protruding from it..

Adam silently cursed himself. He never stopped back home after leaving the office, which meant he did not have the necklace. That was his piece of evidence, for both him and the Watersons, to show this was the true emerald.

"Does this look like what you're looking for?" Mrs. Waterson asked.

Adam nodded. "I could prove it, with a necklace that was specially designed to have that special hook fit perfectly on it."

"Who could have guessed that this would be so important?" Mrs. Waterson said to herself, not putting her hand into a fist, but Adam saw her fingers tighten. She sat next to her husband. "A present from my sister, long gone now. So I have an emotional attachment to it as well."

Adam gave another nod. "I understand. Is there anything I can do to persuade you to part with it?"

Mr. and Mrs. Waterson turned to each other. Mr. Waterson nodded, and Mrs. Waterson turned back to Adam. "I can't say that I would never part with it. My sister's memory is wrapped up in the emerald, though it does not bring me the comfort of having my actual sister back would. But it still means something to me."

She understands what I'm going through, Adam hoped.

"And it is a valuable jewel in and of itself," Mrs. Waterson continued. "So I will sell it to you, but only for..."

At first, Adam could not hear the amount. He asked Mrs. Waterson to repeat herself. Then he realized he had heard her the first time, but his mind refused to accept the number. Adam cleared his throat.

"I realize that the emerald is valuable, and I did not expect to get it for free. But even with a highly favorable appraisement and doubling it for the emotional value..."

Mr. Waterson repeated the same number his wife had spoken moments ago.

It was impossible, Adam knew. The price they were asking for had too many digits to it. The emerald could not be so valuable. Didn't Grace say something about the sapphire possibly being more valuable? Certainly, the diamond might be pricey, especially if Grace had been right about it being five karats. But Adam did not expect to hear a price like this for the other three.

Adam stood and put out his hand. Mr. Waterson stood as well and shook it.

"Let me go home, crunch some numbers and think on it," Adam said.

But he could crunch those numbers in his mind on the drive back to Palmyra. So long as the Watersons demanded such an outrageous price, the emerald would never be his.

Chapter 25

Numbers. Numbers on spreadsheets, in files, on receipts.

Numbers were haunting Adam. Recently, numbers had been his only source of comfort. But today, numbers haunted him more than usual.

One number hung over him, the number the Watersons had told him at the end of their meeting yesterday. The amount was absurd. The emerald had emotional value, to be sure, but its financial value could not be so outlandish.

And in every case Adam worked on, he found himself comparing the amount he would need to buy the emerald to the dollar amounts on every page of every assignment.

He saw no way to get the money. He had calculated the numbers the previous night and...

Couldn't think about those calculations now, Adam decided. He needed to keep focused on the numbers on the screen in front of him.

He worked through another twenty minutes of spreadsheets before another thought distracted him.

What was the point of the Watersons making the price so high? It was not only that it priced Adam out of the possibility of buying the emerald, but it also priced most people out of the market. Those who could buy it would have access to more valuable jewelry, gemstones that warranted the cost. Why not tell him it was not for sale and be done with it?

Something was amiss, but whatever was out of place did not matter. Adam feared he would have to accept never getting his hands on the emerald.

A sandwich appeared on the workspace next to his keyboard.

"It occurred to me you walked in this morning without your brown bag," Nate said from over his right shoulder. "So even though you canceled on me, I figured you might still need some food."

"Thanks," Adam said. "What do I owe you?"

"Nothing, unless you want to explain what has you so droopy this morning."

"Droopy?"

"I concur," Tessa agreed, and Nate turned his head to his left side to see her. "By the way, here's a dessert from the bakery. Unlike Nate here, though, I'm not playing favorites. Everybody gets one."

She handed Nate a chocolate chip brownie, and for a moment, Adam again pondered how Tessa bought these gifts for everyone in the office. He also wondered why she was so obsessed with giving them out. But then his mind was quickly brought back to his biggest problem by her words.

"So," she asked, "if it's nothing too personal, is something wrong? You've looked as if you have ten-pound weights pulling down the sides of your mouth since you walked in today. I'm a bit ahead of schedule one my queue if you needed to send two or three files my way."

"Thanks, but no, that's not it," Adam said, and then described his meeting with the Watersons last night.

When he ended the tale, Nate asked, "What was the actual cost they were asking for?"

The words feeling like acid in his mouth, Adam answered.

Neither Tessa nor Adam said a word for a moment, but Nate finally spoke. "That's insane. I'm not even all that into jewelry..."

"No girlfriend, huh?" Tessa teased.

Nate turned to her. "Not for a while," he said before returning his gaze to Adam. "I don't know what to tell you. I know those jewels are important to you, but if they own the emerald, you can't force their hand. They can set whatever price they want."

Adam nodded. "I know, I've been trying to accept that ever since I left their house." A beeping sound interrupted him.

"Sorry, guess my lunch break is over," Nate said, tapping the screen of his phone. As he walked to the other side of the office, he added, "I'm sure a solution will appear. Have faith."

Adam jerked his head to his screen again and realized he had worked through his usual lunchtime. Well, with a sandwich and a brownie in front of him, he may as well dig in now, and worry over files, reports and emeralds later.

He unwrapped the sandwich. Nate must have known something was upsetting him, seeing as he bought the double-bacon cheddar burger. But Tessa rolled up a chair next to him before he began to eat.

"Want some?" Adam asked. If she took the time to buy dessert for everyone else, Tessa might not have eaten her lunch during her break, he figured.

But she shook her head. "No, I'm good. And I have ten minutes left before my break ends." Then she lowered her voice. "Look, I know you didn't give us a word-for-word account of your conversation last night, but am I right that you didn't negotiate with...who are they again?"

"The Watersons."

"Right, them. Did you discuss any options at all?"

"I pointed out that even a favorable appraisal would only be a fraction of that total. They repeated their, um, offer, and that was that."

Tessa frowned. "I don't want to hurt your feelings, but, for someone who understands the numbers behind finance, you're a little naïve in these sorts of situations."

I'm still new at hunting lost family heirlooms, Adam thought to himself, but he remained quiet.

"You didn't want to get into an argument, but you could have counter offered, or suggested payments over time made directly to them. Something to avoid interest on a bank loan. You could have discussed joint ownership, or renting the emerald for a time, especially if you find the other two jewels you need."

"That last idea wouldn't work," Adam said, shaking his head. "Grace and I never talked about temporarily holding the jewels. We always focused on getting them back to stay. I intend on doing that. Or, at least, I did."

Tessa pursed her lips. "Noble goal. But sticking to a noble goal may cost you getting the emerald. Especially when you are openly admitting the emerald and the other gems are each one-of-a-kind. That will give someone who owns one of them the leverage to drive up the price, even to unrealistic amounts. You were lucky with the ruby and the sapphire, but the Watersons have forced you into a position of weakness."

Adam did not need to be reminded of anything she was saying, but he sensed Tessa's intentions were good, so he let the comments pass.

Tessa appeared lost in thought. Adam's stomach was begging for a bite of the burger, but Tessa spoke before he put his hands back on it. "You want it now, don't you?"

"Of course, if I could. But at best, any idea I can come up with would cripple my bank account for years. I'm not trying to cry the blues here..."

"Most people can't afford what you're talking about," Tessa interrupted. "At least, not without large risk. But sometimes the easiest solutions work best." She leaned back in her chair, eyes looking straight at him. Her smile widened. "Yes, I know how we can best handle this. Do you trust me?"

Trust. Adam remembered when that small voice within told him when he should trust Rylee, and when he should not. He had not heard his conscientious inner voice since, so he trusted his gut.

"I think I do."

"That will be enough. I'm going to trust you, too. I'll explain later, but tomorrow after work, if the Watersons are available, drive me to them. I know how to handle this situation, and you'll have the emerald back before Saturday."

Adam shook his head, not in disagreement but bewilderment. "What did you figure out? What did I miss?"

Tessa stood, turned and flexed her right arm, showing one of the dollar bill signs tattooed over her arm muscles. Still smiling, she explained, "Money talks."

Chapter 26

The clock mercifully reached five.

Adam, knowing he sounded too eager, stood up from his desk and called over to Tessa. "Are you ready?"

"Do you have time for me to-," she hesitated. "I need to run one quick errand before we go. I never had the time over lunch. Can you give me fifteen minutes?"

Adam nodded. "I'll be by my car."

He said goodbye to Nate and Mrs. Douglas and spent several minutes standing in the office parking lot. It seemed like an eternity as he watched his coworkers drive to their homes. He had not arranged for a specific time with the Watersons, so he had no concerns over being late. But he was nervous. If anyone had asked him, he was not sure why he trusted Tessa with this. She was being coy about her intentions.

Rylee used negotiation to get the sapphire. Could Tessa be intending the same thing? Or did she know the Waterson family? But in either case, why wouldn't she tell him what she intended?

His nerves, he realized, came from knowing he was about to see the emerald again, and most likely be denied it. But if there was even a one-in-a-million chance Tessa could somehow pry it from the Watersons, Adam was compelled to take those odds.

Getting the jewels was the only thing that mattered anymore.

Adam finally saw Tessa's sedan pull into the back parking lot, next to his vehicle.

"Everything okay?" he asked as she stepped out.

"We're good to go," she answered.

Tessa sat in the passenger seat and soon after they were on their way.

They made a little small talk, mostly about day-to-day struggles in the office. But as they approached the I-83 Bridge, Adam asked what had been bothering him.

"Are you ever going to tell me your plan?"

"I don't recall ever saying that I have a plan."

Adam jolted toward her, then remembered he was on I-83, over the Susquehanna River, a half-mile outside of Harrisburg at rush hour. He turned back to the road.

Tessa laughed. "Just needling you. But honestly, it's best if you don't know until the last moment."

Adam shrugged. "Whatever you say." He knew there was little risk to this. He had nothing to lose in his wallet or his social schedule. There might be an emotional burden if this did not work, but what was one more to Adam?

As he drove them into Lemoyne, Tessa started making the observations about the town and some homes they passed. She pointed to a two-story house with an enormous yard and a two-car garage. "If I ever move to the West Shore, I might choose a place like that."

Adam glanced at the home before the car passed it. At one time, he believed he and Grace might have moved up to that style of home. Grace's goals may have been to help others, but her plans required becoming successful business people. There had been a chance they could have lived an upper-class lifestyle in the coming years. Not any more.

He noticed Tessa gazing at him. She smirked, raised her eyebrows, but said nothing.

Adam did not understand what that was about, but would not try to figure out his co-worker right now. They had arrived at the Watersons' home.

After parking on the street, they rang the bell and were soon greeted by Mr. and Mrs. Waterson. They shook hands, with Adam taking care of the introductions.

"Is this your second wife?" Mr. Waterson asked.

Mrs. Waterson slapped his arm and said something about how rude the question was, but Adam hardly cared. His offense against Adam was making it impossible to buy the emerald, not any insinuations.

For her part, Tessa took the question in stride and extended her hand. "I'm a co-worker of his, who is interested in seeing if we can resolve the situation here."

Mr. Waterson took her hand. "I apologize. But we're not budging on the total."

The Watersons welcomed Adam and Tessa into their home and let them sit in the living room. The married couple rested on separate chairs on one side of the room, while Tessa and Adam sat next to each other on a couch. The emerald sat on the center of the mantle over the fireplace on the wall between them. It had not been there before, Adam remembered. He wondered if they were taunting him with it.

"Well, has anything changed?" Mr. Waterson asked after they had given their guests glasses of tea and exchanged some small talk about the weather and the local news.

"First, if you don't mind," Adam said, "May I attach the emerald to the necklace? So we all know it's a sister piece to the other jewels?"

Mr. Waterson turned to his wife. "Certainly," she said. "But even if it fits, it is still mine."

Adam nodded, and Mrs. Waterson took the emerald out of the display and handed it to him. He opened the jewelry box, where the necklace sat with the ruby and sapphire attached and three other clasps remained empty. He attached the emerald to the first clasp.

He twisted it in. The corkscrew disappeared into the clasp and snapped into place like a perfect jigsaw piece. Adam looked up at the Watersons. He had hoped seeing the emerald with the other two jewels would soften their stance.

"I can see this must be part of the collection you mentioned to us," Mrs. Waterson said. "I sympathize. The memory of your wife, and her love for her father, are legitimate reasons to pursue each of these jewels."

That's a set up for rejection if I ever heard one, Adam thought.

"But the emerald was in my family for many years, too. I agree with my husband. Again, I can't say I'd never part with it, but we need reimbursement for it. The price we established stays the same."

"And what was that price again?" Tessa asked.

The Watersons turned to her, gawking as if confused to find she was still there. Mr. Waterson spoke the number. It was the same, and it still gutted Adam to listen to it.

Whether or not he ever tracked down the onyx, the emerald had been placed far out of his reach. And if someone charged this much for the emerald, what would stop someone else from charging just as much for the onyx or diamond? He started to take the emerald off of its clasp.

Tessa grabbed his hand. "Don't," she hissed. Then she turned back to the Watersons. "I hope you are a man and a woman of your word."

She reached into her purse and pulled out a leather wallet. She opened it and pulled out a bill, setting it on the coffee table in front of them. And another, and another, and another.

Adam's eyes did not focus on the bills at first, but now he saw clearly. Those were thousand-dollar bills. And Tessa was counting them out one by one. Most of the time, her eyes stayed on the Watersons, but she glanced at Adam and winked.

She had to stop somewhere earlier, Adam remembered. It must have been the bank. But how could she afford this?

Adam lost track of how much money she had pulled out. But after more bills piled up than he would have hoped for, she finished. Mr. Waterson stood from his chair, picked up the pile of thousands, and counted them himself. At first, he was pale from surprise, but now a greedy smile spread across his face. Adam glanced over at Mrs. Waterson. Her smile showed less joy and more avarice. Their poker faces were gone.

He confirmed it was the right emerald: the shape, the silver setting, the way it fit in the custom clasp. But he was being had. By extension, so was Tessa.

Mr. Waterson carried the bills over to Mrs. Waterson, who started counting herself. Adam whispered to Tessa, "You understand we're being taken."

"Yes," she breathed, so only he could hear. "Financially. But there is an emotional price you shouldn't have to pay. We need to take it from them. I gave them their money, now close the box."

Adam snapped the jewelry box shut and locked it. The Watersons were too distracted to notice.

"Are you sure?" Adam asked Tessa. "This is my burden. I don't want you to give up your life's savings for this."

Tessa stifled a chuckle. "Trust me. This is hardly my life's savings. I'll explain another time."

At last, the Watersons finally finished counting the money. "Our transaction is complete. Thank you."

* * *

At first, Adam was a rude host driving home. He had given up hope of recovering the emerald, even with Tessa's encouraging words earlier in the week. He was speechless for several minutes as he accepted the truth: he possessed it now. Though he still had no leads on the onyx or diamond, he was more than halfway to completing the collection.

If only Grace could know that.

But even when he found his voice, Adam did not want to speak. He had a question for Tessa, but he understood it was none of his business.

Fortunately, Tessa was not so reticent.

"There are many ways to show a lady your appreciation," she said, "but feel free to start with words."

"I'm sorry, thank you," Adam said as they merged onto I-83 to drive them back to the office. "I'm not sure what to say. Again. The same thing happened when we got the sapphire, too." That was true, but Adam remembered he actually reacted the opposite way with Rylee. He repeated "thank you" like a fool to her, instead of his silence now. "I was certain I'd never get my hands on the emerald."

"I tried to clue you in on the way there. You didn't seem to pick up on it."

Adam thought back. "The fancy house that interested you? That was your hint?"

Tessa nodded. "But you're distracted. You don't care about money. You care about getting the jewels, so I can't blame you for not picking up on subtle hints." She winked at him.

"This is all a pleasant surprise," Adam admitted.

"And you want to know how I have so much money."

Adam mulled over what words to use. "Look, if you make more than me at work, I don't resent it. You've been there longer than me. But that doesn't account for how much you paid the Watersons."

"It doesn't," Tessa said. "It didn't come from anything illegal or unseemly either, in case you were worried about that."

Had Adam not been so distracted by their success at buying the emerald, he might have become suspicious. He was glad he had never found the time to analyze her obvious wealth.

"Okay, I'm curious. But it's none of my business either."

"I'll tell you what," Tessa said. "Why don't we have dinner tomorrow evening. I'll tell you my secret, as long as you don't spill it to anyone, at work or anywhere else. And you can tell me anything about the other gems. Maybe I can help you with the last two."

Well, without her, today would have been a failure, Adam reasoned. Having a rich friend to help had its benefits. "Sure. Should I pick you up at your place? I don't know exactly where you live."

She winked again. "Oh, let me pick you up. I'll drive."

Chapter 27

A few minutes had passed since Tessa's text appeared on Adam's phone, so he expected to see her out in the parking lot by now. He did not know exactly where Tessa lived, but it was somewhere in Hershey, so it should not have taken her too long to drive to the apartment complex.

Adam was willing to pick her up or at least meet her at the restaurant, but Tessa dismissed his chivalry and insisted on getting him. She never said at which restaurant she had made reservations.

She must like to keep everything mysterious, Adam thought.

He checked his phone again. No new messages and the most recent text was twelve minutes ago. Maybe she was still getting ready when she had contacted him. Either way, it was nice enough outside. He could wait.

He glanced at the phone one more time. No calls or texts. He could not remember the last time anyone had made a video call to him. Then he did.

Grace. One night before she died.

Adam took three deep breaths. He would never stop mourning her, but he also would not let the sadness ruin his time with Tessa tonight. Tonight Tessa and he will celebrate getting the emerald, which remained in the safe alongside the ruby and sapphire. If he and Rylee would have celebrated like this instead of meeting in the apartment...

No point worrying over past mistakes, Adam decided.

Adam glanced around the parking lot again. He remembered what Tessa's sedan looked like and still did not spot it. This explained his surprise when, from the edge of his vision, he saw Tessa step out of a red sports car.

He had noticed the sports car when it entered the lot seconds ago, but did not realize Tessa drove it. Between its flashy color and European styling, it was hard to miss.

Tessa was even harder to miss in her figure-hugging black dress. The outfit also revealed two more tattoos, one on the inside of each shoulder blade. An infinity symbol was visible on one side and a bell with immense flowers around it on the other.

Adam walked over to her, feeling underdressed in his slacks and button-down shirt. "I have to admit, you are full of surprises," he said to her.

"I figure the cat will be out of a bag soon anyway," Tessa said. "May as well flaunt it since I've got it." She gestured to the car. "So, may a girl give you a ride?"

* * *

Grace and Adam had their share of expensive dinners over the years. A small share, but those special dates happened occasionally. Their honeymoon, their anniversary and when they found the ruby were the only ones Adam could recall, now.

Even on those dates, he had never been in a restaurant like the one he sat in now, across from Tessa at a high-top table.

"You look like a deer standing in the middle of 422 at midnight," Tessa whispered.

"Sorry," Adam answered sheepishly. "I've never been here before now. I'm afraid if I breathe too deeply, they'll charge me for the air."

Tessa laughed. "Oh, they get you coming and going here. But it's worth it. The shrimp platter is to die for. Literally, in seventy years, I want that to be my last meal."

"So, is that your recommendation?"

"Whatever you please. I said earlier, it's on me."

Adam shook his head but looked through the menu. "I'm still not comfortable with that."

"You will be. I'll explain everything after they take our order."

A few minutes later, Adam ordered a medium-well steak with crab's legs, and Tessa ordered the shrimp platter she spoke so well of. Adam, unable to resist the opportunity, and willing to make this a celebration, ordered a glass of his favorite red wine.

"You drink wine?" he asked.

"Rarely," Tessa said. "And I never drink when I'm driving, not even a little. That's one thing I'm cautious about. I'm a bit of a risk-taker on other things, like spending my money, driving too fast, and..." She let the word trail off as if Adam was supposed to fill in the blank.

Is she flirting with me? Adam wondered to himself. Or is she having a good time and nothing more, while I happen to be here?

"Well, I guess it's story-telling time," Tessa suddenly resumed. "I'll tell you my story, but then I want to hear yours."

"I'm not sure I have much of a story," Adam said. "I don't have an interesting past, while I'm beginning to think you do."

"My story is about my past, and I am aware it was a privileged one," Tessa said. "But the story I need to listen to is about your future. I want to know what the plan is for getting the last two jewels you need."

Maybe Tessa will help buy the other two if they could be tracked down. That was Adam's hope. His second thought was her playfulness tonight was not flirting, but instead her personality away from the office, a side of her he had never seen. It was for the best. Even if he wanted to start a new relationship sometime, Adam was still too much of an emotional mess to consider any real dating now.

"I'll go first," Tessa said. "My father was born into a wealthy family, to begin with, but he also worked hard. Before he met my mother, he was already the CFO at an oil company. And he did not only earn money, but he also understood how to invest it."

Adam nodded but said nothing.

"As I said, I was born into privilege. But I was also born into a hard-working family," Tessa continued. "My mother did a home-based education service. You know those work-and-home jobs which most people never make anything? But then you read about that one-in-a-million person who makes thousands each week?"

Again, Adam politely nodded.

"My mother was that one-in-a-million. She met my father at a business-persons' conference. They both did speaking engagements at events like that. Hit it off-," she slapped her hands, "Wedding bells and boom, here I am."

"Do your parents live around here?"

"No," Tessa answered. "They live and do most of their work in Arizona. I moved here after college. And that is the other part I want to explain...wait, I wish to make one thing clear. Everything I say tonight, and everything we do, you can't tell anyone."

"You said so yesterday. No one at work will know."

"No one at all," she cautioned. "I waited until the absolute last minute yesterday to let you know how much money I have. But there was a reason to tell you. You're not interested in being rich. You want those jewels to honor Grace's memory."

"Of course."

"But other people will beg for money, not because they need it, but because they want the easy life. Other people will resent me because I can have as easy a life as I want. But I don't want to be the target of anyone's greed or anger. I want to be one of the gang at work, but also be able to have my fun during my personal time."

Adam considered for a moment. He didn't care for keeping secrets, but Tessa was entitled to her own, he decided. "I never would have kept a secret from Grace," he started.

"If she were alive, I would have made an exception for your wife."

"But life being as unfair as it is, yes, I will keep this secret from anyone." He remembered the night after he and Grace found the ruby. They had stopped keeping even the darkest secrets from each other. Secrets about his father. Adam would never find another relationship so personal again.

"Not this secret alone," Tessa brought him out of his depressing thoughts. "Everything we say and do tonight."

Adam was relieved the earlier moments weren't flirting. She wanted to live a double-life, which Adam would find exhausting and deceptive. He did not judge her for her lifestyle, it was her own choice. But he would hate to be one way in public and one way in private.

She also acted a bit paranoid. No reason to be involved with a double life.

"It all stays a secret," Adam confirmed.

"Thank you. So, my parents had no problems with buying me whatever I wanted when I was in school. I am their only child, so they completely spoiled me. Until I finished college, then the work ethic kicked in."

"Did they cut you off financially?"

"No, but they forced me to work. If I had a full-time job, they would continue to send me money every month. They don't care if I'm at a grocery store or in the oil business. They want me to work. As long as I'm employed, they'll take care of me."

"So you're satisfied to be in a low-level, punch-in and punch-out job. Not too much extra time taken out of your life, and the pay doesn't matter."

"And I wanted to work in a place that could be a constant reminder about how to use my money responsibly. Someday, everything that my parents have will be mine, but so will all the decisions. I won't stay in an accounting firm forever, but I figured that would be a good place to learn some lessons I'll need down the road."

Their food arrived. "Of course, I'm not too responsible," Tessa said with a grin. "I appreciate a fun night out. I enjoy getting whatever I want."

Adam's eyes had been on his food when the plate was placed in front of him, but then he looked back up at Tessa. There was a different smile this time, one which he would have read as flirtatious had he not already decided that could not be happening.

Unless he had guessed wrong.

A wealthy woman with a guy who had settled to live in a small apartment? No, he must have been imagining it.

* * *

There were no more double-entrees at the dinner table while they ate their food and discussed the two remaining jewels, the onyx and diamond. As Adam had guessed, Tessa offered to help pay for them if they could be found and were up for sale. But, beyond checking in at her favorite jewelry stores, she knew no leads on where to find them.

Tessa took care of the check and did not hide the fact that she was a generous tipper. They left in her sports car, and Adam asked a question that popped into his mind.

"If it's not private, what are your other two tattoos for?" Adam asked.

"I'll tell you, but please keep them secret too."

"I'm a man of my word."

Tessa smiled. "The bell is supposed to be a wedding bell. At least, that's what the artist said. But marriage isn't a priority of mine, so I think of it as a celebration bell. You know, how in the past when a holiday began, or a war ended, they would ring bells throughout the town. So, to me, it is a sign that life is to be celebrated."

"And the infinity symbol means you want to celebrate all the time?"

"You're catching on."

Adam was enjoying the conversation so much–or so inebriated from the red wine–he almost missed Tessa putting on her right turn signal. "Um, you go straight down this road for a few more miles.."

"Not for where we're going," Tessa said with a smile.

They changed course, and Adam guessed their destination would be obvious soon. But after several blocks, he was still unsure of what was happening. They certainly were not going to his apartment, and though he had never been to Tessa's home, there were few residences in this direction. As they travelled farther away from the actual town of Hershey, Adam could not remember anything notable about where they headed.

"So, is this going to be a surprise?" Adam asked.

Tessa took her eyes off of the road and gave him a look of confusion. "Maybe you're not catching on." Then she smiled again and turned back to the road. "I can't believe how naïve you are. I know you don't pick up subtle hints sometimes, but I dropped enough clues for how tonight will end. I hoped this dress would shout it."

There was no denying it, Adam had noticed the dress. But he did not want to make any assumptions about Tessa's intentions from it. A tiny black dress, he assumed, only meant Tessa acknowledged the importance of finding the emerald. She was dressed up for the occasion. She could not mean...

But she pulled up to a motel on the outskirts of town, and then Adam realized she meant it. Those words earlier were not little jokes from a woman having a nice evening.

In an instant, he remembered this place. He had never been inside before, but Grace had mentioned this motel. Something less than flattering. Something about wanting to make her bed-and-breakfast chain the opposite of this establishment. Better run, more appealing, a reputation for committed couples instead of, well, for what Tessa intended.

"I grant you, not the ritziest place," Tessa said, and it was obvious weather and time had worn the building, and the owners had done little to restore it. "But I don't want either of us to do the walk of shame tomorrow morning where neighbors might see us. I doubt anyone we know will spot us here."

No one will know, Adam's mind echoed. He suddenly realized he had been naïve. His mistake with Rylee weakened him to this temptation. He had believed a few platonic relationships with female friends proved he was now beyond committing another illicit act, but tonight it seemed irresistible. Now, he realized, he was more vulnerable than ever.

He shouldn't, yet he wanted to give in.

Adam mustered what little resolve remained in him. "Are you sure? I mean, you and I, we're just coworkers."

"I know," Tessa answered, reaching out and stroking his hair. Adam did not want to admit he liked her touch, but he did. Too much. What had happened to him?

"Trust me, this doesn't happen too often," Tessa whispered. "I'm not like that. But when something important occurs, something really important, adults should be free to celebrate it as much as they can. The emerald is important to you. We should celebrate it."

Adam listened for the voice inside, the conscience which had guided him in the past and tried to stop him from being with Rylee. There was only silence.

Even without the voice, he understood from a factual point of view this was wrong, another mistake.

Another pleasant mistake.

With that thought, Adam's resolve disappeared.

Part IV

The Bottom
of the Well

Chapter 28

Who am I becoming?

The question echoed in Adam's mind for days. The query returned less often over time, but he never found an answer for it.

He first asked himself the question after Tessa dropped him off at his apartment on Sunday morning. She must have believed that was less suspicious than walking out of his place or hers. Still, the moment her sports car disappeared from view, something worse than guilt overwhelmed him. That was when he first wondered if his identity changed.

Three days had passed since then, leaving him as an exhausted man trying to find motivation for work on a Wednesday morning. The shame, which had started as a sharp dagger in his soul, became a throbbing, dull pain, but it never faded away. For two days he and Tessa had exchanged knowing glances in the office, but no words or smiles. Then, yesterday, she would not make eye contact with him.

They had made no promises, so Adam knew he should not be disappointed or disillusioned. In fact, he was not disappointed or disillusioned in Tessa at all. She could live how she wanted to live.

But he was disappointed in himself. In the daytime, he did extra exercises, hoping to shove away his frustrations with his shortcomings with each pushup. He spent two nights fighting sleep, trying to figure out how he allowed himself to fall again. Why did he give in without an effort this time? At least with Rylee, he tried to hold back. With Rylee, he experienced false happiness for a few days before the guilt affected him. Now with Tessa. . .

Adam stopped tightening his tie, remembering how he sat up with the start in the middle of the night when he thought those things the first time. Then he realized he was comparing one-night stands. And now he was comparing them again. A man should not behave this way. At least, not a mature one.

He knew that many other men–from high school, college and work–would not be agonizing over these encounters. Two women–both attractive, both respectable–chose him. Many men would be proud. Some would have bragged to others. But that's not who Adam was.

Or was it? Or was he becoming someone he did not want to be?

Adam hoped not. He remembered Grace saying that she didn't want any other man, only him. She meant she would choose him over any other man, but he thought she also meant she wanted him to remain the quality of man he had always been.

He could no longer say he was that kind of man, nor a guy who had made one mistake and worked his way through it. He was flawed. Somewhere within, something wrong festered within him.

Maybe it originated with never meeting his father, Adam mused as he dressed for work. Yes, he had a step-father, but he did not come into his life until Adam was already twelve years old. He never felt as close to his mother's second husband as he should. No, the image of how a man should act had always been a vague one at best.

And yet, when Grace shared life with him, none of this behavior existed in his mind. He understood how to treat her as an equal partner in their marriage, and how to treat other women as friends and with respect. When Grace died, Adam's clarity of thought deteriorated. He had since recovered from that, but now he was losing any moral compass he once possessed.

He never wanted to forget Grace, but he wished he could wipe away all the agony of her death and all memories of his mistakes since then. But none of it would quite leave him. Instead, the thoughts would become sharper. The worst thought of all was they were about to step up into a new level in their marriage at the moment tragedy stole her from him.

They had become more open with each other–they truly held no secrets. The finances were not up to their hopes of running a bed-and-breakfast and raising a child, but they were close enough to take the first steps.

And they had found the ruby.

Adam started out the door but stopped and shook his head. He possessed the emerald and the sapphire now, too. He should be excited about that, and yet his heart carried guilt instead of gratitude. Even so, he promised himself he would find the onyx and the diamond. He would complete the necklace.

He would honor Grace with his actions, even if had failed so far.

* * *

It had been a frustrating day at the office. The work itself had not taxed Adam. The cold numbers themselves provided comfort.

But there was tension Adam could not escape. He had not spoken with Tessa, had not been within twenty feet of her, all day. Yet, there was an additional weight within, knowing she worked in the same room and he had no way to communicate with her.

At least he and Rylee had briefly talked about what had happened between them. Adam still carried guilt from that, but they had stated where they stood as a couple afterward. With Tessa, there was this mystery again. She obviously did not want anyone else to know about what happened, and neither did he. But was she bitter with him? Confused? Adam was not sure.

He closed the last file of the day and shut down his computer. He needed to fill out a handful of forms in writing, but otherwise was done with his assignments. But then he heard footsteps behind him.

Adam turned and saw Tessa, but she was not walking towards him or even looking at him. She walked through the back door of the office.

Adam guessed she left for the day a couple minutes early and filled out the last of the forms. He tried to put her out of his mind. But then the door opened, and Tessa re-entered the office carrying two large bags.

"Surprise, everyone!" she shouted. "Dinner is on me tonight. Foot-long subs for everyone. Save them for lunch tomorrow if you already have plans."

"Tessa," Ms. Douglas called from her corner office. "You're not supposed to be doing that on the clock."

"It is exactly thirteen seconds after closing time."

"Oh, well, in that case, I'll take a turkey hoagie."

Tessa walked over to their boss to give her a sandwich. Adam was struck by two things. First, Ms. Douglas must have grown up somewhere else. Everyone in central Pennsylvania knew the proper name for foot-longs was "subs". But more importantly, Tessa still refused to make eye contact, even when she walked by him to reach Ms. Douglas.

After giving Ms. Douglas and two other coworkers their subs, Tessa walked back the way she came, right by Adam's desk. He looked to her face, hoping for a smile, even a forced one. Would he hear a joke, or a quip, or even a rude word?

There was no glance or speech. Tessa did, however, pull a sandwich out of the one bag and set it next to Adam. She wandered to the other side of the office.

All Adam wanted was to go home, so he did. Taking his sandwich out to the car, he drove back to Palmyra.

On his way, an incoming call to his phone interrupted the radio station. He glanced down a fraction of a second to see who called, and at first dismissed it as a spam phone number. But before declining the call, he glanced again and recognized the digits. It was the number for the Lebanon newspaper, one of the media outlets he had reached out to for advertising and possibly for a story about the jewels.

It was also possible an intern was on the line to sell him a subscription, but if that were the case, the end-call button was right under his thumb. Adam accepted the call. "Hello, this is Adam."

"Mr. Thompson, I am Lucas Evans. I'm a reporter at The Lebanon...,"

"You're calling about the jewels, aren't you?"

"Yes," Lucas said, and from his tone, Adam could tell he was not offended by being interrupted. "Do you have some time to talk? I'd like to do a story on where these gems came from, the local connections, and whether you believe you're close to finding the remaining three or not."

"Two. I just found one this weekend."

"Even better, then. Do you have a moment?"

"I'd love to talk with you, but I'm driving right now. Actually, could you call me back tomorrow, about a half-hour later than this?"

"Sure. My story is due by next Monday, but that still gives me plenty of time."

"Good. I'll look for your call."

At last, some much-needed good news. An opportunity to put the search for the jewels out into the media and public eye. It would have been nice to be interviewed at the beginning of the search, but Adam would have to make the most of it happening now.

But Adam did not want to talk yet. He wanted to be in the right frame of mind, and the cold shoulder from Tessa had him in anything but the proper spirit. Adam also wanted to talk from the right place when he shared the history of the jewels. Then he realized the apartment might not be the right place. It still felt so empty without Grace. The office would not be appropriate either, and the reporter will call back after hours, anyway. He would think of somewhere else where he would be more likely to stay in friendly spirits.

Adam arrived at the apartment complex and entered his place. He tossed his bag with the sub in it on the kitchen table. That was when he noticed a folded up paper fall out. It was not a napkin, but a notepaper, the same shade of off-white used in the office.

He grabbed and unfolded it. There were a few lines written inside, and even had Adam not already figured it out, he would have identified the writing as Tessa's.

"Burn after reading. I can stand working in the same building as you, but I can't talk to you anymore. We can't let anyone even guess what we did. I am not blaming either one of us, but unless we need to speak for our job, we need to disconnect completely."

Adam sat the note on the dinner table. He wandered around the apartment for a few minutes, trying to process his thoughts. Not talking to each other at all might tip off a co-worker that something had happened. And what difference did it make to Tessa? If she got a reputation she didn't want here, she could move wherever she wanted. Maybe she was not as worldly wise as she thought.

He understood there would be no proper relationship with Tessa. What churned his insides was not disappointment. But the sickening sensation was different from when he made the same mistake with Rylee.

Then he realized what ailed him. Tessa was ashamed of him, of what they had done together. Who could blame her? She had not lashed out at him in anger, and her note did not convey any malice. But Tessa no longer wanted to be associated with him in any way.

Shame. That was what plagued him the moment he and Tessa parted last weekend. It was far worse than guilt.

She should be ashamed of him, Adam realized.
He was ashamed of himself as well.

* * *

Though he did not remember hearing a sound, Adam woke at two in the morning. After failing to fall back asleep after a half hour, he stood and stretched. He wondered what he could do at this hour.

He walked to the kitchen and poured himself a glass of water. His body was awake, but his brain only caught up with it now. That meant he was too awake to go back to bed soon.

Adam realized it had been a long time since he had looked at the old suitcases that had once belonged to Grace's father. They had provided no useful leads for over a year, but maybe the faded ticket stubs and smeared receipts would bore him back to sleep.

He opened up one suitcase and set it on the kitchen table. He idly flipped through the papers, most of which were even more yellowed than he remembered. They all looked familiar, and all looked useless.

"Oh, here's a new one," Adam mumbled to himself. "Oil change and tires rotated twenty-two years ago. Don't remember that. Bet I find a failed auto inspection before I find. . ."

Adam stopped speaking and perked to attention. Sometime in the suitcase moved. He only noticed the motion at the edge of his vision, but was certain something shifted.

Then he saw it. There was a corner of a black-and-white photograph sticking out of the lid of the suitcase. Adam gently tugged on it, pulling down to reveal a picture that showed no people, but five rough stones.

The lateness of the hour and Adam's all-around depression kept him from understanding what he saw at first. But then it hit him.

These were the stones that Grace's father cut into the five jewels. Grace had said that they were cut from valuable stones that had been family heirlooms. The coloration was hard to interpret from the black-and-white picture, but Adam soon identified ruby, sapphire, emerald, onyx and diamond. None of them were particularly large, and all of them were rough. These were what Grace's father used for his creation.

Adam flipped the photo over, hoping to find some more information, but all he saw was a number.

"1898."

Those stones were in the Davis family for generations, Adam realized. And the date did not mean they necessarily obtained them in 1898. They may have been heirlooms even earlier than that.

Adam thought some more about the date. Photographs in that era were much more expensive and time-consuming. The Davis family, or the members of the family at that time, chose to take a photograph of the jewels without even including any people. They must have been precious to them.

He could not say that he really cared about what Grace's ancestors thought of the stones. But Adam could say this gave him a new appreciation for his task. He may have married into that family instead of being a blood relative, but this was new evidence that he was right to find all five of the jewels.

Chapter 29

"No, I can't be certain either the onyx or diamond is owned by someone local," Adam said into his phone as he walked. "But since the other three were all found nearby, I'm optimistic."

"Other than social media, do you have any contacts outside of central Pennsylvania?" Lucas asked. "People who might have eyes open for you?"

Adam tried not to think of Rylee, considering where he stood right now. It seemed so inappropriate. But he answered Lucas's question. "I know people in other states, and they know about the jewels."

There was silence for a moment. Adam continued his walk, stepping off of the path and onto the bridge.

"Do you have any plans for a celebration event when you find all the jewels?"

Adam stopped a few steps onto the bridge. What did he have planned for when he possessed all five gems? He was supposed to put them around Grace's neck. That was what she had said when they found the ruby. Did he have any way to celebrate now? He hardly knew any friends left to invite to a celebration. Nate was a possibility, but who else could he even talk to anymore? Michelle? Brandi?

"Are you still there, Mr. Thompson?"

He spent so much time questioning himself Adam had almost forgotten the phone interview. "No plans yet. I don't want to get ahead of myself."

"Understandable. Well, that's all the questions I have. I'll look for the photo of the three recovered jewels you sent to my email. The story should run this weekend. Thanks for your time."

Adam thanked Lucas and put his phone in his pocket. He resumed walking and stopped in the middle of the bridge. The Quittie flowed underneath him. It was a creek, never to be confused with a majestic river, but from this spot, the waters appeared majestic to him.

Grace and he became a couple here.

It was not where they first met. Neither of them remembered when they first spoke to each other, though they were sure it happened in elementary school. But it was here, during their senior year, where Grace had made her move.

And it was also here where he had surprised her by spending the evening of their first anniversary at this same spot on the bridge. It seemed as if they kissed and whispered for hours, though Adam's memory exaggerated. But he did not imagine the emotional intensity of the moment. He had been nervous he would disappoint Grace, that he had not come up with any fancy way to celebrate their first anniversary. Instead, she gave him love more passionate than he ever imagined. The kissing and touching, though so intense he still remembered the heat, did not account for all the passion. It was the realization she would have always taken him. Over any other man in the world, she would have chosen him.

Adam closed his eyes and listened to the water rush. For a moment, he felt as if Grace stood beside him. Adam tricked himself, he knew. But he needed to allow himself to be fooled. He needed to believe Grace waited for him to open his eyes. Maybe the Grace from years ago, talking to him and asking him out. Or Grace as she should have been today, telling him she missed him and could not wait to share life again.

He still heard only the water, but in his mind her voice spoke. Grace encouraging him to chase their dreams together. Not only the jewels, but making a family, opening the bed-and-breakfast, and dreams they had not yet imagined.

He opened his eyes. The trees, bushes, walking path, bridge and creek remained the same as they were minutes ago, and all those years ago. He heard the current of the water and a few birds chirping in the distance.

But there was no Grace.

It hurt less here, though, Adam realized. The pain of loneliness existed alongside the guilt and shame of his actions in the past few months. But there was a distance. It had been an exhausting day of work avoiding Tessa, but being in Annville now put space between Adam and that problem. Rylee remained in Chicago, with only a smattering of terse text messages connecting her and Adam anymore. That distanced Adam from his guilt there. Now, standing on the bridge set the emotions farther away. He was still aware of them, but they would not crush him here.

Nature helped keep the dark thoughts away for a time. Walking along the path where he and Grace had walked so many times when they dating made it easier to endure the twenty-minute interview with Lucas. But mostly, it was here where Adam found it easier to remember how wonderful his relationship with Grace had been.

Thinking back on when Grace first showed interest in him, Adam was able to see life as it was before college, before engagement, before marriage.

Before death.

Before Adam became who he was now. A time when Adam believed he deserved Grace.

Then it was simple. Drive around town together. Share a pizza. Catch a movie. Sit in a parking lot and talk for hours. He realized their time together was amazing then, but only now did he realize how precious each second was.

Adam wished he could stay here, on the bridge, for hours. But the park rules said he needed to leave the nature park by dusk, and the last thing he wanted was to deal with a citation. Besides, he could not stay still. If he meant to honor Grace's memory, and the memory of all they had shared, he would not allow himself to waste time finding the onyx and the diamond.

He frowned and strolled back off the bridge. By the time he reached the path which ran along the banks of the creek, he realized he stood with his head down and shoulders slouched. He righted himself and looked to see if anyone spotted him sulking.

No one watched. Still, he sensed the weight of the last fifteen months become more burdensome as he left the bridge, creek and park behind him. His heart returned to the heaviness it had suffered from earlier today, the weight increasing with each step away from the bridge. Even his lunch break with Nate had been awkward, with Adam unable to tell him what plagued his mind and Nate seeming uncomfortable.

The loneliness weighed him down like a force from the outside of his body when he drove home, while guilt and shame gnawed at him from inside his heart.

It was almost like when he had taken the sapphire and emerald, and his foolish trysts which followed. An evening at the Quittie should have made Adam happy again, or at least restored some peace for his soul. But the brief relief only made the returning pain sharper.

It doesn't matter how much I'm hurting, Adam told himself. I'll never see Grace again. But I will work hard enough to prove I deserved her. I will recover the last two jewels.

Chapter 30

"Not there. Let's sit in the corner."

Adam wasn't sure why Nate made the request, but he changed course and sat at an isolated table in the coffee shop. Already with his cold brew in hand, he leaned back. These Thursday lunches with Nate were invaluable. They did not allow him truly to escape from his problems, but the difficulties of life seemed a little more distant for an hour.

That was true of his visit to the Quittie last week, too. But there he stood alone. Here, he had company.

Nate sat across from him. "I think we need to talk."

"We always do."

"I mean about something important."

Adam leaned forward, setting his drink on the table. He remembered their lunch gathering a week ago when Nate seemed distracted. "Something from work?"

"No. Yes. It's tied into work, but so much bigger than that."

"What's happening?"

"Remember, you told me to call you out if I started to see problems."

Adam froze. Was he sinking back into the fog of depression and not realizing it? He suffered from emotional confusion and would not argue that point. The three gems in his possession brought no joy, and he made relationship decisions he could not have dreamed of a few months ago. But he had asked Nate to say something to him if he slipped into depression.

"I did," Adam finally said. "Do you think I'm fading?"

"Not in the same way as last year. Look, I hate to tell you this at all, but I need to bring up something from...,"

"Your baseball team. Go ahead."

"So, I listened to our life coach, Jonas, but not applying much of what he told us to my life. So, after winning a big tournament, I made a foolish decision. And because of it, I can tell you've made a similar mistake. I can tell by how you carry yourself in the office. And the way Tessa does."

This time the words paralyzed Adam for even longer. How did Nate know? He was certain Tessa had not talked. She had made such a point of not being spotted, there was no way she revealed their night together. But even if Nate had figured out something happened between them, he could not know what.

Nate must have mistaken Adam's silence as permission to continue.

"There was a girl, Maggie. I was attached to her for years, but without romance. We were best friends, but no more. After we won the regional tourney, we went for it. Stupid teens that we were, we did it in right field of our ballpark. We thought night time would keep us hidden, but someone caught us."

Adam's brain was trying to keep up with Nate's story while trying to figure out if he should be humiliated or not that Nate deciphered his past. Then he remembered something. "Was that the 'big catch' you made that you acted so ashamed over?"

Nate nodded. "Even if we hadn't been caught, it was a mistake. We didn't stop caring about each other, but things were never the same. It was hard to speak with her anymore. Neither of us were carefree around each other.

The burden we carried is like what I see with you and Tessa. We both needed to go through the process of forgiving each other, and ourselves. The shame overwhelmed me."

"Are you saying I should be ashamed?" Adam asked, deciding not to deny the truth.

"All I'm saying is, hold on."

Hold on for what, Adam wondered, but then he spotted the waiter carrying their food to their table. Adam ignored his sandwich and focused on Nate. Once the waitress left, and Adam confirmed no one still had taken a table near them, he spoke.

"I know I told you to call me out if my depression returned. But even if you know what's going on in my private life, you don't need to throw it in my face."

"But this can lead back to depression so easily," Nate said, holding his wrap but not eating it. "Once I realized what I had done to Maggie and our friendship, I got low, almost to the point of depression. And I wasn't mourning anyone like you are. One day, it will have its consequences. It may only be emotional, but it will be no less painful."

He and Rylee had already disconnected, Adam thought. Tessa did not want to be in the same office as him anymore. Nate was right, there were consequences. But he had heard enough.

"Your advice is duly noted," Adam said. "You're not blabbing to anyone else, are you?"

"Of course not," Nate said. "I know as well as anyone the pain of having my private life exposed. Well, Maggie suffered the ridicule worse. I guess the girl always does."

"What happened to her?" Adam said, his nerves calming enough finally to take a bite.

"That was the summer before our freshman year at college. We attended different schools. Between semesters, we would wind up in the same place by coincidence once or twice. We would say hello to each other, then walk away. I haven't seen her in three years."

That made Nate pause, and they both ate silently. Adam thought about Rylee and Tessa. What if life was going to be this way for the rest of his days? A second genuine love might come around, but he could not imagine that now. He would compare everyone to Grace, and eventually, Adam would find a shortcoming preventing him from a long-term relationship.

But he had proven to be weak enough in the face of temptation to cross lines from which he had always distanced. Knowing he had violated his own principles, and the principles Grace had lived by also, he felt unworthy of true romance, anyway.

To Nate's eyes, he assumed, Adam looked as if he ate while mulling his thoughts. But he feared he might be falling into another depression. Adam felt none of the fog which had plagued him after the fire, but he was now missing both Grace and the man who he used to be.

"I'm sorry if I'm opening up old wounds," Nate said as they finished their meals. "But I know you're hurting. If I continued to be silent, I would have failed you."

"What gave me away, apart from Tessa and I giving each other the cold shoulder?"

"Your drinks for the last few weeks. You never flavor your cold brew when you're upset."

Adam glanced at his near-empty drink. He had not even realized it, but he was drinking his cold brew straight and bitter.

At least, he had not noticed the bitterness on the outside. The bitterness within grew again. But now, it was directed at himself as much as anyone else.

"I was lucky," Nate continued. "Peter, our team captain, forced me to see my behavior as wrong. Then Maggie forgave me, and she helped me forgive myself. Otherwise, I would have stayed in my depression and may have continued in even more empty relationships." Nate focused again on Adam. "Don't go down that path. Any mistake eventually catches up with you. Repeated mistakes can ruin you. You don't want to fall apart without Grace."

Now the bitterness redirected toward Nate. For him to call out his indiscretions was one thing, but speaking of his pain was too much. Adam stood and threw his empty cup on the ground, resisting the urge to throw it towards Nate's head. The plastic did not shatter, though Adam wished to break something.

"I already have fallen apart without Grace! And I'll cope with it how I want, and with whoever I want!" Adam stomped out of the cafe, striding down the road at a brisk pace, as if he could outrun Nate's words. Somehow, hearing him say it, even though Adam was quite aware of his condition, turned Adam's pain into a knife in the heart.

Adam slid his security badge and entered the office. He walked over to his workstation, but on his way, he noticed Tessa scowl at him. After he sat, Adam could see Nate enter. His co-worker looked at him with sullen eyes.

Adam turned to his screen and ignored them. He did not know why his resentment grew towards Nate. Every accusation and warning rang true. Maybe Adam had turned hostile, not because of Nate calling him out, but because he had no way of making things right again.

There was no life coach, team captain nor ex who was still communicating with him.

Yes, he had fallen apart without Grace. He had no other way to live.

Chapter 31

Numbers were again Adam's best friend.

It had happened before when Adam was lost in the fog of grief. When all he experienced was loneliness, the stoic numbers on his screen helped numb the pain. When he was frustrated over the asking price for the emerald, numbers had turned on him. But again, numbers became the only thing on his side while he faced loneliness again.

This time, he faced a different loneliness. Grace was still gone, of course, but he had finally accepted her death. That her official status remained "missing" made no difference to Adam. But now all his other connections disappeared as well. Once, the numbers gave him a sense of comfort throughout the office. Now, he felt protected only by his workstation.

He dared not turn his head away from his screen. He would not glance at Tessa or Nate. If Tessa still suffered from guilt, that was her own business. Yes, Adam still carried guilt also, but they needed to cope with the shame alone. But Adam would not look at Nate, either. Something about their conversation last week had shattered his trust in him. He was unsettled by how Nate had known about Tessa and him. Maybe he never should have talked with Nate about how much losing Grace pained him. Whatever the case, Thursday lunch conversations were finished.

Along with every other conversation he might have had. Adam came into work, did his job, and drove home. He gave his best effort, but did not care about the long-term ramifications. At some point, he would find work elsewhere,

Adam decided. But a job search could wait. His emotions were so overtaxed he did not want any transitions now.

At least with broken work relationships, there were ways to begin again. He needed to find another business with an open position and make new connections.

He would never be able to start over with Grace. And he could not start over with his best man or his wife's maid of honor. Adam was unable to think of anywhere where he would not be alone.

He glanced at the clock in the corner of his screen. Thirty minutes until the weekend. He told himself to focus on this last file, and then he might find temporary relief.

Adam would soon go back to his apartment. He still missed having Grace there, but at least he could accept loneliness where he was physically alone. It someone hurt less than loneliness surrounded by others.

* * *

Adam laid back onto the bed. He wanted to vent to someone, anyone. Work had been frustrating. He was disconnected from all his coworkers. But now, at home, the memories of other broken relationships surfaced. His friendship with Rylee had atrophied, and Michael... how could he look Michael in the eyes again? Maybe Michael had moved on and found someone else, but still, sleeping with your best friend's ex is a death knell to a friendship.

For a moment, he considered talking with Brandi. She possessed a compassionate heart. Maybe she would be willing to listen to his troubles. Then he considered how easily he might let out the nature of the mistakes he committed to lead to his anxiety. Brandi had never shown any interest in any relationship, so he doubted the mistake would ever be repeated with her. If he revealed his affairs, though, she might no longer trust him. No reason to confide in anyone who did not already know.

Michelle? No, he decided. Adam did not know her well enough.

His mother? He did not want to disappoint her.

His step-father? A joke.

Adam finally forced himself to rise and pulled the two old suitcases out of the closet. He looked at the photograph of the original stones again, hoping to glean some clue from it. Grace had said that the diamond may have been given to a relative of hers. But there were no names hidden anywhere in the photo.

Adam shuffled through every legible paper, despite remembering them all from before. He never found a lead in any form that he or Grace had not noticed a year ago.

He checked the time on his phone. Adam had endured twenty minutes without thinking of her. That was both good and bad, he supposed.

Adam placed the suitcases back in the closet and laid back on the bed. There was no music playing and no television on in the living room. Everything darkened at sunset. Adam did not bother to turn on a light. He suddenly realized he had never eaten dinner, but he still felt no hunger.

Nate had delved too far when they last ate together, but he was right. Adam knew he was falling apart without Grace. But that would never change. He was without Grace, and he could never be put back together. Any hope of being whole again vanished.

The light disappeared, minus a few parking lot lights which glimmered in the window. Adam wanted to let out a scream, hoping all his frustrations and ruined dreams would exit with the sound. He almost felt like a cliché out of a movie, and even though there was no one to embarrass himself in front of, he kept the primal sound within his lungs.

A movie. Adam remembered their movie date, a few months after they were married. He remembered how Grace forgave the rude girls in the theater. Adam recalled how she thought the woman in the movie should forgive the man who cheated on her. He remembered her saying she would forgive him, even if he cheated on her.

Grace was dead, so what had happened was not cheating in the strictest sense. But Adam knew he had done the wrong thing, twice. If Grace somehow knew, how could she truly forgive him?

He turned onto his side. He did not want to further rattle his mind with questions he would never answer. But he saw the faint silhouette of the jewel box and asked himself another impossible question. Would it still have mattered to Grace if he found the last two jewels?

His phone buzzed, and the light from the screen flooded out the darkness. Adam picked it up off the nightstand and read the text message from a number he did not recognize.

"I found your number on a social media post you provided. My name is Emma. Are you still looking for a lost onyx? There is a chance I've found it. Do you know where

Pinchot Park is? I may have spotted it at one of the homes near the lake."

Adam remembered exactly where the lake was, in northern York County. Should he reply? No, not until morning. He was mentally exhausted and needed to relax. Putting his guilt and frustrations aside, Adam closed his eyes in a vain attempt to find sleep.

He needed to convince himself finding the gems would still matter to Grace. Adam was forced to do this.

Chapter 32

Adam repeatedly told himself not to get his hopes up and repeatedly failed.

He had already driven to Pinchot Park and could see the lake within the park from here, so he had time to review the facts several times. The message was vague, so it may not be the onyx. But it encouraged him more than the spam messages he received from people trying to sell him any random valuable stone or gem. The chances of finding the onyx relatively soon after the sapphire and the emerald were minuscule. Nevertheless, nothing was stopping the jewels from appearing near each other...

And on and on.

But Adam's hope was not only in the possibility of finding the fourth jewel. He hoped this was the one moment that might pull him out of the darkness that had been thickening ever since Grace's death. He had hoped for the same thing when the sapphire had been found, and when the emerald had been purchased. There had been quick moments when sunlight seemed to break through the clouds, but the shadows needed only a few days to snuff it out.

He could say the same thing for his time with Rylee and Tessa. Not the women themselves. They helped him when they had nothing to gain by it. Adam still appreciated their efforts on his behalf, even as he carried the guilt from their encounters afterwards.

Adam refused to look back on those nights again.

Then he remembered he was truly content after finding the ruby, but that was different. Grace was there.

Grace and he had one of their best days together when they found the ruby. He might never be free from this pain, even if he found the onyx today and the diamond soon after.

As he found the address and pulled into the driveway, Adam reminded himself he was not doing this to make himself proud. He was trying to honor Grace's memory. But when he realized what building he drove up to, he forgot for a moment any of his larger goals.

The building in front of him took his breath away. It was two stories tall and built in a style from over one hundred years ago. The house conveyed the charm of a comfortable home, yet large enough to house well over a dozen people.

"My apartment would fit in one of this guy's closets," Adam whispered to himself.

Adam tore his gaze away from the home and looked around the lawn. There were a few trees, but well-manicured grass occupied the acres around the house. He was not sure where the property ended since no other homes stood nearby. He guessed the line was somewhere around where the grass ended and the trees, the same variety which surrounded the lake, began.

Putting his back to the house, Adam looked down at the lake. It was visible along with the thick trees, down the slope of a hill. The area was idyllic, as relaxing as anywhere Adam had been for ages. Admittedly, it was a hot, humid August day, so the weather was not quite as perfect as it otherwise looked. Still, these were nice surroundings. If Grace lived today, he thought, this might have been the perfect spot for her...

"Hey, you," someone shouted. "Want to get going on this?"

Adam turned to the side of the house and saw a woman waving him away from the house. As he walked to her, she yelled again, "It's over here."

He could not quite catch up to her since she turned and strode over to the woods. Then Adam saw a well, a few yards beyond the treeline. When the woman stopped by it, Adam was finally saw her clearly. She had black hair, bobbed to her shoulders. She stood two inches shorter than Adam, but with her hands on her hips and a grimace, she had already taken charge.

"Hello, I'm Adam."

"I figured that out already," she said. "I think your onyx is down there. Maybe."

Adam already felt awkward about this encounter. "Okay. Um, I took it from your message that this isn't your home, so can I..."

"Okay, pay attention because I don't plan on telling you twice. An old geezer owns this home, but only spends less than half the year here. It must be nice to be rich. But he needed someone to watch over the place and a few other spots up here while he lives in another home. As I said, rich. I'm the caretaker for the outside of this property. I never go into the house, but I'm responsible for making sure everything is okay out here. I'm here each Saturday before hitting the clubs at night. And don't judge."

Adam didn't care if she was a clubber and was not sure why she brought it up only to tell him not to think about it. He noticed her stylish clothes did not match her work as a caretaker. If he judged her, it was for not saying anything involved with how to find the onyx.

"But if none of this land is yours, are you sure I can take the onyx if it is on this man's property?"

"If it's here, it's down this well," she said, pointing. "And the well is over the property line, into public territory. Not by much, but by the letter of the law, this well does not belong to the owner of the home. I figure if you can get it out and you're sure it's yours, there's no reason you can't walk away with it."

"What makes you think it's down a well?" Adam asked, hoping he had not wasted the hour driving here.

The woman sighed. Adam finally remembered her name, Emma, which he had seen on her message yesterday. "Why do you need to know all the details? Look, I saw something glimmer down there last Saturday. The sun shone at the right angle to shine through the branches and hit the bottom of the well. I had already seen people sharing your posts about the jewels, so I wondered if that glimmer might be one of them." Emma pulled out her phone. "I took a picture, if you want to see it, too."

Adam looked at the screen. It seemed to be blank at first glance, but there was a sharp reflection of light in the corner.

"That is very little to go on," Adam said.

"Calm yourself," Emma said, though Adam was not agitated. At least not yet. She flipped to the next picture. "When I noticed the little star, I took another picture with the flashlight on."

"And you didn't show me that picture first?"

Emma echoed those words back to Adam in a mocking tone, then added, "Just look at it now."

Mud covered the well's floor, but near the circular edge, there was a small spot of darkness which presented a different hue than the mud. It again sent a reflection back to the lens.

"It could be the onyx," Adam mumbled.

"Speak up."

"But it would make more sense for it to be something else. A coin or something like that."

"Definitely not mud, though," Emma said.

"Would an onyx reflect like that?" Adam continued to think aloud. "Maybe the silver setting would."

Adam walked to the edge of the well and pulled out his phone. He turned on the light and looked down the shaft. When held at the right angle, a small pinpoint of light returned to his eyes.

"Why would it be down there?" Adam asked.

"Are you asking me, or do you just enjoy talking to yourself?"

"It's more fun than talking to you," Adam muttered.

"What did I do to make you think I'm deaf?" Emma replied, but Adam's mind wandered.

The diameter of the well was shorter than his height was but wide enough that he could, in theory, stand within it. The sides of the well were constructed with rough stone. So, in theory, he would have a handhold.

No more theories. Adam needed to find the last jewels, and one might be in this well.

At this point, what else did he have to live for? Time to put his exercise routine to the test.

"If you call someone for help, make sure they keep all their equipment on the public side of the property line so I don't have to explain this to the owner of the mans-," Emma gasped, then screamed. "What are you doing?"

Adam was already completely under the top of the well. All four limbs pressed against the stone, his phone with the flashlight still on tucked into his belt, he descended a few inches at a time.

"If you break your neck, they'll accuse me of killing you!"

Thanks for the sympathy, Adam thought.

He moved down another foot. This well was no deeper than twelve feet at most, Adam estimated. He descended a little more. It was still dangerous, but Adam was more tired of searching for the gems than by working his muscles against the well wall.

He found a foothold, then a handhold, and repeated the process. Eventually, he had to reach to the other side of the well to continue safely. Relatively safely, anyway.

"I swear, I only told him that something might be down there," Emma yelled from above. "I never even mentioned the idea of climbing to the bottom."

In the back of his mind, Adam realized she was recording herself as evidence if he injured himself. Not the most unreasonable action, he knew. But when his right foot touched the soft ground, he realized he had made it to the bottom of the well.

"Don't worry," he yelled back to Emma. "I can't fall any further."

What he assumed was Emma's shadow blocked what little light came in from the top of the well. "I'm sure you'll find a way," her voice echoed

"You're not much of a cheering section," Adam shouted back.

Adam looked to the ground and realized what his anxiousness had cost him. Though he had room to stand in the well, and probably could find a way to climb back up, it was difficult to reach his hands to the mud. He tried to kneel, but as he did, he blocked his flashlight from showing him where the reflection was coming from.

He grasped around where he thought he saw a flicker of light. Slime oozed between his fingers. Only now did he wonder what bugs or animals might live here.

"Are you still breathing? I'll call an ambulance or a coroner. Your choice."

Adam was about to give a retort, but then he noticed something, or rather, the point of something. He tried to grip the object, but it slipped away. Adam grasped a few more times, and finally, he pulled it into his palm. He brought his hand up to his eyes, ready to clean it off and to be sure if this effort warranted the danger. Then his flashlight flickered out.

At first, his disappointment focused on how he could not be sure if this was the onyx. It felt right in his hand, but he had no guarantee without a clear view. But then he realized he could not see the protruding portions of the rocks for a climb back to the surface.

"Hey, would you mind shining your light down here?" Adam shouted. "My phone battery is dead."

He did not hear an answer right away. Adam put the object, and some mud, in his pocket. He would need both hands to ascend.

There was some sunlight from above, but it did not help Adam on the floor. He reached around, hoping for two safe places to grab.

And then the darkness vaporized into man-made light.

"Never say I didn't do anything for you," Emma's voice echoed.

She better not hope I do anything for her, Adam thought to himself. But light was light, and it made the climb much easier. He was particularly cautious, knowing his muddy shoes were a liability now, and his muscles were worn from the descent. But soon he reached with his left hand to the rim of the well's wall. He pulled himself up and over, though he received no further help from Emma.

He fell to his knees on the uncut grass around the well. His muscles ached in ways he did not remember them ever experiencing before. He tried to catch his breath.

"So, is that it?" Emma asked.

Adam laughed. He roared. He was not in the mood to be playful in the slightest, but the absurdity of it all finally reached his brain. A vague lead, followed by a few photographs, led to him risking his own life, or at least his good health, to pull a random object in the mud.

"I have no idea yet," Adam answered when he recovered. But actually, he did. The item had felt as if it were the right shape. And there was a point poking into his palm, which he hoped was the end of the corkscrew hook. He reached into his pocket and pulled it out, holding it up to the afternoon sun.

Both he and Emma were silent. Some mud was still smeared on it, but there was no question about what Adam held.

A vertical middle facet. Smaller points on the ends. Silver setting. This was Grace's onyx.

Adam snapped his fist around it, as if Emma was trying to take it away. But she smiled coyly. "Remember, you never would have found it here without me."

What was it doing in a well? That riddle came without an answer, but he did not care. He had four of the five jewels now. He might do the one thing for Grace that he had focused on for months. Finding all five became a realistic task.

"Ahem," Emma said, striding over to him. "First, you're an idiot. You're lucky you weren't trapped down there. But, second, you have your fancy rock. Time for payment."

This woman irritated him, but she was right. The first two jewels, Adam had been lucky. No payment had been required, just donations to causes, and he was free to choose the amounts. For the third, Tessa had been there with two lifetimes of cash available. This time, Adam would have to pay for it himself.

"How much?"

"I'll take five hundred dollars."

That would hurt, but Adam could afford it. It was an exorbitant price considering Emma never owned the onyx. But a finder's fee was understandable considering the place where she spotted the onyx. But he only had two hundred dollars in cash in his pocket and had left his checkbook at home.

"Okay, I can send you a check..."

"Oh, you can't pay today? Then make it one thousand."

"What? Who carries that much money on them?" The image of Tessa pulling absurd amounts of money out of her purse appeared in Adam's brain, but decided not to mention her.

"I'm letting you take the jewel without paying me first. Thus, interest. Three-hundred dollars per day."

It's like she wants me to hate her, Adam seethed. But instead he said, "Fine. I will drive back down here tomorrow with a check and put it in your hands before you have any other ideas."

"Agreed. Meet me back here. After this nonsense, I don't want to bother taking care of the grounds today, so I'll be back at the old man's house tomorrow, anyway."

Adam almost screamed at "nonsense" but kept himself in check. He wondered for a moment if he should avoid paying her at all, but decided against it. With the check, he would have a paper trail showing he had paid Emma for her help–if whatever she had provided. At least he would protect himself in case Emma was the suing or vengeful type.

That would hardly be surprising.

Chapter 33

Again, Adam had a new jewel to connect to the necklace and secure in the jewelry case. Again, he did not receive the joy he had anticipated.

Checks for colossal sums can create that effect. One-thousand dollars would not liquidate his bank account, but it would hurt for a long time. Adam could visualize himself paying his college loan on his fortieth birthday.

He should have haggled more. Maybe he was too intent on getting the onyx home to realize the cost. That was also why he had risked descending into the well without thinking through the situation. His judgment on nearly everything remained clouded.

But he had agreed to this, and if Grace were living, she would not want him going back on his word. Still, he doubted if she would have agreed with several of his decisions in the last few months.

The check secured in his wallet, Adam walked from the bedroom to the living room. True, life overall was smoother now than two months ago. He regularly updated his bank account, so he knew this payment would not ruin him, even if it stung. The apartment was clean and organized again, and Adam took the time each weekend to make sure it stayed that way. As his albeit foolish climbing in the well proved, he was back in peak physical shape.

But each of those issues were surface changes and nothing more, Adam understood. The important things were as much of a mess as ever. Even during this unexpected success in finding Grace's jewelry, everything seemed wrong.

Because what he did was wrong.

Adam walked outside, hoping a breath of fresh air would bring fresh thoughts along with it, but this did not distract him. As he entered his car, his mistakes forced themselves into the forefront of his mind.

Rylee. Tessa.

Before starting the engine, he took a moment to consider: if Grace could speak to him from the grave, would she have forgiven him?

There was the slightest chance she would have understood with Rylee. Or at least said it was wrong, but excusable under the circumstances. Or that it he had stabbed her in the back with the worst betrayal possible.

Tessa...no. Neither relationship was ever romantic, but at least there were powerful emotions with Rylee. Tessa was a co-worker, nothing more. And now neither of them could even talk to each other.

But she had offered to pay for the remaining jewels if they could be found. Adam considered contacting her about this payment for the onyx. Tessa might keep her word on that.

Then he shook his head as if someone else were in the car and asking him these questions. He and Tessa never exchanged a sentence with each other anymore. He would only make things worse by asking her for money.

As he started the engine and pulled out of the parking lot, Adam recognized the actual damage of his indiscretions: ruined relationships.

And Adam knew no way to undo this. Time reduced the sharpness of the pain and made it easier to send a text here and there to Rylee or Michael. But time never changed anything of substance.

When Grace died, he lost the love of his life. When he failed to adapt to life without her, he lost what few friends he had. Adam had lost his connections to those he cared for and felt no strength to forge new bonds with anyone else.

By the time he was midway between his apartment and Pinchot Park, Adam was convinced only one purpose to his life that remained.

The diamond.

That thought gave Adam a brief, strange surge of happiness. At least he still had one purpose, and a kind of purpose most people would never experience. Even better, he was eighty percent of the way to his goal. Only one of five gems still remained.

Then the happiness reduced to a sliver of its initial size. The diamond will most likely prove to be the hardest of all the jewels to recover. They already knew the challenge when Grace first opened her father's files and they began this search.

Grace.

He had dishonored her with how he had lived his life since her passing, not to mention making himself a fool in the eyes of those who knew him. But he would find the diamond and bring honor to her memory by bringing the jewels together, as they were meant to be.

As he turned south on Route 177, he stopped wondering over the greater purpose of his life and pondered where the diamond might be. It was supposed to be in the hands of Grace's relatives, even though Grace never knew of any other family after her parents died. Did "family" mean something symbolic? A friend her father trusted so deeply that he considered the other person a relative?

He analyzed what that possibility might mean before frustrating himself. Adam would still have no idea where to search, whether he sought a relative or friend of the Davis family.

Another possibility, if family meant literal relatives, was to call every Davis in the region. Reach out to every Davis who used a social media account on any website. It bordered on spamming, but Adam did not care about the ethics of the internet for now. The search for the diamond was all he had left.

As he pulled up the driveway to the house–no, Adam decided, more of a mini-mansion–he remembered he still needed to finish up this business with the onyx. The question of how the onyx ever wound up in the bottom of a well still nagged at him. One more thing that forced him to contemplate the past.

In the past there was pain. Losing Grace, giving in to Rylee and Tessa, losing friends because of his foolishness. It was time to anticipate the future. Once he handed this check over, the diamond must become his focus.

When and if he found the diamond, he hoped he would find happiness there. If not...better not to think about that either, Adam decided.

He stepped out of his car and looked at the giant building again. It seemed crazy one man lived in it and not a family. It easily could have held fifteen people. Despite having scolded himself for looking back, Adam could not help but think this might have served as the perfect building for Grace's dream to run a...

"About time you showed up."

Emma's voice itself sounded quite pleasant, almost like a song, yet her tone made it screech in Adam's ears.

"Is there any chance you'd reconsider?" Adam asked, certain there was not but determined to try. "The thousand you asked for at first was more than fair."

"Look," Emma said, stepping up to him in a grey t-shirt and jean shorts, "you have what you wanted. Is it crazy that I'm asking for what I want?"

No point fighting this battle, he decided as he reached for his wallet. Adam put the check in her hand.

"You could have just mailed it," Emma said as she scowled.

"And you could have not charged me interest for paying you one day after I found the onyx."

"I found it."

"I climbed into a well to get it."

"No one told you to act so impatient."

How obnoxious is this woman? Adam asked himself. *She sure looks nice though.*

It was not the same voice he had heard before, not the guidance he had received with gentle wisdom. The unfamiliar voice echoed from the same part of his mind, but it sounded grittier, rougher, crueler.

While Adam paused in confusion at his thoughts, Emma shook her head. "Just forget about everything else. Our transaction is finished. You took the onyx. I've got my money, and my work here on the grounds is done. I'm heading home. Goodbye, won't miss you."

She brushed by him and strode her way to the car on the road.

Sometimes it only takes a few words to bring a woman back.

What a horrible intention to pursue. So degrading. I've been making mistakes lately, but only brief lapses in judgment. I still respect women.

Come on, look at her. Let her channel that aggressive energy into pleasing you.

She seems to despise me for some reason. And even if she were interested, I can't make this mistake again...

All that arguing? Tension. She wants you. And you want her.

Adam felt himself slip again. Emma was about to open the door to her car. If he held back a few more seconds...

This won't cost you any relationships.

True. He had no relationships left to lose. And she was shapely.

Something inside him snapped, and the voice laughed.

"Why don't we make our meeting worthwhile?" Adam called to her. He could not believe the words as he first spoke them. But once he finished uttering the question, his heart seemed trapped by them. Some part of him sensed how wrong this was, but the rest of his being committed to taking this chance.

Emma's hand rested on the handle of the car door but did not open it. She glanced back. "I'll regret asking, but what do you mean?"

"Let's be in private for an hour, and I'll show you."

I'm not the man I used to be, Adam told himself. He realized he should not be doing this, but he could not resist.

No, this was not about resisting. Emma had shown no interest. He created this temptation.

Because Adam wanted to make Emma fall the same way he did.

Stop acting so confused and upset. She'll give in, too.

But while the voice inside Adam's head spoke, he also heard Emma's voice from the car. "What an arrogant bastard you are."

"Guilty as charged," Adam answered.

Emma opened the door and stepped into the car. But midway through the action, she stopped and stayed motionless for two seconds.

See?

She stepped back out of the car, turned around and walked back to Adam. She gave him the first sincere smile he had seen. "Oh, why not? Arrogant bastards are the most fun." She slid her arm around him. "The same man who owns this house also has a small cabin south of the lake. He pays me to check on that, too. It's a half-hour closer than my place, so hop in your car and meet me there in twenty minutes."

"What good does someone else's cabin do us?"

Emma's smile was wicked. "When he left, he forgot to lock the door."

Part V

The Jewelry
of Grace

Chapter 34

Adam punched the dashboard as the traffic light shone red. The impact did no damage to the car, and he felt no pain in his fingers.

That was what scared him.

Fear was the last thing he needed now, with all the other emotions threatening to crush him from within. Until this moment, guilt, shame and loneliness were the three choking his soul. Dealing with a fourth draining emotion would be too much.

He committed the same mistake again. No, "mistake" was the wrong word. This was more of a habit now.

He had time to change his mind, driving to the cabin. Even before that, he should have kept his mouth shut when Emma had meant to leave the mansion. But he laid with her, anyway.

Just as he did with Rylee and Tessa. Each time, the temporary high from the tryst became briefer, and the guilt afterward became heavier.

Adam had been emotionally drained by a year of mourning when he was with Rylee. It should not have happened, but he knew he was weak then.

He should have stood his ground with Tessa and said no. But he barely contemplated refusing her offer.

Now he had been with a stranger, after initiating the encounter himself.

His descent continued, and that frightened him. He feared what the next step downward would be.

When he had punched the dashboard, he experienced no pain. He feared, the next time this happened, he would be beyond feeling guilt over his misdeeds. He would commit the crime, and no longer understand he had done anything wrong.

The light finally turned green, and Adam drove onto the exit ramp to merge onto I-83. It was getting late at night, and the road was empty. He needed to speed back to his apartment and sleep before he started the work week tomorrow. If he could find any sleep.

Emma had left the cabin almost immediately. Adam did not care where she went or why she was so quick to leave. At least, he told himself that. As he questioned whether he cared, he punched the dashboard again, a dangerous reaction while driving over seventy. This time, it did hurt.

Am I going to transform into the opposite of what I was when I was with Grace?

The question lingered. He could not think it through with any coherent logic. But he was sure of the answer. Yes, he became everything he was not when Grace lived.

And it was time to stop fooling himself. If Grace knew from beyond the grave his behavior, even after "death do us part," she could never forgive him.

Adam considered himself less than a man now. Or maybe a fallen man at best. More of an animal. He may have learned how to make his life appear better on the outside, with the apartment in better shape and his finances straightened out. But on the inside, he possessed more characteristics of a beast than a person.

Over the last twenty minutes of his drive, Adam's mind numbed. He refused to think about any woman anymore. He could not think about anything anymore. Emma, the jewels, his job, what future years might hold, none of it. Only muscle memory allowed him to drive without incident. He became a blank slate until he parked at the apartment complex.

His mind remained empty as he walked into the vestibule and unlocked the main door to the first floor. He turned down the hallway to his apartment.

Adam saw her golden hair. It was disheveled and shorter than before, but still nearly reached her shoulders.

She turned towards Adam as he approached, picking up speed with every step, and then he saw her blue eyes. Her gaze brought his mind back to its senses. The other women, his job, the gems, everything else in the world remained forgotten, but one word echoed through both his mind and the hallway.

"Grace!"

He feared he saw an illusion, a trick of his memory. But he caught her by her shoulders, and the sensation sent electricity through his nerves. Grace stood here, in front of him.

Only now did he realize how exhausted she appeared. She looked as if she might pass out, so he held her without hugging her, being cautious since he did not know Grace's condition.

She smiled. "Your eyes," she said, while her gaze filled Adam with one emotion he lacked for more than a year.

Joy.

Then Grace took a deep breath. "I had to look into your eyes," she repeated, "when I knew I would make it back."

Grace put her arms around Adam, and he finally embraced her with his full strength. "I don't care what happened, as long as you're here and you're staying here." Tears covered his face.

"I'll be with you forever," Grace said. Then she pulled back an inch. "Now, don't be scared or angry, but I'm afraid I'm going to pass out from my trip here. Please, let's go inside and let me sleep. I'll explain everything as soon as I can, but I..." She started mumbling, then raised her voice again. "I need some sleep. More than some. I've been through a lot."

Adam could not imagine what Grace lived through, but for today, details did not matter. Impossible as it may be, she was home again. He unlocked the door. "The landlord changed the locks a few months ago," he whispered, hoping Grace had not been trying for hours to unlock the door. He was about ready to carry her to the bed, or at least support her, but Grace found enough energy to walk there on her own, albeit slowly.

"I so wanted to see our home again," she whispered. "The living room looks nice. You even made the bed. The place looks nicer than I expected."

"It wasn't always," Adam answered. "I'll turn down the sheets."

"Don't bother," Grace said, falling onto the bed. Onto her side of the bed, Adam realized with a grin.

"Do I need to call an ambulance? Are you sick? Hurt?"

"Trust me, no. I've been in hospitals enough." Grace brought a hand to her mouth. "Oops. Don't worry over that. I'm fine, I'll explain everything. It was a lengthy trip back, that's what has me worn down. I'll explain it all when my head is clearer."

Adam, now slightly recovered from his shock of seeing Grace, could not help but be a little concerned. Her comment about hospitals had his mind racing. But before he asked his questions, Grace spoke again. "I brought two bags. Could you bring them in from the hallway?"

Adam nodded and rushed back out the front door. He grabbed the two suitcases, not the same ones Grace had taken with her over a year ago, and carried them into the bedroom.

Grace already slept. In one sense, seeing her slumber was a beautiful vision to Adam, as he watched the peaceful rhythm of each breath. But then, his concern for her health emerged. He took her wrist and checked her pulse. He was no paramedic, but he found the normal vibration. Adam placed his wrist across her forehead. No fever.

But he sensed heat. Not the warmth of illness, but the fire he experienced only with Grace.

Adam sat next to her on the bed, and for several minutes did nothing but watch Grace sleep. He had never seen any image more wonderful. Each rise and fall of her chest restored part of Adam's hope for their future. He did not recognize the clothes she wore, a simple top and white capris, but he did not care where they had come from.

Ever so quietly, Adam changed into his sleep outfit. Without turning down his side of the bed, he laid down next to Grace, and slid his arm around her. She remained asleep, but turned towards him and put her arm around his shoulder. He kissed her forehead as exhaustion crept over him.

Somewhere in the back of his mind, he knew he needed to call the office and tell them there was no way he would come in tomorrow. He had taken so much time off recently, he would have to give a convincing reason, but he had one. A reason his boss and coworkers would never believe, but Adam did not care.

Grace was alive.

Even amid his joy, Adam sensed darkness in his heart. Truths lurked, ones that threatened to ruin this moment. But Adam refused to focus on those.

Grace was alive!

Chapter 35

Grace did not wake until noon, leaving Adam to observe her breathing throughout the morning. She looked healthy, and each breath seemed normal. Still, he worried about any health problems under her skin.

He had called Ms. Douglas earlier, letting her know what had happened and that he wanted to take a week off to help Grace readjust to being home. His boss told Adam he saved enough time to take off, but he would be out of time for the rest of the year, and while it was his time to use, his reason sounded unlikely. Adam switched to a video call and showed Ms. Douglas the image of Grace sleeping in their bed. Befuddled, Ms. Douglas told Adam to do what he needed to do, and they would see him next Monday.

Adam was no less confused than his boss. He wanted Grace to wake up. He needed to talk with her, to find out how she had returned and why she had disappeared for so long. But he waited. Regardless of what had happened, she needed her rest now.

Other, darker thoughts pestered in the back of his mind. Adam fought them back. He could not deal with other problems now. Grace and Grace alone was all that mattered now.

When Grace first aroused, Adam gave her a piece of toast and orange juice and let her regain her bearings.

"It's so nice to wake up here again." She looked around the bedroom. "You didn't change much. Our wedding photo is still there. I like it."

"Are you sure you're feeling okay?"

"Exhausted. It will take more than one night's sleep to regain my strength."

"Can you tell me what happened?"

Grace sighed. "What I was awake for, yes. I'm afraid I can't figure out all the answers myself."

"Awake?"

"Honey, this will be hard for you to hear, but I slept in a coma while I was missing."

"Oh, dear-,"

"Easy, easy," Grace calmed him, patting his knee. "I'm here now."

Adam tried to catch his breath. "Okay. So, something happened in the fire. Were you hit by falling debris?"

"No," Grace answered. "This will sound a little confusing, but the fire is unrelated to my injuries. I only learned about the fire in the last week."

"The Pine hotel burned over a year ago."

"I know. But for me, less than a month has passed. Let me start at the beginning, the day after I last spoke to you. I received a phone call from someone who lived in Paradise, Orson Davis. He said he was a relative of mine. I didn't know if he told me the truth, but he wanted to meet as soon as possible."

"Is this man a suspect?"

"No, please, let me finish," Grace said, placing her hand on his knee again. The touch calmed Adam, but only slightly. "I walked to the conference like I had planned the night before. After the morning sessions, I met up with him at a restaurant near the hotel. He seemed to know my father from the way he talked about him. It turns out they were distant cousins. Orson looks as if he must be many years

284

older than my father would be now, and his skin is darker. I
had already known my ancestry came from Germany, but
Orson told me that there was also a line that actually
connects me to the Middle East."

"Do you think he found information on you or your
father online?"

"Okay, I'll skip to the spoilers: Orson is a wonderful
man. He didn't hurt me. Quite the opposite. After our lunch,
we arranged to meet again, because he needed to tell me
more about my family, and he had something for me. If he
ever told me how he knew I was nearby, I've forgotten it. But
I remember how the lunch ended. While walking out of the
restaurant, I got careless and stepped out in front of a car. I
realized it at the last second, and then everything was
blank."

"It hit you?"

"No. I don't remember the accident, but according to
Orson, I tried to step back out of the way. The car swerved
and missed me, but I fell back and hit my head on the curb
at full force."

"And then you fell into a coma," Adam wept. He knew
the tears were irrational. Grace laid in their bed now. But
thinking of her suffering and how he did nothing about it
brought back the old pain.

"I guess the next thing I should tell you is what
happened that I can't remember. We need to take Orson at
his word on this, but the hospital papers in my bags back up
his story. I was in a coma for nearly a year. My physical
health otherwise stabilized, but I couldn't wake up. So I was
in a hospital most of the time I was gone."

"I'm so sorry. I should have been there."

"How would you have known?"

"Well, for starters, why didn't the police notice your name on the hospital records? They listed you as a missing person."

"Well, that's where this gets tricky. To make sure he could take care of me, Orson signed me in under my maiden name."

"So you both used the same last name, from their point of view," Adam reasoned. "The police told me you had left your ID and phone in the hotel room."

"I'll never be so forgetful again."

"Had you ever told this Orson your last name?"

"I don't remember for sure. But either way, he told me afterward he did it to cover me under his insurance."

"Oh, yeah. I guess I should have been seeing dozens of claims in the mail. But how did he take care of you? You're not a dependent of his."

"I didn't need to be. I haven't told you much about Orson. This is all so much to take in, even after days of pondering it. But he really is a retired general. And he's saved and invested so much money–you'd like him–he could pay for my treatment on his own."

"An entire year's worth?"

"I saved copes of the claims and receipts," Grace nodded. "The hospital staff said he watched over me all the time."

"All?"

"I don't think they meant it literally. But he was a constant companion, I am sure of that. But the hospital staff was suspicious."

"I'm glad they were. You carried no ID. All he had was a random rich man's word."

"Well, Orson had his own identification, so he could prove who he is. Proving that we are related or that I would approve of letting him make medical decisions was harder. But then, three weeks ago, I finally showed signs of consciousness. I don't know if there's such a thing as a correct number of days to be in a coma, but the doctors said I woke just in time. Another month, or even less, and I would have suffered permanent memory loss. Even so, when I first realized where I was, only smatterings of images returned. But once my mind cleared, the staff requested my Social Security Number to verify my name, and a DNA test to prove I was related to Orson."

"And?"

"The Social Security check was quick. The staff was not happy to find they had been given my maiden name, but since he did care for me, their anger passed. As far as the DNA, the connection is distant, but we are, in fact, related. The results came in the day I left North Carolina. So apparently have both European and Middle Eastern blood in me. Kind of makes me feel more worldly," she smiled.

"But why didn't he reach out? Or a hospital staff member? You wore your wedding ring, didn't you? Orson must have known you had other relatives. Even if you didn't, this is why missing person bureaus exist. He should have contacted the police."

"Orson said he did. He showed me proof."

"How? I never heard anything from him."

"Orson told me he called you several times while I was still unconscious. He wanted to tell you everything that happened and encourage you because he was certain I would return. But you never returned his calls."

"I never received them." Adam defended himself. "That was exactly what I was looking for. All I wanted to know was where you were. At least, until I gave up hope. And yes, I gave up. I'm sorry."

"Don't be. If his calls didn't get through for whatever reason..."

"Are you sure he called, and he's not making it up after you woke?"

"He showed me his phone log, shortly after my memory cleared and I asked him the same questions you're asking now," Grace said. "I saw your number a dozen times. I can't prove he left any voice mails, but I know he called your phone."

Adam thought back. It was possible Orson found his number through a reverse-number search online, but why would Adam have never received these calls?

"Don't worry over it, Adam. Everything worked out. Well, except that they cut my hair somewhere along the line. It still feels a little short to me."

"I'm still uncomfortable that you were in the care of someone we hardly know, relative or not. Especially since he says he called when I never...,"

Then he remembered. During the fog of his depression, Adam had become so withdrawn he only bothered with messages from work and the police departments. Everything else, be they telemarketers making sales or acquaintances offering encouragement, were ignored and deleted. He never had Orson's number, so when he deleted all the other voice mails, he also deleted Orson's attempts to reach him.

"He must have called from one of the other numbers," Adam mumbled to himself. "I should have kept answering them, listening to all the messages. His messages must have been in there somewhere, but I never listened to them. Orson must be one of the people I refused to listen to. But he never called the police, either?"

"He said that the police weren't family, and the police were not going to pull me out of a coma. From his point of view, they didn't need to know," Grace said. "Try not to worry about this. He did exactly what he said he would do. Orson restored me to you. He even bought me the new suitcases and gave me a gift card for extra clothes for my trip back up here. You may never have answered his call and he may never have tried to reach you through someone else, but Orson did the most important thing. He put me back here with you." She yawned. "There's more to say, but maybe it would be best to wait until tomorrow."

She snuggled up into bed. Adam laid next to her, though adrenaline, fueled by his confusion, kept him wide awake. Was this Orson a kind man, whom age prevented from making logical decisions? Was he someone wiser than everyone else who handled this the right way? Or was he doing something unethical or illegal behind the scenes?

Adam shook off that last thought. The DNA test showed Orson is Grace's relative, and over more than a year, nothing had happened to their bank account.

Something needed to be explained to make every piece fit together. Still, Adam found rest by putting his arms around his wife and reminding himself of the one thing that mattered.

Grace was alive.

Again, the dark thoughts cast pale shadows over his happiness. But Adam stroked his hands over Grace's back and pushed the memories away.

Grace was alive!

Chapter 36

Grace slept in the next morning as well, though not as long as she had the morning following her return. Adam still felt palpitations each time he gazed at her. Sometimes the rush came from the excitement of having her back, sometimes from the concerns he still held about her health.

Over the morning hours, Grace filled in some details from her stay, but nothing that answered the more disturbing questions Adam wanted to ask. He knew no more significant facts about Orson. Apparently, he was related to Grace, but that did not prove they should trust him. Orson should have done more to reach him, like trying social media channels. The hospital staff should have sought him out, too.

There will also be paperwork to do somewhere, now that Grace was no longer a missing person, and the police had never been informed.

But while he listened to Grace, and coaxed her to eat a little more, Adam decided to not pursue those issues today. She needed a break from drama of any kind.

In the early afternoon, Adam wanted to check how much energy Grace regained. "Do you want to go outside, do anything, get some fresh air?" he asked. "You haven't been outside the door since you arrived. Do you have enough energy for a quick walk?"

Grace smiled. She was sitting on the sofa in their living room. "I might, but that's not what I want now. There are two different things I wish today. First, I want you to sit here next to me."

Adam slid in next to her, putting his arm around her shoulders. "And?"

"And, I want you to put golf on the television."

Golf. It had been so long since he had looked forward to watching golf. He had forced himself to put it on the television or phone every so often to catch up on a few highlights, but he could not enjoy it. The television or phone would be turned off and his mind would wander.

Again, thoughts lingered in Adam's mind. Again, Adam pushed them back.

Now, with Grace here, he was determined to enjoy her presence again and be able to enjoy everything else, too. But she never enjoyed golf.

"Why would you want me to put on a sport you never appreciated?" he asked. "If we're going to put a show on for the first time...well, the first time since you've returned...wouldn't you rather-"

"I'd rather watch something the man I love loves," Grace answered.

No reason to argue, Adam thought, though he was still a touch concerned Grace was not showing much energy. He turned on the television and then realized he did not know what day of the week it was. With Grace's return, he had lost track of time. It was almost as if the last two days had existed out of time.

But the television menu screen reminded him this was a Tuesday, a day where live golf events were rarely played. "I'm not sure that much is on. Sure you don't want a romantic movie? There are always dozens of those on cable."

Grace shook her head and nuzzled into his cheek. "No. Find a golf event."

After a moment, Adam found a channel showing a replay of a professional golf tournament that had taken place

292

the previous weekend. He and Grace spent fifteen minutes in silence. Adam thought Grace was asleep, but she spoke as a commercial break started.

"On the bus rides back here, I desperately missed you. I could only imagine how terribly you missed me. I wanted to call, but I also needed to see your eyes. I needed you to see me right in front of you so you would know it wasn't a hoax. But in those hours, I realized how much I missed this. The quiet times, alone. You following this stupid sport, me sitting next to you with nothing to say because I will never care about golf."

She lifted her head, then kissed Adam. "And it's all so perfect."

* * *

"I know, it would have been wiser to call you once I recovered," Grace said, leaning in towards him from the foot of the bed. "But as I said, I needed to see your eyes, up close."

Adam caressed her cheek. "All that matters is you are here now." He kissed her on the forehead. "I still feel as if this can't be real."

"Oh, it's real," Grace said, smiling. "But there is one more thing that will make it more unbelievable. You haven't opened my box yet, have you?"

Adam tilted his head. He had forgotten. Before they watched the golf match together, Grace had said she had two things she wanted to do today. "What box?"

"Open the tan suitcase. There will be an olive box inside." Grace stopped and brought her hand to her stomach. "And, could you make a little more to eat? I don't want to pass out when I tell you this."

"Are you sure you don't need to go to the hospital?"

"No, this is just my hunger returning. Everything is fine."

Adam strode to the kitchen and grabbed two cheese sticks and a slice of sweet bologna. He hoped more protein would be what Grace needed. He still was not sure if Grace might not need medical attention, or if she remembered everything with this old general correctly. But he had always trusted Grace before she had disappeared, so he trusted her now.

It did not help his confidence, though, that after resting on the sofa to watch the golf, all Grace wanted to do was lie back in bed. Or rather, sit and talk some more. A little physical effort on her part, even the slightest display of strength, would have eased his nerves. He tried to convince himself she was in a rut, being tired leading to more being tired, as almost anyone experiences from time to time. But he could not be sure.

When he returned to their bedroom, Grace sat up in bed, smiling. Adam handed her the plate with food on it. As she ate, Adam grabbed the tan suitcase in the corner of the bedroom. He opened it and found the box Grace had described.

"Before we look inside, are you certain you wouldn't want to walk while the sun is still shining?" Adam asked.

"Be patient," she said as she ate. "I think one more good night's sleep and I'll be back to normal, or at least closer to it. But I need a little more energy to tell you about our surprise there."

Adam looked at the box. It felt heavy enough to tell something rested within it, but he had no guess what it held. "Is this going to be a game? Are you going to give me any hints?"

Grace shook her head. "It's too important to turn it into a game." She swallowed the last of her food, drank more water, and turned back to Adam. "Open it."

Adam turned two latches on the box and lifted the lid. His eyes saw it right away, but several seconds passed before his brain understood what he was holding.

"I told you it was important," Grace said. For one of the rare times, Adam could not look at his wife. As his mind finally caught up to what was happening, he was too stunned by amazement at what he saw.

The diamond. Shaped circularly on the top, eight facets on the sides, aiming down to a point. It was encircled by a golden setting, with the telltale corkscrew hook on top. It was exactly how Adam had envisioned, but more radiant, more valuable, and more miraculous now that they possessed it.

Gripping the box now that he knew what precious item was inside, Adam looked back to Grace. "Where did you find it? How did you find it? If you were knocked out for a year-"

"General Davis, um, Orson, is not just a distant relative," Grace explained, and she eased the box from him. "He was the one my father trusted with the diamond. That was why we met, before the accident. He must have found out I was nearby, Maybe he saw me traveling between the Pine Hotel and the conference. At any rate, he set up our lunch meeting and gave me the diamond. Then, after I woke, he made sure I had it again to bring back."

Adam's gaze returned to the diamond. This was almost too much to comprehend. Grace being here pushed any level of plausibility, and now she had the last of the gems. How did this happen, and all so quickly?

"Adam, do you still have the necklace? Do you still have the ruby?"

Adam had not given it a thought before, but now he realized Grace did not know the other jewels had been found. He had not wanted to trouble her with those adventures, or misadventures. He ran over to the closet. Adam pulled out the safe, entered the combination and pulled out the jewelry box.

"This is a surprise for you," he said as he opened the box.

Grace gasped. She kept one hand on the diamond's box while bringing the other to her chest in shock. "You did it. You found them all."

"Not all," Adam corrected as he set the jewelry box on the computer desk and pulled the necklace out. "I would never have found the diamond without you coming home."

"We are together, and so are the jewels," Grace whispered. "You and I truly exist for each other."

Grace took the necklace from Adam and attached the diamond to the center. All five jewels hung together, and Grace's hands pulled the necklace taut, letting each gem hang from the clasps.

"Go ahead," Adam said while Grace gazed at the jewelry. "Put it on."

Grace kept the necklace in her hands, but stood up and walked to the bedroom mirror. She held the jewels out in front of her, staring at her image.

"A family in Lemoyne had the emerald. Someone who stopped by the hotel had the sapphire. The onyx...that's an odd one."

Grace did not appear to be listening. She held the gemstones still and started speaking with a hushed tone. "Daddy, I have them back. Wherever you are, I hope this gives you peace."

Adam walked up behind but said nothing. He was not sure how emotional Grace was at the moment, thinking of her father and the jewels so soon after going through her ordeal in North Carolina. But after a minute's silence, he encouraged her again. "Put it on. That's why your father made them."

Grace did not move for a few more seconds. Then she turned to Adam, her eyes still intense with their radiant blue, but the lids above them creeping downwards with exhaustion. "No. This was not supposed to be a gift to me only. The jewels were a wedding gift. They are as much for you as me."

She put the necklace in his hands, then turned to face the mirror again. "I want my husband to put the jewels on me."

It was such a simple motion, putting the necklace around her neck, letting the stones come to rest on her skin. But Adam's hands shook as he latched the ends of the necklace. All those years led to this moment. He let go of the necklace, put his hands on Grace's shoulders, and held his breath.

Grace held her breath too. Then she exhaled. Without another sound, she touched each of the jewels, then brought her hand back to the diamond. She stared at the reflection, as did Adam. Neither spoke for several moments.

In more carefree times, Adam would have said the gems were a bit much for the t-shirt Grace wore, but he never noticed the rest of her outfit. There was more to this than Grace's beauty or the jewelry's value. They belonged together, and now they were united.

Finally, Grace turned to Adam. She fought sleep, Adam saw, and probably a dozen emotions he could not see. But Grace mustered enough energy to say, "I love you."

She kissed him passionately. Adam did not know how long the kiss lasted. It, like everything else now, was a moment out of time. Grace was back, the jewels were recovered, and they still had almost their entire lives ahead of them. Their first mission was already accomplished, and they could soon chase their other dreams.

When their lips parted, though, gravity won its battle with Grace's eyelids. "I'm sorry," she said, her eyes shutting. She reached back for the bed, and Adam helped her into it. "We should, I mean, I want to," she forced out. "I promise, I only need one good night's sleep. Tomorrow, we can, we can."

"It's okay," Adam whispered. "You're back home. That's all I need now."

Grace kept her eyes open a moment longer. "Thank you," she whispered back. "Thank you for doing so much for me, even when you didn't know." For a moment, Adam thought she was asleep. But Grace finished, "when you didn't even know I would make it back."

Then she slept, her breathing falling into the familiar, comfortable rhythm Adam had grown so accustomed to hearing. The jewels were still around her neck, leaning forward off of her skin as she slept on her side.

Though her hair was frumpy and her sleep clothing plain, it was the most beautiful image Adam had ever seen.

* * *

Grace was alive!

The impossible truth returned to Adam again as night fell. The bedroom became almost pitch black as the sun fell below the horizon. Grace turned from side to side a few times but continued to sleep. Still not completely sure about her health, Adam checked Grace's forehead twice, but found no signs of a fever. By now such checkups were more about his nerves than any genuine problems, Adam realized. He gave her a gentle kiss, hoping she felt it in her dreams.

Adam readied himself for slumber. He wondered when they should tell people this news. Had his boss already started spreading rumors? Who would believe them? Adam had been with Grace since Monday morning, and he could scarcely believe it. And would anyone accept the story of the general who turned out to be a relative?

Even Adam still wondered about that man. If he is a relative and he knew Grace's father, why didn't he reach out to them for their wedding? Why didn't he try something more than phone calls to track down Adam when Grace was hurt? He had given the diamond to Grace, watched over her and paid for her care, but none of these good deeds answered his questions. Everything appeared to have turned out okay, but some details still confused him.

Adam laid in the bed next to Grace. He stared at her for minutes. Eventually, he would tell her the stories of how the emerald, sapphire and onyx were found.

The darker thoughts returned, and this time, could not be denied.

Adam froze.

No, no, no, no!

Grace was alive. Grace was always alive!

He no longer lived in days outside of time. The last two months came crashing back into Adam's reality.

He tried to rationalize his actions. Everyone assumed she was dead. He should not have done what he did anyway, anyway, but...

Adam stopped looking for excuses. Legally, she had always been a missing person. But more important than the law, he had made a promise. A vow. Not only had he broken the vow they shared at their wedding, but also the promise he made a few months afterward.

"There is no circumstance that I would ever be with another woman."

No circumstance. None. Even ignorance did not excuse him. Adam had given Grace his word.

Rylee. Tessa. Emma.

Adam had failed the woman who mattered most.

Finding the jewels did not matter.

Exhaustion allowed him to fall asleep in the early hours of the morning, but there was only brief rest to be found there. Even in his dreams, he was aware of only one truth.

Adam had cheated on Grace.

Chapter 37

Grace made better time than Adam.

"See, I told you I'm all recovered," she called back to him.

Granted, they were only walking. Still, it encouraged Adam to see Grace healthy enough to stride around the apartment grounds without trouble. The humidity from the previous week had broken, giving this August afternoon the atmosphere of a pleasant May evening. Unfortunately, Grace's show of strength and endurance was the only positive Adam could find.

When they awoke soon after sunrise, Adam wanted to tell Grace about his past mistakes and get it out in the open. But he found it impossible. How could he break her heart so soon after she came home?

"C'mon, you can keep up a faster pace than that," Grace teased, reaching out her hand back to him.

Adam forced himself to quicken his step along the path, but he did not take her hand. "Sorry. I worked out here and there, but exercise has not been a priority for me lately." Even that was a lie. Adam had built his strength so well that he had managed the climb up and down the well. But the thought of that effort, and what it led to the next day, only kept him in his shame cycle.

Grace kept her hand out a moment longer, then pulled it back. "Well, don't forget, my memory is back, too. And I always beat you, walking or running."

That was true, Adam remembered. It seemed as if her memory was intact. But he said nothing.

"No words?" Grace asked. "Not going to jab back with anything?"

Adam became tongue tied around his wife and could not bring any words together. Shame pressed in all around him, and any words sounded like lies in his mind. But so did the silence, and this was already an awkward pause. "I wasn't sure you were ready for friendly picking," he spat out, but it sounded terrible.

"Are you sure...oh, wait, we've finally been spotted."

Adam looked ahead on the path, and twenty yards ahead was Brandi, carrying grocery bags. Upon looking back at them, she dropped them and ran forward.

"I hope you are recovered because-," Adam started before Brandi crushed Grace with a bear hug. Adam barely understood what either woman said, but they filled each word with joy.

Adam was ecstatic to have Grace back, but he envied the happiness she had now. He had experienced it for two days, this time over something worthy of joy, but now it was gone again.

"I thought I saw you a couple of days ago walking into your apartment," Brandi said after she let go of Grace. "But I was sure I imagined it, and I would have felt like an idiot coming over to ask Adam what was happening."

"I don't blame you," Grace said, apparently unaffected by Brandi's grip. "But I'm back and I'm planning on staying around for a long time."

"Do you need anything? I'll cook up dinner for you or something. This must be crazy for you."

"I appreciate the offer, and I'll take you up on it sometime. But now," she looked back to Adam, "I want to take most of my time to reconnect."

"Say no more," Brandi said, raising her hands. "But you know, this would make big news if you wanted to go public."

"We already called local news outlets this morning," Adam said, not sure why he spoke at all. But he felt so off-balance he did not know if getting into the conversation or staying silent was less inconspicuous. "She'll do two or three interviews tomorrow, and a few more the next day."

Grace nodded. "I needed a few days to put my thoughts in order, but I don't want to hide anything. People need some good news, and I hope my story will be that for them."

"Well, when you're ready, I'll be excited to hear how you made it back," Brandi said.

A minute later, all three of them walked back into the apartment building. Brandi walked to her room, and Adam and Grace entered theirs.

Once they were inside, Adam gazed at Grace for a moment. He looked at her blue eyes, wanting to find hope in them. And he did, but it seemed as if it was hope for her. If hope existed anywhere for him, the guilt inside himself shielded him from it.

Without a word, he walked back to the bedroom and sat on the edge of the bed. There was no way out of this except to tell Grace the truth, but he did not know if he dared take that step. It might be a step towards losing her again.

A moment later, Grace walked into the bedroom. "As I said, my memory is back. We raced each other around that path, but we also walked it. Many times. I remember you always held my hand when we walked it together."

Adam looked over his shoulder at her. He wanted to say something, but nothing came out.

"You used to hold my hand almost anywhere," Grace said. "When I first came back, you were ecstatic. Really gentle with me, which I appreciate, but ecstatic. Today, you've been almost morbid."

She's going to figure it out, Adam thought to himself. He wanted to confess before she put the pieces together, but Grace spoke again.

"I was gone for a year. You thought I was dead. Adam, I know you went through hell without me. I've healed. Do we need to do something fun to help heal you?"

She sat next to him and stroked his back. Her touch felt wonderful, but also like a gift Adam should not have.

"This," Adam finally started, but then had to recover and start again. "This will be hard."

"Are you angry with me?"

Adam did not expect that question. "No, never."

"I understand if you are. I should have called the moment my mind was clear. I kept you in the dark for several extra days..."

"That's your way," Adam said. "I can understand why you wanted our first conversation to be face to face, to look into each other eyes-," he stopped and looked into her eyes again. Guilt forced him to state downward.

"Are you worried over Orson? About why he didn't reach out to the authorities?"

"Well, yes, but honestly, that can wait. He kept you safe and you are back now. The questions I have for him are not as important as..." Adam could not finish sentences anymore. He had to speak the truth out loud, but the pain of doing so would be overwhelming.

Adam could no longer bear to look at Grace. He stood and turned away, facing out the window door but looking at nothing.

"I made you a promise," Adam's voice cracked, and he hoped Grace heard. Saying this was difficult enough without having to repeat himself. "I swore something to you and I betrayed you while you were gone."

He heard Grace rise from the bed, but he did not turn to face her. "It's your choice to tell me about it," she soothed. "But it's best for you if you can say it. Don't carry any guilt in your heart."

Adam tried to force the words from his throat, but it was almost enough to keep him from breathing. Eventually, he stuttered a few words. "I promised never-," he had to compose himself again. Still turned away from Grace, he forced more strength into his voice. "I promised never to stray, under any circumstances. But I did. I-." Adam tried to push the words out, but he had already said enough for her to know what needed to follow. He waited for Grace's wrath.

"You slept with Rylee."

Adam was so stunned he turned around, looking into Grace's eyes, where he could not look upon moments before. How did she know about Rylee in particular? Why were her words so calm? Why did her gaze appear so sympathetic?

"You knew? Have you talked with her?"

"Not yet," Grace said, and she reached out for him. But Adam took a step back. He did not deserve any part of her affection. And he still had not admitted to all his failures.

His wife gave him space but continued. "No one knows you as fully as I do. I know your strengths and your weaknesses. You were not meant to be alone. And trust me, I know Rylee, too. She had already broken up with Michael when I left, so when I woke up and realized how much time had passed, I just knew."

She reached for him again, and this time, he let her caress his short beard. "I also know you never would have done it if I had been here. If you had known I was okay. I forgive you."

"I haven't asked to be forgiven."

"You don't have to," Grace assured him. "I told you before, it's easier to forgive when you don't waste time waiting for an apology. But you need to accept my forgiveness."

How Adam thirsted for her pardon. But he refused it. He gently took Grace's wrist and pushed her arm away. So she had interpreted his affair with Rylee in the best way: the two people closest to Grace comforting each other while mourning her. In their compassion, they failed to resist crossing the line. She chose not to see it as the ultimate betrayal.

Adam could have left it at that. But he refused to add dishonesty to his sins.

"You don't understand," Adam said.

"I do, I truly do."

"There were two others. A co-worker, and-," Adam almost choked again. This was the worst violation possible, whether or not Grace had died. "A woman I had only met the day before."

This time, Adam faced Grace when he confessed his crimes. Maybe to forgive him for straying with a close friend, while believing Grace was dead, was easier from her point of view. Grace said she saw that coming. But two additional times, once with a near stranger, must be unredeemable. It was too callous to be forgiven.

He had found Grace again, after more than a year of anger and depression, and now his marriage with her was doomed.

Her face froze, and for the first time since they dated in high school, Adam was unable to read her expression. Finally, the corners of her lips flicked upwards, but Adam could not believe she was holding back a smile. It must have been a nervous twitch because she hated what had happened.

"I am disappointed," Grace said. "You knew better. But, as I said, I know your weaknesses. When you cross one line, it becomes easier for you to cross more. Especially when you were separated from me."

"If this is too much, once you don't need me to settle in anymore, I can go."

"What? No!" Grace shook her head, closing her eyes. "I never want to lose you. I never want to be apart from you again, no matter what you've done."

"After this many mistakes? After these kinds of mis-."

Grace opened her eyes and cut him off by kissing him on the mouth. Adam was too stunned to kiss back, but also too pleased to stop her. Yet, he decided to not accept her touch. His mind still fought it. He no longer deserved any part of Grace, neither her heart nor her body.

When Grace released, but still kept her arms around Adam, she stared into his eyes. Her gaze pierced within his soul. "When I returned, I knew you hadn't been perfect. Now that I'm here, I just want you to be mine. I'm not worried over how you wandered or who you wandered with."

"Maybe you should be."

"Do you love any of them? Don't confuse this with other kinds of love, you know what I mean."

"No. Each time, we both understood it was a once-and-done thing."

"Then, do you hate them? Blame them for what happened?"

Adam shook his head. "No. Everyone makes mistakes."

"Then stop this self-hatred now. Yes, you're guilty of the same offense, which means if you don't hate them for it, you shouldn't be hating yourself."

"That's not so easy."

"Then let me ask something that is easy for you to understand. Do you love me?"

The question caught Adam off guard. He had worried so much over his past he forgot how much he still cared for Grace. That was why his past hurt so much today. "Of course, I love you."

"And I love you. I will never send you away. I will never ask you to leave. Yes, I do have the right to push you away. I'll never approve of what you did, and I won't make excuses for you. All three of these women, sleeping with them was wrong, whether or not you knew I was alive. But there is nothing you can do to make me stop loving you, not even this. You wouldn't be telling me all your affairs now if you didn't understand you were wrong, and if you didn't want to be back only with me. There is nothing that can separate me from you again."

She leaned in and kissed again, softer this time. Adam tried to be stoic, tried to tell himself he should not accept this response, but he gave in an returned the same effort. Still, his mind continued to doubt. Grace should not forgive so fully and so quickly. She should not forgive him. There must still be a price to be paid, and he was sure to pay it later.

As if Grace read his mind, she pulled back, but only a centimeter. "You don't believe I've truly forgiven you already, do you?"

Adam shook his head, his hair mingling with hers as he turned back and forth. "How can you forgive me right after I confess? How can you forgive me at all?"

"Because I forgive the things that are wrong. That is the only way they can be made right again. You need to have to accept that, or else my forgiveness can't help you."

"Help me? But I wronged you."

"Yes, I was wronged by you and them. I have the choice of being vengeful, but I will never do that to you. But, every time you and another woman wronged me, I was not the one who was wounded by your actions. You were." She pulled him close, impossibly close it seemed, and whispered into his ear, "Being away from me, and straying those times, it all broke you. Without me, you couldn't do anything to stop it. But I'm here now. You don't have to stay broken."

Grace was right. Rylee, Tessa and Emma all could make him forget the pain and loneliness for a day or two. Only Grace would ever end them. But she should not have to. "I don't deserve to be anything but broken," was all he said.

"This isn't about what you deserve," Grace said. "This is about what you need. You need to believe I have forgiven you, you need to stop holding on to your shame, and then you need to trust my forgiveness."

"How?"

"We can figure out a fun way to start," she said in her deep lover's tone she had not used since her return. "We still haven't celebrated each other since I made it home."

Adam smiled but held back. He did not merit the kisses from her lips, even the slightest caresses from her hands Grace had already given. He yearned for what she offered, but still, how could he accept a love he never earned? "Why would you want to do that now, after everything I said?"

"Two reasons," Grace purred, tracing under his chin with the gentlest touch of her finger. "First, whenever there's a chance for it, I'll always want to make love with my husband." Another kiss lingered and melted all Adam's resistance. "Second, I want to make you whole."

And she did.

Chapter 38

"Do you know the total monetary value of the jewels?" Lucas asked, notepad in one hand and his phone recording the interview on the dining table in front of him.

Grace, sitting across from him, shook her head. "No, money was not always exchanged for them, so they weren't ever appraised, at least not by us. Maybe my father had them appraised all those years ago, but we never found any papers proving that." She tapped the diamond below her neck, between the other gems. "We know this is the most valuable, but there's no way to put a number on it. Quite honestly, finances don't affect their value to us."

"Good," Lucas said. "I had hoped I wouldn't have to delve into the money aspect of this. If you don't know the values, I don't have to write too much on that subject."

"What are you hoping for?" Grace asked.

"To find out what the last year was like for you. And for you," Lucas raised his voice, directing his words to Adam, who listened from the living room couch. "Not only where you were, when you were there, how you got lost and came back. I want readers to know how it felt to be reunited."

"They can't," Adam said.

Both Grace and Lucas turned to him.

"Only someone who has lost their spouse and been reunited with her can understand," Adam explained.

"He's right, somewhat," Grace said. "But the best I can describe it is that being reunited was our first date, our engagement, our wedding and anniversary all together, and then some. Anyone looking at me the day I came home would not have been able to tell. I was so exhausted, but it was the greatest moment of my life. Seeing and holding Adam again meant everything."

She had spoken similar words today and yesterday. Grace and Adam had agreed they should limit the interviews to these two days, yesterday and today. Let the media hear about what had happened, but do not let the interviews dictate their lives.

Grace endured interviews by two newspapers, one radio station and three television stations in the last thirty hours. But Lucas Darnold of the Lebanon paper was the only reporter who had come to their apartment. Other print writers interviewed Grace over the phone, though television hosts conducted their interviews in the gardens in Hershey for a pleasant background.

Adam appreciated the personal touch Lucas gave by being in their apartment, though it was not heavy on his mind.

What remained in his thoughts was Grace's plans for the next two days, something she had told him after getting out of bed. There had not been enough time between interviews for Adam to press the matter.

Her forgiveness of him had been so quick, and he believed her: Grace was not holding a grudge for his dalliances. Adam had to hope, sometime in the future when Grace was having a challenging day, she still forgave him. Maybe she had not considered everything when she spoke so kindly to him two days ago. He wished there was something he could do, something tangible to make the forgiveness remain. But even so, he did not plan to forgive himself anytime soon. He was a lucky man to have a wife like Grace, but that did not transform him into an exemplary man. She knew the worst of what he had done. He would feel better if he also told her everything that had happened, not just the mistakes but each step that led to them. Those discussions took place during breaks between these interviews.

There was a chance that those discussions could rouse her anger. But honesty and openness had helped him so far.

Either way, it was still hard to imagine she wanted...

"Well, thank you for your time, and letting me into your home," Lucas said, closing his notebook and shutting off his phone.

"Humble though it may be," Grace said, rising.

"My place isn't any larger," Lucas said. "Small-town journalism isn't the job for anyone who wants to live in a mansion. Not that a reporter's lifestyle is much of an issue for me anymore."

"Why's that, if I may ask?" Adam said. He opened the front door to show Lucas the way out, but he was curious. Or wanted a few extra minutes to process what had happened in the last week.

"This will be my last story for the newspaper. Next, I am going out on a limb and chasing a dream."

"We've already caught one dream," Grace said. "I hope you catch yours."

"Well, if you ever want to help, buy a copy of *Jonas's Team*. It just went on sale this Monday. Non-fiction section."

"You're an author? Congratulations," Adam said.

"I'm starting work on a second book about what's happened to the players on that Central team since the last time they saw Jonas."

"Hold on," Adam said, "Are you talking about the Central baseball team from about five years ago?" He closed the door. No more idle chit-chat. He wanted to know.

"Yes. I reported on that team. Great baseball squad. But the amazing thing about them was this life coach they listened to, Jonas. He taught them all sorts of lessons, for baseball and everything else, and did some inexplicable stuff..."

"Like heal an injured player? Or predict the results of games and specific moments a day before the game was played?"

Lucas nodded and scrutinized Adam. "I don't recognize you from that team. Were you a fan? A relative?"

"It's Nate, isn't it?" Grace said to Adam. "This is the team he's always talking about."

"He tells a new story from Central's regional-championship team all the time, and I think Jonas was the name of the man who guided them off the field," Adam said. "I'm not a baseball guy, but from almost two years of talking with Nate, I may know as much about that season as you do."

There was silence for a moment. Lucas looked lost in thought.

"Mr. Darnold?" Grace asked. "Are you okay?"

"Do you mean Nate Stoltzfus?"

"Yes," Adam said. "Did you talk to him for this book?"

"I did. He was one of the first. It's...he has a cousin. I didn't mention her in this book. I should type something about her in the next one." Lucas shook himself. "Sorry, didn't mean to let my mind wander. I'll send you an email when the story is ready to run, both online and in print."

Adam opened the door again. "Let us walk you back to your car."

They left the apartment and the building. When they reached Lucas's car, Adam thanked him again, but Grace addressed the writer one more time.

"Just in case you need to hear this. If I'm overstepping my boundaries, I'm sorry, but it sounds as if you lost someone you lo...cared about."

Lucas nodded. "I haven't seen Lydia since before that crazy baseball season ended. We both had other things we needed to do. Neither of us is finished with those issues yet."

"I'm in no position to promise you anything," Grace said. "But if you're hurting, remember us." She put her arm around Adam. "We're the proof any relationship can be restored."

Lucas nodded. "Thanks. I think I needed that." He sat in his car, but before closing the door, he added, "And I need people to buy my book, too. Don't forget."

Adam and Grace, holding hands, walked around the apartment complex and nearby field, as they had before.

"Each of the reporters has been nice," Grace said.

"They have. But Lucas seems a bit different. More interested in the people than the story."

Grace nodded. "I hope he finds his Lydia."

"I'm happy I found my Grace."

She stopped, forcing Adam to halt as well. "We've only just begun."

"A whole lifetime together."

"Yes, but that's not what I mean," Grace said, with her suggestive smirk. "I mean, we have two days to, how should I phrase it? Heal you," she said with a wink.

"Are you serious about this plan?"

"I already made the reservations for tomorrow night. As for the next night, well, that was taken care of before I ever made it back here."

Chapter 39

Everything was out in the open. Grace's story was no longer a secret from the world, and Adam's failings were no longer a secret from her. It was a reprieve to not hide any secrets, so he asked his question with only a hint of trepidation.

Well, more than a hint.

"I never will stray again, and I never want to," he said. "Never. But if anyone knew how quickly you forgave me, they might think you're giving me a free pass for everything I've done wrong."

Grace shook her head, adjusting her sunglasses as she drove. "It's true if you were a different sort of man, you might have misunderstood this as permission to fool around. Or, at least, that you got away with it. But remember, I never would have married you if you were that kind of man. And I don't care what anyone else thinks. It is my prerogative to forgive, and I am, fully and permanently."

Adam sat askew in the passenger seat, half-turned towards Grace. Over the last two days, otherwise full of interviews, he had found time between to tell Grace the details about his misdeeds in her absence. For thirty minutes, Grace would explain to a reporter how she became unconscious for a year and, to use a term he heard in movies, "fell off the grid." Then, for the next hour, Adam would explain to her the details of how and why he strayed from the straight and narrow path.

Through it all, the interviews for the public and the explanations in private, Grace wore her five jewels, as she did now. The gems gave her an extra glow, but also reminded Adam of the cost it took to get them. Their presence gave him happiness and shame at the same time.

Grace never demanded for him to reveal the details of his low points in her absence. Adam was not sure she wanted to know any more than she already did. But Grace seemed to welcome the chance for Adam to release the burdens. At certain points in the story, he expected anger, or at least criticism. But Grace simply listened with understanding, rarely interrupting. She did not wince when he recalled the moments he caved to another woman. The only time she questioned his actions was when he put his safety at risk by climbing down the well for the onyx. Then, her eyes teared up with concern for him. When he had finally told all there was to say last night, Grace took him in his arms and kept repeating, "Never forget, you are forgiven."

Adam believed her. Grace had forgiven him. But he must be an embarrassment to her. Adam could not forgive himself for that. All this made her plans for today and tomorrow more surprising.

"I know your forgiveness doesn't mean you don't care that I gave in to temptation," Adam said. "I'm still shocked you forgave so quickly."

Grace glanced at him, then turned back to the road.

"'Don't waste time waiting for an apology,' and all that," Adam said before she repeated her mantra. "But even so, shouldn't I prove myself to get out of the doghouse?"

"The only way you could have been in a doghouse would have been to pretend what you did was okay," Grace said. "That never happened. But even then, the one thing you would need to do is realize you were wrong."

"I still feel as if I need to do something for you. Buy a fancy gift. Build something."

"Of course you should do something for me. And I should do something for you. We're married. That's how marriage works, putting each other ahead of ourselves as much as possible."

"I don't see how what I did couldn't have hurt you more."

"I never said it didn't hurt," Grace answered, though there was no edge in her voice. "But I can hurt and heal without holding a grudge. I just love you more than your mistakes could wound me."

"It still seems I should earn...,"

"You'll never need to. I look forward to each act of love you'll show me. Finding the sapphire, emerald and onyx are all expressions of your love. But none of them are needed to earn my love back. My love isn't earned, and you never lost it."

"Well, even with that degree of forgiveness, this idea of yours surprises me."

"I hoped it would." The seductive smirk returned.

"I'm not even sure what you have planned for tomorrow is even legal."

"It is, but don't worry over tomorrow now. There's going to be enough going on today. And both days should help you, too."

"Help me what?"

"Me forgiving you? That was only the beginning," Grace said as she turned up the hill. For a moment Adam felt they drove straight into the sun, which turned the sky from a blue afternoon hue to a pleasant auburn sunset. But then he looked at the Spartan Hotel. By now Grace's coworkers must have heard about her return, with the news coverage it had in the last forty-eight hours. Adam did not remember Grace contacting them, but certainly, word had spread by now.

But telling them she was back, alive and healthy, was not Grace's primary reason for being here.

"I'll admit, even after you forgave me...this is a little awkward. You sure about this?"

"That awkwardness is one reason we need to be here. And I reserved the room two days ago. Let's go, shy guy."

Adam was not sure if that was a dig at him or a tease, but Grace was out the door in a heartbeat after parking. Adam stepped out and grabbed their bag out of the car. They had packed light, one heavy bag being all they needed. By the time Adam made it to the hotel doors, Grace was already inside hugging Michelle.

"I can't believe you're back," Michelle cried. "I was so excited I didn't sleep after I saw you on the news."

"I've missed you," Grace said back. "I've missed everyone."

Adam walked up next to his wife. She let go of Michelle and put her arm around him. "Of course, he's the one I missed the most." She kissed him on the cheek.

"I'm so happy for you, too," Michelle said, giving Adam a quick hug. Then she noticed the bag he carried. "Wait, are you two staying here tonight?"

"I already reserved a room. Can you check us in?"

Michelle nodded. "Yeah, sure." She moved back behind the counter and started typing. Her expression changed to a mix of surprise and slight embarrassment. Adam assumed she noticed which room Grace had reserved.

Michelle looked up from the screen and smiled coyly at Grace. "Oh."

Grace nodded. "Yep."

Michelle put her fist out. Grace gave a fist-bump back. Adam blushed.

"Wait a moment, until I process your card and you can go, I guess, do your thing," Michelle said, reflecting a knowing smile, as she returned to her screen. Adam experienced simultaneous embarrassment and excitement. But Michelle's next look was of confusion. "You used your credit card, right?"

Grace nodded, and Adam recalled her reserving the room online. He remembered Grace using their card.

"Don't worry about it," a voice from the back office called to them. "I canceled the payment and put it on the house. The room, any food or drinks you want, anything and everything. You lovebirds enjoy your evening."

"Thank you, Mr.-,"

"Don't get used to it!"

Adam, Grace and Michelle all laughed at the gruff manager. Michelle handed Grace their key card. "I'm inspired by you. By both of you."

"Thank you. After I've had some time, I want to work here again."

"Monday the twenty-sixth, six in the morning, don't be late!" the distant voice called out.

* * *

"You do the honors," Grace said, handing Adam the key card.

"Should I carry you across the threshold?" he asked.

"No, we're two years too late for that," Grace answered with a smile.

Adam swiped the card and held the door open for her. He followed her into their room for tonight.

The Honeymoon Suite.

Reds. Pinks. Lavenders. Scents that could turn the most distracted mind to love. A spacious bed.

And a roaring fireplace with a fancy, soft rug in front of it.

Grace strutted to the bed, ran her hand along it, then turned back to Adam. The five jewels reflected the light from the fireplace as she smiled. "I need to prove something to you tonight. Not for my sake, but for yours."

"You don't need to prove anything," Adam answered, setting the bag, stepping to Grace and taking her in his arms. "Though I seem to recall, I owe you your fireplace fantasy."

"Yes, you do," Grace smiled. "But that's just a side benefit."

"Before you make your grand point, please admit something to me. When you worked here, you shared some of our bedroom secrets with Michelle, didn't you?"

"What exactly happened and those kinds of details? Never. That's for you and me only. But I've never hidden the fact you and I had a strong love life. And that's the point. That is part of the reason we will do this here and now."

"Part?"

"Okay, fine. Part of it is my fireplace fantasy. But the rest of it is for you. Remember what happened between you and Tessa."

"I don't want to think about any other woman."

"But you need to understand something. Tessa was ashamed of what she did with you. She wouldn't go to our home or yours because she did not want to be seen. She has money to go anywhere, but she chose the dumpiest place in miles to avoid being seen. Even before it happened, she felt shame over you. And now you are carrying shame about yourself. But I never will."

"Even after everything I did? I know you forgave me," Adam quickly added. "But still you wouldn't proudly show me off."

"I just did," Grace said. She nuzzled up against him, and Adam realized she was right. Both Michelle and her manager already knew exactly what was happening in this room tonight, but Grace drew their attention to it.

"Do you love me?" Grace whispered.

"Of course, I love you."

"I know, but I wanted you to hear yourself say it. And I love you," Grace whispered. "You are my husband. You are my lover. I will never be ashamed of either of those things. What actually happens in private is no one else's business. But I will never be embarrassed of having others know how much I love you with my heart, with my mind, with my soul, or with my body."

She kissed him. He wanted to say more. He wanted to say, though he had failed her before, he would love her as he did now for the rest of their lives. But one look into her blue eyes told him she already understood.

I don't deserve her, Adam thought.

They kissed passionately. Adam assumed the time for words tonight was over, but Grace broke the silence one last time.

"Now, let's do what we should have done two years ago."

Chapter 40

Adam felt a mix of conflicting emotions in his heart, in his mind and his gut. The memory of their night in front of the fireplace endured, but as Grace drove them to their next destination, his spirit darkened.

He had already questioned this action in the morning when they packed and left the Spartan Hotel. They had made no reservations or appointments where they were going. Why not go home and start readjusting to life together? Grace had made her point: she had forgiven Adam, even though he did not deserve it, and she was not ashamed of Adam, even though most other people would be.

Grace insisted, although she did not explain why she was so determined to drive him back to Pinchot Park. Ultimately, Adam would give Grace whatever she wanted, if it was in his power. But her plan pushed his boundaries. Maybe legal boundaries, too.

The car glided onto the driveway of the impressive home where Adam had found the onyx. The home where he met Emma, the last and most incomprehensible of his mistakes. Adam had told Grace all about what had happened, and even though the tryst did not take place here, a haunting sensation shuddered through him. Why bring him back to here when she meant to help Adam through his guilt?

Grace exited the car and looked at the home, for the first time, Adam realized.

"He wasn't kidding," she said.

"Who?" Adam asked as he stepped out.

"Orson."

"What does he know about this place?" Adam looked over the house again. In the mix of the fading afterglow and growing tension inside him, he sensed a degree of envy. A home like that seemed too large for one man. If he and Grace ever started a family, or...

"Silly me," Grace said, going back to the car and opening the passenger door. "You haven't read this yet." She pulled something out of the glove compartment and handed it to Adam. "I took the liberty of reading this before I reserved our room at the hotel. Once I saw what Orson wrote, I learned what our next step had to be."

Adam saw the envelope, written out to both of them. It was already open. Grace walked up to the front door, then turned to a couples' swing on the front porch. "Take your time," she called out to him.

He walked over and sat next to Grace. She was as gorgeous as ever, not even needing the jewels around her neck to display her beauty. He ran his hand through her hair and down her back. She smiled, kissed him, and then glanced at the letter in his hand. Adam read silently,

To Grace and Adam,

I know you will still have questions when you read this. I will answer all questions in due time, but that time is not now. Now is the time to prepare for the future.

Grace, take Adam back to my Pennsylvania home. The address is on the other side of this letter. That home will be yours. You can live there. You can love there. You can remodel the building into the business you've dreamed of running. It will take time before this transaction is made official, but my son, Jonas, will take care of the paperwork in

*my stead to make sure it goes to you. This is a free gift of
love. Not merely a gift for you to use, but for you so share
with others.*

*Adam, you feel betrayed by me. I understand your
anger, but I did what needed to be done to keep Grace alive
so she would return to you. This will be difficult for you to
understand, but you needed to be away from her while she
was ill. Only by being separated from her would you ever
understand how much you needed her.*

Jonas will come when the time is right.

General Orson Davis

It was too much to take in all at once. So many
questions remained unanswered, and others now joined
them. How could Orson know what Adam needed? Did he
know Adam had strayed? Did Grace ever tell him about her
dream of running a bed-and-breakfast that was aimed for
lower-income couples? Even if she had, why give up a
mansion for someone he scarcely had the chance to know?
And could this Jonas be the same one mentioned by Nate
and Lucas?

Then it occurred to Adam that maybe Orson was not
giving up the mansion. It was easier to believe this was all a
joke, a prank and a deception than accept the letter at face
value.

"He can't mean it," Adam said, turning to Grace. Or
turning to where Grace had been. She stood by the door. He
continued, "No one gives away a house, especially one like
this. And he says we can start planning a bed-and-breakfast.
We can't even go in the door. The woman who takes care of
the grounds isn't even allowed."

Grace stood and smiled. After a few seconds, she reached into her back pocket while winking, and pulled out a golden key. "This was in the envelope, too." She placed it in the lock.

It was such a mundane thing, a key opening a lock, and yet Adam was stunned as Grace turned the knob and opened the door. He hopped to his feet, ran through the doorway and inside the estate.

The house was dark, of course, except for the mid-afternoon light shining in the western windows. They walked through an entryway and into a sizable living room, which ironically featured a marble fireplace. Adam did not take time to linger. He buzzed through the rooms. A kitchen, set between a large dining room and a smaller, more intimate one. A bedroom downstairs. The master staircase leading to four more bedrooms on the second floor. There was also a small library, a den and a game room, though those rooms remained mostly empty, so they could make them into whatever someone wanted.

Correction, Adam realized. Whatever Grace and he wanted.

That was a tough, though pleasant, thought to wrap his mind around. This home was going to theirs if Orson kept his word. Granted, he had it in writing, though he doubted the letter would stand up in court if it came to that.

Adam looked around the upstairs landing, then realized he had left Grace behind downstairs. He ran down the steps at a pace he had not run since Christmas when he was eleven years old. He found Grace looking around the smaller of the two dining rooms, tracing her hand over the table.

"It has a traditional quality to it," Grace said, though Adam could not tell if she spoke to him or herself. But as he caught his breath and looked around the room, he realized the inside was similar to the outside. It carried a style from a century ago, but everything appeared to be in pristine condition.

"But in a way young people would enjoy," Adam added.

Grace looked over her shoulder at him. "You say that as if we're not still young."

"Sorry," Adam said. "I guess I'm already thinking of our clientele. Trying to bring newlyweds here."

"But older couples, too, on milestone anniversaries," Adam added, still scarcely believing their discussion.

They spent the next two hours going around the home, getting a feel for everything there. It was not designed as a bed-and-breakfast, but the changes did not seem to be major to Adam. Especially if they received the property for free, since then the money they saved and any future loans would go to those alterations.

After walking through the last of the upstairs bedrooms, Adam almost believed this was happening. He was not sure which surprised him more: Grace's quick forgiveness or Orson's generosity. Adam had done nothing to deserve either, and yet he received both now.

They descended back downstairs. "Did you notice how large the porch out back is?" Grace asked. "I didn't see any furniture, I guess because Orson doesn't leave any out while he is in North Carolina. But a few tables back there would make for a nice open-air dining area."

"Grace, are you sure?"

"And out front, with the swing and the view of the lake..." her voice trailed off before she found it again. "We can make this a romantic place for everyone."

"Grace," Adam started again. "Do you think we can trust Orson? This is so much, I don't know, so much house!"

Grace laughed. She placed her palms on Adams' cheeks and kissed him. "You're cute when you worry over nothing."

"Nothing? You don't find it odd that the man is handing this to us? That he is making no requests or demands?"

"Actually, I do. But not as odd as taking care of me for a year without asking for a reward. That's what you've missed. I find it hard to accept Orson did not connect with you in that year, but he took care of everything. Had you known, could you have done anything to end my coma any sooner?"

It was the same question she had asked earlier in the week. His answer did not change. "No, I suppose not."

"Well, we know we can trust him with my life and my health," Grace said. "So I'll trust his word that this home will be ours." She pointed to the door which led to the lone downstairs bedroom. "And let's turn that into our bedroom. The guests will be upstairs."

"It will still be an expensive undertaking," Adam said. "The biggest expense, the mortgage, will be eliminated if everything goes as Orson promised. But with alterations, monthly bills, advertising..."

"Don't ruin the moment," Grace said, walking to the bedroom. "I know there are still challenges, even with everything Orson is gifting to us. But let's focus on the gift."

Adam nodded and followed her into what they hoped to convert into their master bedroom. It was nearly as large as their entire apartment. The bed, though sizable, did not take up much room relative to the floor space.

Grace lowered the shades, though the sun was already set. She turned on a dim lamp, then stood at the foot of the bed and turned back to him. Grace raised one eyebrow.

She looked irresistible. Grace had said before they started this trip, she planned on this. Adam thought she was a little crazy at the time, but he had not read the letter yet. This bedroom was theirs now.

Even after last night, Adam hungered again. Unfortunately, he also felt the guilt that had hung over him in the last few months. Though they were together again, he could not shake the sense he was taking something he should not, something he did not deserve.

Grace noticed the hesitation. "It's our place," she encouraged. "The issue here isn't if we have permission," Grace said. "We do."

"And it's not about you forgiving me," Adam said. "Or being ashamed of me. You forgave. You told me you weren't ashamed of me."

"You're the man after my heart. You never need to worry about those things. So unless you're too tired...,"

"Of course not."

"Then what is it?"

"I don't know. I can't describe it."

"I can," Grace said, and she walked up to him and reached under his shirt with her right hand, and then placed her left hand over his forehead. "You know I have forgiven you here," she said, tapping his temple. "You know I am unashamed of you here." She tapped again. Then she rubbed her hand over his chest. "You have not accepted it here."

Adam almost said there was no difference, that he was forgiven whether or not he accepted it. He almost said it was better for him and her if he did not claim her forgiveness. He almost said he needed to hold on to the guilt and shame. But none of those words left his lips.

Grace continued, "You are still carrying a weight you no longer need to bear. Neither you nor I will ever forget what happened, but we cannot be held back by it. I have done everything I can do. But even with my forgiveness, you cannot move forward until you accept it."

Adam found his voice. "The quick way of saying it is that I need to forgive myself."

Grace smiled. "Yes, that's it. Do you love me?"

Why is she asking a third time? Adam wondered. "Of course, I love you. You know I love you."

"Then do it. Forgive yourself."

Impossible. Adam did not deserve it. He was relieved Grace had chosen forgiveness when she was within her rights to punish him, even leave him. But...

"It's the hardest step," Grace said, again reading his mind. "And it needs to be the last one. But it's the most important. Let the burden go. You've learned your lesson, and you have me back. There is no way guilt or shame can help you. Let them go."

He held on, despite her encouragement. He wanted to be completely free of this nightmare, but he could not allow himself to be awakened from it.

She's right. Let it all go.

The voice. It had returned. Not the cruel one that had lured him toward Emma. Rather, the wise one from before spoke.

Grace was the one wronged by your actions. If she believes you should be forgiven, and you truly love her, you will forgive yourself.

"I don't deserve it," Adam whispered.

Both Grace and the voice inside spoke in one accord.

"This isn't about..."

...what you deserve.

"This is about..."

...a gift of love...

"...you need to accept."

He had always loved Grace, but now Grace was in his heart.

No, I don't deserve her, Adam realized. But I love her too much to deny her gift to me.

Adam could not tell how much time passed. It must have been longer than a few seconds, and he doubted he left Grace standing there for hours. But it may have been a few minutes or forty-five. No matter how long, he perceived what happened over that span. The burden lifted. The weight dissipated.

He did not keep his promise.

He could not say Grace had been the only one.

But Grace was willing to regard him as if both things were true. Since she was going to give him that gift, he would accept it.

The weight. The guilt. The shame.

Gone.

Only then did Adam realize his eyes had drifted shut, but when he reopened them, Grace was still there with her palm over his heart. Whether it was from gazing into his eyes, or the beat of his heart, or some perception Adam never understood, Grace again recognized what happened within his soul.

"Now I truly have you back," Grace said.

Adam forgot his caution over being in what was still technically Orson's home. With the burden gone, with the cycle of forgiveness complete, his love for Grace increased, stronger than ever. The love he received from her, if not stronger than before, was given with more spirit.

They spent the night expressing their rejuvenated love to each other.

* * *

Before Adam drifted off to sleep, he heard Grace whisper, "I know I'm not supposed to feel it, but I think you made my other dream come true."

Everything in the past week, good and bad, wore on Adam, and he was about to fall into a deep slumber. He could not think of which dream Grace meant.

But before unconsciousness overtook him, Grace took his hand and placed it over her stomach.

Adam smiled as he slept. Grace could not know. But she had been right about everything else.

Chapter 41

The following morning, Adam and Grace swayed on the couples' swing on the front porch of Orson's home.

No, Adam corrected himself. Of their home, and their bed-and-breakfast. Not officially yet, but it would be.

At the moment, he was not concerned with such things. He was in the afterglow again, but this time nothing dimmed the sensation. This was not only the afterglow of their lovemaking. This was the afterglow of true forgiveness–forgiveness he had received from both Grace and himself.

That forgiveness allowed Adam to see everything clearly now, just as the sun, now halfway up the sky, allowed him to see Pinchot Park in the distance. Over the last two months, he realized he had done the wrong thing many times. Only now, with the burden of shame gone, he could understand how he had fallen so far.

He looked into Grace's eyes. They had not spoken this morning. They had not needed words. But he wanted to say the things he was thinking now, to discover if Grace agreed with his thoughts. One smirk from her told Adam she would allow him to break the silence.

"I understand it now," Adam said, as quietly as possible, as if there were a sleeping baby nearby. "Before you came back, I could not figure out why I would give in, if I did the wrong thing searching for the jewels, or in being around women at all."

"And yet the entire time, you knew none of those things could be true," Grace answered in the same soft tone.

"It was how I treated the jewels, and how I treated my relationships with...them," Adam said, not willing to say the names of the other women at this moment. "With the jewels, I thought of them as the only way to honor you. At first, I meant to stay faithful, even after 'death do us part', but then I didn't think it mattered any more how I acted. The total measure of my love for you became whether or not I found the rest of the gems. And I never would have found the diamond, anyway."

Grace, still nuzzling him, nodded, their noses rubbing against each other. "And the other women, you weren't wrong to be around them, to be their friends. You were not making a mistake getting the jewels, but rather in making them too high of a priority. And you were not wrong being around Rylee, Tessa and Emma." Apparently, saying those names was okay, Adam realized. The afterglow endured the utterances as Grace continued, "You wouldn't have found the other gems without their help. But you needed to be wiser around them."

I should have celebrated with a meal with Rylee, the way she first said to, Adam remembered. I should have driven on my own to the dinner with Tessa. I should have, well, not been a jerk with Emma. And while I had thanked Rylee for her assistance in finding the emerald, I could have shown appreciation to Tessa and Emma for their help. But as he recalled each encounter, he felt no guilt this time. These mistakes were no less wrong than before, but Grace was right last night: shame would not do him or anyone else any good now.

Grace had forgiven him, and now, so had he.

"We'll need to head back home soon," Grace said. "And we will have to make a stop along the way."

"Breakfast?"

"Two stops then. Your office, as well."

"Why?"

Grace stood. "First, you're going to explain to your boss why you're not working right now."

It was Monday! Adam had forgotten. It was early enough that he could still call in before his usual start time.

"But, more importantly, there are others who need forgiveness," she said. She walked back into the house. Adam rose, but Grace was already back outside before he made it to the door. She held an envelope, but it was smaller than the one which had held General Davis' letter to them.

"What is that?"

"Something I wrote this morning before you woke. If this place is ours now, Orson shouldn't mind us using his stationary." Grace shut and locked the door. "We will need to install more modern locks. Something electronic with a security system..."

"Now you're getting ahead of yourself."

Grace looked back and kissed him. "You're right. Priorities. And the priority for today is letting all three of them know they are forgiven."

Adam realized she wanted to go back to his office to speak with Tessa. "That might be a little much," he warned. "Not the forgiveness, but you don't know how she will react to seeing you. She might be scared or defensive."

"And she always will be until she knows she's forgiven." Grace and Adam walked down the porch steps and towards the car, but Grace continued to the road to put the envelope in the mailbox. She walked back to Adam. "As for Emma, I've never met her face-to-face, and from your description, she sounds like someone who is hard to talk to. But she needs to know I forgive her, too."

"Emma might not care to be forgiven. She doesn't realize she slept with a man who was still married."

"She will if she sees the news stories that have been all over television and social media the last few days. But no matter her response, I forgive her regardless. And sometimes the ones who are the worst violators are the ones who appreciate forgiveness the most."

* * *

When Adam parked in the lot behind the office, most of his coworkers were already outside waiting for them.

Grace stepped out of the car first, and Ms. Douglas ran up to her and hugged her. Adam missed what they were saying at first until he stopped the engine and stepped out of the car himself. Ms. Douglas was speaking. "If you would have called earlier, we would have prepared a party for you."

"I don't need a big deal made over me," Grace answered, then turning to Nate. "I only wanted to see everyone face-to-face again."

She and Nate embraced quickly. Meanwhile, Ms. Douglas spoke to Adam. "Everything okay with her?"

"She's fine," Adam said. "You wouldn't know she was unconscious for a year."

"Good. Now, you understand all this time off you've had lately will lead to some consequences?"

"I guess I should expect to work Saturdays and holidays."

"Many Saturdays and holidays. Maybe every Saturday and holiday. But that can start next week. Once you guys leave, I don't want you around here until next Monday."

Adam was relieved that he still had time off with Grace. He promised himself to make the most of it, seeing as things were going to become quite busy soon. Extra hours at work and the business of transferring the ownership of the mansion.

Grace had walked over to the doorway where the other accountants and managers were standing. She was greeting and embracing everyone. Nate did not spot Tessa among them.

Ms. Douglas walked back to the building, reigning some employees back to their desks, Adam guessed. But Nate came over to him. "I'm so happy for you," he said, hugging him. Awkward as a hug from another man felt, Adam returned the embrace.

"It's a miracle having her back," Adam said. "Not on the level of the things you talk about in those baseball stories of yours, but a miracle nonetheless."

"Do you guys need anything? Rearranging the apartment? I'm sure there will be some headaches with the bank and tax issues."

"Nothing I'm worried over right now. But thanks for the offer."

"I didn't offer any help," Nate answered with a grin.

Adam almost missed the joke. Through the door window, he saw Tessa looking out to the crowd. She must be ashamed to step out and be near Grace, Adam realized. Tessa might have guessed he had been honest with Grace about what had happened. He had said during their dinner together that he would not hide anything from Grace.

Nate was about to say something else, but Adam put up his hand. He wanted to watch this.

Grace was waving to the door, and Tessa finally stepped out, like a shy child going to her first day of kindergarten. Grace embraced her, almost swallowing up the shorter woman in her arms. Then Grace guided her away from the other workers who still stood outside. They were still too distant for Adam to hear what Grace said. But as Tessa's expression changed from fear, to shock, and at last a smile, he could guess what she had been told.

"You were right," Adam said.

"Of course I was," Nate said. "But which thing are you referring to?"

"Two things. First, about mistakes catching up to me. They did. Not in any physical way, but they threatened to tear me apart."

Nate nodded. "And the other thing?"

Adam gestured to Grace and Tessa, who were hugging again. "Forgiveness is the greatest miracle."

They watched the two women for a moment longer before Nate spoke again. "I must go back to my desk. We are behind on our cases."

"Sorry about that. I realize my emotional entanglements aren't the only way I've hurt progress around here."

"Don't you dare apologize for having Grace back, or for finding the jewels. They are quite the gems, aren't they? But I needed to check something with you and Grace."

"I don't want to rush her out of what she's saying to Tessa. What is it?"

"The news stories said she found a relative in North Carolina, another Davis. It's such a common name, I didn't want to make any assumptions. But is Orson Davis a retired Army general?"

Adam nodded. This might confirm his suspicions. "You recognize the name?"

"I have not met him, yet. But most of my teammates from the Central team have gone down to North Carolina to see him."

"Why?"

"Sorry, I forgot I've never told you these details from the baseball season I'm always bragging about. Orson Davis is the father of Jonas Davis, the one who guided us into being a better baseball team and into letting go of our pride."

"So much has been happening, I never had a chance to check on this for myself, but it seems this is the same family. And, I assume, the same Jonas that Lucas wrote about in his book."

"Apparently. It's unfortunate Lucas's book is already published. Everything that happened to Grace should have been included."

"He said he was working on a sequel. He will probably be in touch again." Nate saw Grace walking over to him now. "This is too crazy. It can't be a coincidence the same family that helped your baseball team also returned Grace to me."

"I'm ready to go back home now," Grace said. "It sounds as if your boss isn't giving everyone any more of a break in the middle of the day anyhow. What are you two talking about?"

Nate, risking Ms. Douglas's ire, explained the connections between Orson, Jonas and the Central baseball team.

Grace smiled. "I'm sure both Orson and Jonas will continue to be a part of our story. All three of our stories, I suspect." Adam wondered if she meant Nate as the third person, or the baby she assumed she was carrying, but said nothing. "Hopefully we can meet Jonas when we close the deal with Orson."

"Deal?"

"Another story Ms. Douglas won't give you time to hear," Adam said. He reached out and shook hands with Nate. That was more comfortable than the hug. "Thanks for calling me out when I needed to be. Sorry I didn't listen."

Nate shrugged. "I didn't listen until it was too late, either. Lunch next Thursday?"

"As always."

When Nate walked back to the office, and Grace and Adam were back in the car, Grace took his hand. "You know what I need to do next."

Adam nodded. "In some ways, Rylee will be the easiest."

"And the hardest."

* * *

"She is going to lose her mind when she sees your name," Adam said, leaning in over Grace's shoulder.

"I know exactly what will go through her mind," Grace answered, leaning back and giving him a quick kiss.

A few days ago–even twenty-four hours ago–Adam thought it was impossible to love Grace any more than he already did. The unmerited forgiveness she had shown him made him want to be with her all the time. But with him, and even now with Rylee, there was a relationship to be saved. Grace was in the right both times, and he and Rylee were in the wrong. But Grace wanted those relationships to be restored more than she wanted justice.

But what Grace had already done today surpassed that. There was no relationship to salvage between her and Tessa, or her and Emma. Yet she went out of her way to show each of them the same forgiveness. Even with people she had never seen before, Grace showed compassion.

How could Adam respond to a love like that with anything other than more love?

"Now, she's looking at the phone," Grace said, turning her attention back to the computer screen in their bedroom. "She's not sure if she should answer. She's nervous it's a prank. Now she's excited that I might be alive." The phone continued to ring. "But now she's afraid I am angry with her because she doesn't realize I'm calling her to forgive her."

The computer's screen remained blank. "Or maybe she left her phone at home," Adam said.

"I doubt it. She almost has enough courage, and then finally hits the button and-,"

Rylee's face appeared on the screen. There was a second's hesitation, and then she screamed. "It really is you! I didn't know if those stories were true or hoaxes!"

Adam did not have the best view of the screen, but he was sure there were tears already rolling down Rylee's cheeks. Grace cried as well, but still spoke clearly to her friend. "It's me. I've wanted to reach out to you but..."

"Everything must be so crazy for you," Rylee finished. "I am so overwhelmed with joy. The world was not the same without you. Even out here, I felt your absence. Now, the world is alive again."

"Are you still in Chicago?"

"New apartment, but yes. There is so much to catch you up on when we have the chance. Wait, are those the jewels?"

Grace touched the diamond below her neck. "Oh, these?" she teased. "Yes. I don't know how much you heard, but I was given the diamond before my accident. Adam found the others, and I know you helped in finding the sapphire. Thank you so much."

But even as Grace thanked Rylee, Adam saw their friend's face sag. She glanced up, and Adam guessed, for the first time in the call, she looked at him. "Um, yeah, I guess I did. But, you shouldn't be thanking me for anything. Actually..."

Rylee probably would have continued with an awkward apology, but Grace interrupted her. "Let me make this as easy as possible. I know. I've forgiven Adam, and I've forgiven you."

"You didn't even give me a chance to say I'm sorry."

"She never does," Adam said.

Rylee giggled for a moment. "If you mean it, deep-down-in-your-soul mean it, then you're the second one to forgive me."

"I do," Grace said. "Wait, who else would have cared about you and Adam?"

For the first time, Grace put up her left hand in view of the camera. There was a diamond ring on it. "Michael and I reconciled. Well, more than reconciled. We have a date and a venue picked out. A country club, actually. Adam would love it."

Now, Grace screamed. "I am so ecstatic for you! I've been waiting for years for you two to finally to make it official. You will be so happy."

Rylee lowered her hand and frowned again. "Grace, I know things can never be the same between us."

"They can be better. I'm not going to let the past hold us back."

"Trust me, she means it," Adam quipped.

"Do you believe we can be the friends we once were?" Rylee asked. After Grace nodded, she continued. "Because then, I want to ask you something. Something rather bold, all things considered."

"Are you ever any other way?" Grace said. "Ask. I know I'll say yes."

"There's no one else who should be next to me at our wedding. Despite what I did, would you be my Maid of Honor?"

"Oh, that? No."

Adam froze. Rylee froze on the screen. Had Grace finally been pushed past her limit?

"I can't be anyone's Maid of Honor," Grace explained. "I'll be your Matron of Honor."

The women laughed, and Adam breathed a sigh of relief. Grace was limitless.

After the laughter died down, Rylee took a deep breath. "I am looking forward to seeing you face-to-face again. I mean it. But one problem still hangs over us." Rylee glanced away again, and Adam could tell this time she looked at someone off-screen. Then, Michael walked into view.

There was silence for a moment. Adam had no idea what to say or do and stood mutely in place. He had not seen his best friend since before Grace had disappeared and had not so much as sent him a text message since he had his breakup with Rylee.

"I'm sorry," Rylee cried again. "We got back together soon after, well, soon after Adam and I happened. Eventually, I couldn't keep secrets from him."

"You did the right thing," Adam muttered.

Michael put a hand on her shoulder, and glaring at the screen, spoke. "We have to talk, alone."

"Michael, I'm sorry," Adam started. "I am in the wrong and I..."

"Not you. I need to talk to Grace."

In a moment, Adam stood in the living room. He tried not to listen to what Grace and Michael said. They occasionally raised their voices, though Adam could not call it a shouting match. But Michael had a right to his anger. Grace had a right too, but had chosen not to act on it. If Michael chose to, well, it was all Adam's fault.

Adam refused to fall back into a shame cycle over his mistakes. They were as wrong as they had ever been, and Michael was free to react to his relationship with Rylee in whatever way he chose. He hated to lose a friend over a stupid decision, but he would accept the consequences and go on with life.

The voices stopped, and Grace walked up to him. "Here's the quick version," she said. "Not everyone is as forgiving as I am."

"No one is."

"But he forgave Rylee a long time ago, and after talking with me, I think he believes that you are different now than you were when you were with her. I hope one day he can completely forgive you, but for now, I persuaded him into giving you a little forgiveness."

"What does 'a little forgiveness' mean?"

"It means, in eight months, we will both be in Illinois. I will still be Rylee's Matron of Honor," Grace said, placing a consoling hand on Adam's shoulder. "But Michael will only allow you to attend the reception, not the wedding."

Chapter 42

Adam looked out over the eighteenth green from the second-floor outdoor deck of the reception hall. The last golfers of the day walked off of it and went into the clubhouse, one floor beneath where he watched.

This was a nice country club Rylee and Michael had picked for a reception–nice meaning extravagant, even as country clubs go. He did not play on the course, but walking the grounds and watching other golfers take a few swings made for an enjoyable afternoon.

Not enjoyable enough to make him forget why he was the only person already here hours before the reception.

Eight months had passed since Grace's return, and since they had learned about Rylee and Michael's engagement. Even that had not been enough time to finish everything that happened in their reconnected lives.

Along with adjusting to day-to-day life together again, Adam worked extra hours to make up for the time off he had taken. Grace was now an assistant manager at the Spartan Hotel with extra time commitments and responsibilities. All the while, they prepared their new property to become a bed-and-breakfast.

The actual paperwork was completed, and it was, in fact, Jonas Davis who took care of all the paperwork for his father, Orson, to complete the deal. Adam was anxious to see Jonas, but he was only to be heard. Jonas called and faxed in the paperwork to the real estate office. Adam hoped to one day see both men and finally learn why everything happened the way it had.

But there was too much happening to dwell on that. Grace had taken three flights here, to Illinois, to prepare for her part in the wedding as Rylee's Matron of Honor, and to reconnect with her friend. The times apart reminded Adam of the year he was separated from Grace, which allowed miniature versions of a shame cycle to begin anew. Each time, Grace would gently remind him his mistakes cost something, but he was forgiven. She would always be his wife as much as she had been on their wedding day. The shame would evaporate.

Now here, awaiting the first wedding guests to arrive as the sun set, Adam experienced one other consequence of his actions. Today, he should have been Michael's Best Man. Instead, another college friend took that place, and only Grace's words on his behalf earned Adam a place here at the reception at all.

Despite Grace repeating her request otherwise, Michael forbade Adam from much as attending the actual ceremony.

Adam looked back through the windows and saw some wedding guests arriving inside the hall. Then he spotted the bridesmaids, other friends of Grace's and Rylee's in college. After a quick check to make sure his valuables rested in his suit pocket, Adam walked back into the reception area as Grace entered on the other side.

Grace ran over to him as best she could, her hair long since reaching its usual length to her elbows, but her lavender dress not concealing her baby bump. They hugged and kissed.

"It was beautiful," Grace whispered. "Not as beautiful as our wedding, of course, but beautiful."

Adam did not know what to say for a moment, but mumbled, "I should have been there."

Grace pulled back an inch. "You know what I'm going to tell you."

Adam nodded. He memorized the words, after all the times Grace had said them in the last six months, the times his regrets resurfaced. Still, hearing her say them again made them less condemning and more comforting.

"Our mistakes will always have consequences. They will always cost us something. It cost you a special place today." She pulled him closer again and lowered her voice to the slightest whisper. "But there is nothing you can do, no mistake you can ever make, that will cost you my love."

They kissed again. Adam put his right hand over her stomach. "And I pray they never cost me her."

"Our little Iglesia? Never. I know she will always love her daddy."

* * *

Though Grace sat at the main table for the reception, Adam was seated at the table farthest from it. He spoke with several people he remembered from college and enjoyed the evening with some old acquaintances. A woman asked idly if anyone knew the designer of the wedding dress. Adam could not say who made Rylee's dress, but Grace had told him the bridesmaid's dresses were designed by Lydia Stoltzfus. When he spoke the name, he remembered that was also Nate's last name. Could she be a relative? The cousin Lucas admitted to desiring? That was a long shot, but so was the chance Grace would recover from a coma and be related to an Army General.

It stung Adam to listen to someone else deliver the Best Man's speech, but he consoled himself when he realized how fortunate he was to be there at all. They ate a fine meal, drank good wine, and laughed at college stories through the night. As the minutes ticked on, Adam allowed himself simply to be happy for Rylee and Michael, to be grateful his friends loved each other so much.

Even if their feelings towards him were far different now.

He danced to two songs with Grace when the music started, though the motions were a touch awkward with her stomach becoming more prominent. That awkwardness was nothing compared to the moment when he noticed Michael glanced at him, while he danced with Rylee. He gave Adam a terse nod, then turned back to his bride, and never looked back.

Adam had known Michael long enough to understand the message. Michael had not forgiven him, but he would not press the matter any further. At least, not today.

After the bride and groom left, and half of the other guests departed, Adam and Grace held each other on the deck. A few other celebrators conversed out here too, but they kept a distance away.

"You have them?" Grace asked.

Adam reached into his pocket and pulled out the necklace with all five jewels hanging from it. They never intended for Grace to outshine Rylee on her wedding day, but now that she was gone, Adam needed to see Grace wearing the gems now.

He attached the necklace around her neck, kissed her shoulder, then stepped back to stare at Grace. Even in the low lighting on the deck, she radiated beauty. He could scarcely believe they were together here now. Grace's presence remained unfathomable. It was even harder to believe her forgiveness had endured through these months.

"This isn't how stories like this are supposed to end," Adam whispered.

"We're not at an ending," Grace said, placing her hands on her stomach. "We're at a new beginning. After all, next month is our third anniversary. We will celebrate fifty more. Fifty more uneventful ones, I hope."

"But, we're at the part of the story where the villains have been given their comeuppance, and the heroes are free. This is when you should have cut yourself off from me and found someone else. Instead, you forgave me and even persuaded Michael to forgive me enough to let me be here."

"If I wasn't going to redeem our marriage, what would have been the point of ever coming out of the coma?" Grace slipped her hands off of her stomach and onto Adam's shoulders, swaying to the music. Her natural elegance, the dress, her made-up hair, the jewels, and her baby bump made her the most gorgeous creature in all the world.

Adam's lover. Adam's wife. Adam's world.

"I don't deserve you," he said.

"No, you don't," Grace answered with a straight face. But then she smiled. "But you'll always have me."

The reception, other guests, mistakes of his past and even their plans for the future were forgotten for a moment. They embraced and kissed passionately, ignoring whistles from drunk college friends.

When they pulled back, Grace whispered, "Always us."

Adam touched each of the jewels. For a moment, he wondered if the tale of those gems had ended. He had often speculated about the odd way he found the onyx. Will they ever know how or why it fell into the well? And the sapphire was given to him because the previous owner also believed Grace was dead. Would she come back to recover it?

And was there more to Grace's background than even she realized? How exactly did her family tree trace back to Orson?

The questions remained unanswered, but his thoughts disappeared as Grace spoke. "Each of those jewels means something to me. Each one is a treasure. But I always told you," she said as she lifted her left hand, with her engagement and wedding rings catching the faint glow of the light. "This is the most important jewelry I own."

Adam took his left and placed it with hers, lining up their rings, as if molding them into an infinity symbol. But he realized it was not the rings that made Grace forgive him and take him back.

He placed his hand over Grace's heart. "I will always see this as the true jewelry of Grace."

Epilogue

Emma read the letter a second time. It shocked her.

A week earlier and she would have found it odd and forgotten it. Forgiveness from a woman she had never met. Such a strange concept. It almost made her forget that now she did not need to watch over the old man's home anymore.

This Grace found out she slept with her husband. Had this letter not been in front of the home she tended, Emma would not have known Adam's wife was the woman on the news for reappearing out of nowhere.

It was a relief to know Grace did not wish for vengeance.

But that was not what shocked Emma. Her surprise came from the timing of the letter's arrival. She had found it this morning, in an envelope with her name written on it, one day after she completed a book that was given to her by a friend.

In her bedroom now, she pulled out her copy of the book. Supposedly, the story was authentic, though parts of it forced Emma to suspend her disbelief. Injuries healed with a touch. A man who seemed to know everyone's secrets, and everyone's future.

And yet, many people swore the book's veracity. Eyewitnesses posted their videos on the internet to back up the story's claims. But those witnesses also backed up, not only the amazing wonders of the story but its dominant theme.

This mysterious man taught everyone possessed value. He said everyone's worth remained permanent, not increasing with success or decreasing with failure. He even guided his followers–a team of baseball players–to forgive unconditionally.

It sounded like the way Grace forgave Emma, without even meeting her.

This outrageous compassion, and not the nearly impossible events, compelled Emma to finish the book in two nights.

She looked at the hardbound cover.

Jonas's Team by Lucas Darnold.

This Jonas, if he was real, had never posted a video of himself. There were no social media accounts by him, though in her search to find out more about him, Emma had discovered many scam accounts.

But Grace was real. If Jonas also was real and right in what he taught, and if Grace's forgiveness was part of that teaching, it meant everything to Emma.

She did not have to be cruel to others anymore.

She did not need to overcharge for any service she gave.

She did not need to surrender to one-night stands.

She did not have to lie.

Emma could live an altogether different life.

Looking back, it was the lie she that most troubled her. Adam and Grace should know who owned the onyx before, and how it wound up in the bottom of the well. The jewels were important to them, so Emma should seek them out at their new home once they moved. She should tell them the rest of the story.

And Emma could be honest with them. At least, she hoped so. Old habits die hard or, more often, do never die. But her future did not need to mirror her past. She had been

certain her value came from what she took, no matter how she grabbed hold of it. If she got it the wrong way, she neither expected nor requested forgiveness. She did not make it a habit to give forgiveness to others. But maybe there was a better way to live.

Emma looked at the book in one hand, and Grace's letter in the other.

Jonas. Grace.

Emma slipped the letter back into the envelope it came in and put the envelope inside the front cover of the book.

Only one thing mattered now. She needed to find both Grace and Jonas.

Her life needed to change.

***Grace, Adam, Nate, Lucas and Emma
will return in***

The Fire of Life

Coming 2023

***Read how Nate and Lucas met
Jonas Davis and became intertwined in
Orson Davis's story in***

The Pride of Central

**Available now
on Amazon**